THE GAMES PEOPLE PLAY

BOOK 4 IN THE JOSEPH STONE CRIME THRILLER SERIES

J R SINCLAIR

Copyright 2024 © J R Sinclair

All rights reserved. This book or any portion thereof may not be reproduced or used in any manner whatsoever without the express written permission of the publisher except for the use of brief quotations in a book review.

This is a work of fiction. Any names or characters are fictitious. Any resemblance to actual persons, living or dead, or actual events, or organisations, is purely coincidental.

Published worldwide by Voice from the Clouds Ltd.

www.voicefromtheclouds.com

This book is dedicated to the simply amazing team in the ACU department at the Churchill Hospital in Oxford who looked after me with such incredible care and attention during my chemo immunotherapy treatment. You will all always be in my heart!

CHAPTER ONE

IN THE BUILDING SUNSET, a curl of smoke rose from the tiny log cabin's chimney. Above it, the autumn leaves glowed every shade of red and orange, a tapestry of illuminated jewels. Gabby sat perfectly still among them, balanced in the crook of the tree —an unseen panther ready to pounce.

A sense of excitement built inside Gabby as her breath steamed in the crisp air. She watched the silhouette of a man moving about inside.

It would only be a matter of time now.

She double-checked that her action camera had actually been turned on to capture the kill. Proof was everything in this game.

Gabby forced herself to slow her breathing. God, she loved this part of the hunt—when she was closing in, especially when her intended target was clueless about what was coming their way.

Despite her efforts to stay calm, her heart rate sped up the moment the door opened and Ryan, an art student in his early twenties with a mop of blond hair, emerged. He headed around the side of the cabin towards a small pile of logs stacked against the humble structure, totally oblivious to her presence above him.

Of course, he hadn't figured on anyone tracking him here.

You so underestimated me, Ryan.

She raised the pistol, setting the sights between his shoulder blades as he gathered up the logs. Then Gabby stilled as she breathed out and took the shot.

The man's eyes widened as the foam dart hit him square in the back and bounced off.

Gabby immediately punched the air. 'Got you, sucker!'

Ryan stared down at the blue foam Nerf dart now lying by his feet. Then his eyes briefly flicked back to the cabin, his lips thinned. Finally, he looked up, scanning the canopy until he spotted her.

'Bloody hell, you almost gave me a heart attack,' he said.

'Says the loser,' Gabby replied. She made an L-shape with her fingers and brought it up to her forehead, just to underline the point.

'Yeah, yeah, yeah,' he said, but also smiling.

Gabby grinned back at him, and then leapt down the branches with the agility of a cat. For the final couple of metres, she pushed off the trunk, bounced off a fallen bough, and landed on the ground in a crouch.

Ryan clapped as she stood and did a little curtsy.

'I see you're keeping those freerunning and climbing skills sharp,' he said.

'Of course. I'm not about to let them go rusty, especially when I can put them to such good use at moments like this one.'

'Tell me about it. But how did you find my hiding place, anyway?'

'Oh, when none of your mates would spill the beans, I just asked your tutor at the Ruskin School of Art where you were holed up.

Imagine my surprise when I learned you'd practically leapt at the chance to be the artist in residence in the cabin studio at Wytham Woods. I hadn't even heard of it until your tutor helpfully filled me in on the details. The perfect spot to vanish from the rest of us.'

'Not so perfect, it seems. But you do realise you might be taking this assassination game a bit too seriously?' He held his thumb and forefinger apart just the barest fraction.

'Says the guy I just took down,' Gabby replied. 'Anyway, admit it. You love the adrenaline hit just as much as I do. But I swear I get an even bigger high than when taking part in a Parkour run with you.'

'Seriously, better than free running a course over a rooftop with me?'

'Well, you wouldn't understand the rush for a huntress after a successful pursuit, would you.' She smirked at him.

He shook his head, chuckling.

Gabby turned off her camera that had recorded her *kill*. 'Seriously, I knew I had to go the extra mile when it came to taking you down. After all, everyone is still talking about how you shot Geoff in the student union bar during the Assassins' Syndicate game last year. He's never been able to live it down since, especially as you won the tournament by beating him.'

'I have to say, that was one of my best hits ever. He really didn't expect me to leap up from behind the bar. I'd been waiting half the night just to take that shot.'

'He didn't stand a chance, just like you didn't tonight. I totally owned your arse.'

'Not that you're competitive or anything.'

Gabby grinned. 'Tell me about it. But thanks to tonight, I'm one step closer to winning the prize pot.'

Ryan nodded. 'Yes, that ten thousand pounds is definitely within your reach now. Just two more targets to go.'

She nodded as she reached for his jumper and pulled him closer. 'Don't worry, I'll split my winnings with you.'

'You don't need to do that, although you know I could certainly use the cash.'

'You and me both.' Gabby stepped back and looked at him through her fringe. 'So, have you missed me?'

Ryan pulled a face at her. 'We've only been apart a week since the game began.'

She looked into his eyes. 'Far too long. Anyway...' She reached forward and ran her finger down his chest. 'Aren't you going to invite me into your humble home so we can make up for lost time?' Gabby grinned at him. But of all the reactions she might have expected, it wasn't the tense expression that filled his face.

'As much as I would love to do that, sorry, no. I'm on a roll with a piece I'm working on.'

Gabby's lips pinched together. 'You're seriously going to turn this down?' She swept her hands down over her perfect figure. 'So you can paint?'

'It's just I'm on a roll and if I stop now—'

A crash came from inside the cabin. As Gabby turned, she had the brief impression of a woman's face quickly ducking down from the window.

A storm of emotions swept through her. 'Who the hell have you got in there with you, Ryan?'

He held up his hands. 'Look, I can explain.'

'The fuck you can.' Pure rage burned through her veins as she strode towards the cabin door.

But Ryan quickly ducked back and shoved his arm across the doorway. 'You can't go in there.'

She glowered at him, clenching her hands into fists. 'Who the hell is it? You owe me that!'

Ryan just shook his head. 'Not here, and not like this. I'll come and find you tomorrow. Then we'll talk this through properly.'

Gabby put her hand on her hips. 'What, so you can finish your work that you're on an absolute *roll* with?'

He gave her a helpless look and spread his hands.

'Oh, you absolute shit, and I thought we had a real future together. And you do this after everything I've done to support you. Well, that's it. I want nothing more to do with you, Ryan. You can also kiss goodbye to any idea of me sharing the prize pot with you.'

Ryan reached out, but she shook him off.

'Goodbye and good riddance,' Gabby said. She turned on her heel and stalked into the wood now glowing with the golden light of the sunset.

As Gabby went, an ache was building in her chest. It felt like her boyfriend had torn her heart from her breast and trampled it into the ground.

But even then, part of her wanted to hear Ryan's footfalls running after her. A hand on her shoulder. An outpouring of sorrow and guilt. And eventually she would forgive him. Of course, she would.

But none of that happened.

All Gabby heard was the soft click of the cabin door closing. When she glanced back, Ryan had disappeared inside. Just like that, all her hopes for their future together shattered into splinters. She smeared away the tears blurring her vision.

This pain was so unfamiliar, so shocking, so soul shattering. This sort of thing never happened to her. In the world Gabby knew, she literally had men throwing themselves at her on a daily basis, and not once had she betrayed Ryan. But now it seemed there'd been one rule for her and another for him.

A pulse of fury rose through her, burning and hot. Even though she hadn't seen the woman's face, she still had a pretty damned good idea who it was. The bitch had wormed her way into Ryan's life and stolen her man away. This was all her fault.

Arms pulled even tighter around herself, she started to head back down the track to where she'd left her car.

Gabby became so lost in her inner turmoil, so numb, she'd barely tuned into her surroundings. Then a rustling sound came from somewhere close by to her right. Her heart lifted, despite her anger. Had he come to his senses?

'Ryan?'

There was no reply.

When Gabby glanced into the shadows growing in the woods as the sun started to dip, she spotted the black-and-white striped face of a badger staring back at her. It quickly turned and lumbered away into the undergrowth. For some reason that only heightened her sense of loss and made her heart ache even more.

Now, with each step, the adrenaline ebbed away, and despite the lingering warmth of the mild autumn day, a deep chill took hold.

Gabby shivered as she huddled into her thin jacket, hands thrust deep into her pockets, one of which rested on the Nerf gun. If it hadn't been for the bloody game, she would have been none the wiser about any of this. But now that she knew, Gabby was already certain there was no going back. Ryan had crossed the line, and she would never be able to forgive him. She was too proud for that and would never stoop to being a doormat for any guy.

As Gabby headed along the track, she caught the first glimpse of the Swiss Chalet in the wood. The building had always caught her imagination as something straight out of a fairytale. It had even sparked a fantasy about her and Ryan's future together. One day she'd imagined that once they'd graduated and she had earned a proper salary, they'd have had two houses—an idyllic cottage in the country with its own studio for Ryan to work in, and a flat in London she could use during the week whilst she worked in Parliament before heading home for the weekend.

It was then she heard the crack of the twig from the woods to her left.

Gabby didn't bother to even look this time, as it was obviously another badger. But this time, the sound stopped dead, almost like... He'd come after her, after all!

She whirled around, instantly ready to accept his apology. But this time when she looked, there was no sign of anyone or anything in the woods.

'Ryan, if that's bloody you, be a man and talk to me so we can sort this out.'

Once again, no reply, no movement.

A cool whisper of wind stirred her hair, sending a fresh shiver cascading down Gabby's spine. She screwed up her eyes as she searched the gathering gloom. Then she finally made out a shape standing almost stock still. Was that a figure beyond the next tree, or just a trick of the dimming light?

For the first time, another thought struck her. What if it wasn't Ryan?

A deep sense of fear took hold then, as fresh adrenaline powered through her system. Gabby was closer to the car than the cabin. If she made a run for it, hopefully, if a person really was stalking her through the woods... But then that thought trailed away and she almost laughed out loud as she realised what was actually happening.

Another player in the game had found her, and there was still a chance they could snatch victory from her hands. But only if they managed to assassinate her like she had Ryan. And God, she needed that prize money now more than ever to rebuild her life after he'd sucked her dry.

Her mind was already racing as she put a plan together. Okay, she'd make a run for it.

Without pausing, she broke into a sprint towards the safety of her car. All those months of freerunning and climbing, toning her muscles and sharpening her reflexes, meant she was at the top of her game.

Catch me if you can, she thought.

As she ran, any doubts that she was being followed were swept away. She heard someone break into a run in the woods to her left, twigs breaking under their thundering footsteps, as they no longer bothered to hide their presence.

Even though she knew this was all part of the high-stakes game, this didn't make it any less frightening. It already felt way too real.

But just ahead, next to the high-pitched roofed Swiss Chalet, stood her Fiat 500 and its promise of sanctuary. That sparked hope inside her. She could still escape and survive to play another day.

Game on!

Blood pounding in her ears, Gabby reached her car. She fumbled with her remote and glanced back to see a hooded figure racing towards her. Elation surged through her as she pressed a button on the remote and the car's lights came on as the doors clunked and unlocked.

'Better luck another day,' Gabby called out as she grabbed the door handle, getting ready to leap in.

A whooshing sound and something smacked into her hand. Gabby looked down to see her palm pinned to the Fiat's door by a short barbed arrow.

A split second later, her body registered the pain and burning as a fire blazed through her hand. Gabby's scream echoed through the silent woodland around her. White spots of light swarmed her vision as she attempted to pull her hand free.

Almost casually, the figure advanced, a crossbow raised in their hand.

Fury, almost as intense as the agony she was in, surged through her. 'What the actual fuck? This is meant to be a bloody game, and you've actually bloody shot me with a real weapon!'

The person came to a halt, their face hidden by the shadows of their hood as they aimed the crossbow directly at her head.

'Don't be so bloody stupid, you fucking psychopath.'

When the person didn't respond, Gabby's anger was swept away by real terror.

The person squeezed the trigger.

'Please don't—'

Gabby had the briefest sensation of what felt like a hot rod of molten iron being punched into her right eye. Total darkness filled her mind as her consciousness faded away.

The figure lowered their weapon, looking down as the dying woman shuddered and stilled before them. They smiled in the darkness. It had been a perfect assassination.

The person bent down and lifted the length of chain hanging around Gabby's neck, and took hold of the blue plastic token dangling from it. With a quick yank, they tore the pendant free from the chain, and slid the memento into their pocket.

Then they reached up and turned off the action camera clipped to the strap of their small rucksack. Yes, they were going to enjoy watching that back and reliving this glorious moment.

The figure turned and ran away, back into the wood. Unnoticed, the plastic token fell from their pocket as they leapt over a fallen tree, leaving behind the only clue to what had happened.

CHAPTER TWO

Joseph leaned against the workbench, taking a moment to admire the culmination of several months of handiwork in his boss's garage. The noise of the compressor was deafening in the confined space even with the doors wide open, as Chris Faulkner, suitably masked, sprayed a grey primer coat on the car with steady, measured sweeps.

It was hard for Joseph to believe that the vehicle before them was the same wreck his boss had bought after it had been totalled in a track racing accident. It had certainly taken a lot of painstaking effort to smooth out the numerous aluminium panels. But now, like the proverbial phoenix rising slowly from the ashes, the dented wreck they'd started with had gradually begun to resemble an Aston Martin DB5 again.

With the last spot painted around the rear light cluster, the DCI finally released the trigger and the air compressor rumbled to a welcome stop.

Chris slipped off the protective mask and met Joseph's eye. 'What do you think?'

'A work of bloody art,' DI Joseph Stone replied. 'You should seriously consider jacking in this detective lark, and opening up your own body shop.'

'No, car restoration strictly falls into hobby territory for now.'

'Then the good residents of Oxfordshire will be relieved to hear you'll be keeping your beady eye on the criminal fraternities for a while longer yet.'

Chris gave Joseph a straight look. 'That sounds like you're getting dangerously close to taking the piss.'

'Would I ever?' the DI replied, giving him a perfectly innocent look.

Chris snorted before returning his attention to the DB5. 'It's good seeing her well on the way to being fully restored. Did you know there were only just over a thousand of these ever made?'

'Seriously? So she's rare then?'

'Let's just say it was my absolute duty to keep one of the few vehicles on the road.'

Joseph gestured to their previous project, Chris's fully restored Triumph TR4 sitting behind it. 'So what about your other motor, then?'

'The TR4 isn't as rare as the DB5, but she's still another slice of motoring history. And, as you know, an absolute blast to race round a circuit.'

'Right up to the point I rolled her.'

Chris scowled at Joseph. 'Which, as we both know, was no fault of yours. We have Jimmy Harper to thank for that, and him and his acquaintances trying to fix the race.'

'Aye, but it doesn't make me feel any less guilty about it. I was the one driving her, after all.'

'Look, the same would have happened if I'd been at the wheel. Besides, look at her now!' Chris gestured towards the immaculate TR4. 'She looks as good as the day she left the factory. Probably better, in fact, thanks to a decent paint job. Besides, as I keep telling you, I don't own these cars to just let them gather dust in here. The TR4 was built to be driven, just like the DB5. And the odd mishap is a price worth paying for that kind of motoring heaven.'

Joseph, who'd heard this lecture from his boss a hundred times, nodded. 'If you say so. But even I have to admit, she looks pretty grand.'

Chris cast an admiring eye over the car. 'She certainly does. Anyway, I think it's time to call it a night. What do you say to a pint of my latest batch of home-brewed stout? It may not be Guinness, but it doesn't embarrass itself either, and to the point, I'm actually prepared to serve it to a real-life Irishman.'

'Then sign me up, although maybe just half a pint, as I have to cycle home. I know from experience just how lethal your homebrew is.'

Chris smiled. 'If a job's worth doing, it's worth doing properly.' He headed to the back of the garage where the Aston's engine had been lowered by a hoist onto a workbench. Next to that was a rack of shelving. On that sat an impressive selection of kegs containing the fruits of the DCI's brewing efforts.

Joseph watched as Chris, with the care of a chemist handling nitroglycerin, opened the tap on one of the kegs and poured out a small glass for his guest, and a much larger one for himself.

The DI held the stout up to the light, admiring the dense creamy foam on top. 'This certainly has more than a passing resemblance to the black stuff of my mother country.'

'But the real test is in the tasting,' Chris replied.

'Very true.' Joseph took a sip, trying to ignore his boss, who was watching him like a hawk. His brain registered the very smooth and velvety taste.

'Well?' Chris asked.

Joseph smacked his lips. 'There are definitely toasty notes of dark chocolate and coffee beans in there. Really excellent, and if you were so inclined, I'd be more than happy to take a few bottles off your hands.'

'Bloody hell, that's high praise coming from you.'

'You better believe it. Very well done indeed, Chris.'

Stouts in hand, they went outside to relax in the DCI's garden. Together, they looked out across the valley over Farmoor Reservoir perfectly mirroring the last of the oranges and mauves of the stunning autumnal sunset as it faded. On the horizon stood a hill capped by Wytham Woods. A flock of crows flew towards it, getting ready to roost for the night.

Joseph soaked in the view. 'I've said it before and I'll say it again. You've got a stunning view from up here on Cumnor Hill.'

'It's not bad, is it? At least I got to hang on to this after my divorce.'

'I've never heard you talk about that before,' Joseph said.

'It seems like a lifetime ago now. My ex-wife was my first girlfriend back at school in Bristol, and we got married far too young. Some make a go of it, and we did until we hit our early thirties and then...' He shrugged. 'But at least I was able to start over here in Oxford when I transferred from the Bristol nick.'

Joseph nodded. 'And you certainly landed on your feet here with this house. If I owned this old stone cottage, I think I'd be set for life.'

'You mean this place might tempt you away from your life on your narrowboat?'

'Well, that has its charm too, and I'm certainly very much part of the community there.'

'Which counts for a lot,' Chris replied, taking a sip of his stout. 'Damn, this really is good.'

The DI gave him an amused look. 'If you say so yourself.'

His boss grinned. 'While I'm thinking of it, there's something I need to ask you.'

Joseph cast a sideways glance towards Chris, worried that he'd somehow learnt of his private investigation.

'About what?' the DI said, trying to keep his tone relaxed.

'What's this I hear about you dating none other than our very own prestigious SOCO, Amy Fischer?'

A wave of relief swept through Joseph. 'Oh, Jesus, who's been talking?'

Chris grinned at him. 'Pretty much everyone, although no one's graffitied it in the loos at work yet.'

'Thank God for small mercies.'

The DCI raised his eyebrows at him. 'Well, if you date a colleague, what do you expect? Mind you, I did have you rather labelled as a confirmed bachelor, just like myself.'

'So did I, but that seems to be the way of these things. There you are, happily getting on with your life, when out of nowhere you suddenly find yourself involved with someone.'

'Well, I'm happy for you both, especially in our line of work. That makes holding down a relationship tricky at the best of times. The frequent long hours really don't help.'

Joseph looked at his boss. 'Sounds like the voice of experience?'

'A story for another time.'

The DI watched Chris's look grow distant as he relived some painful past event. It seemed that Joseph didn't have a monopoly on painful divorces.

'Anyway, enough about me,' Chris finally said, returning from wherever he'd been in his head. 'There is another thing I wanted to pick your brain about regarding work, to check I'm not imagining things.'

'Fire away,' Joseph replied, already tensing in case someone had spotted him using the Holmes 2 system for something he deliberately hadn't logged to a case.

'It's about Derrick. Have you noticed anything about his behaviour recently?'

Joseph immediately became guarded as he arranged his face into a smile. 'Off the record, he's as big a pain in the arse as normal, if that's what you mean?'

That didn't even elicit a small grin from his boss. 'If that's all it was, I wouldn't even bat an eyelid; that's just part of what makes the man tick. But even for our esteemed DSU's normal behaviour, the guy seems to have a hair trigger these days. The smallest thing sets him off on a major tirade.'

The DI just shrugged. 'So, his usual sweet self, in other words.'

Chris's forehead wrinkled. 'Then maybe it's just me, but I swear something is wrong. The problem is, whenever I try to broach the subject with him, let's just say it doesn't end well.'

'In that case, my advice to you is to give him the same wide berth that you would an unexploded bomb.'

This time, Chris chuckled. 'Sage advice, as always.'

Joseph grabbed the opportunity to steer the subject into safer waters. 'This stout really is excellent.'

Chris nodded, gestured to Joseph's glass of stout that seemed to have magically evaporated over the course of their conversation. 'Fancy another?'

'Not if I want to pedal home in a straight line, I don't. But I've got to dash. Places to be and all that.'

'A date with Amy?'

Joseph tapped the side of his nose. 'That's for me to know and for you to wonder about.'

'Fair enough. But maybe take those bottles of the stout with you.'

'I don't mind if I do,' Joseph replied, as he stood, relieved he'd managed to shift their conversation away from Derrick.

The problem was, that subject was seriously dangerous territory. Their DSU had very much become the centre of the DI's obsession for the last few months. That also had everything to do with where Joseph had to stop off on his way home.

Until he was ready, and had the evidence to back it up, he wasn't prepared to share those suspicions about the big man with anyone else, even Chris.

CHAPTER THREE

WITH NIGHT DESCENDING RAPIDLY, Joseph pedalled through the tree-lined streets of North Oxford, trying to avoid skidding on the piles of leaves building up in the gutter. The problem was only half his attention was on the road. The other half of his mind was well and truly on Derrick, especially after hearing Chris had noticed a change in the big man's behaviour, as well.

For Joseph, the feeling that something was seriously off about the DSU had grown throughout the Burning Man investigation. He'd become increasingly convinced that Derrick was somehow involved with the Night Watchmen, a well-organised and resourced crime syndicate. The NCA's subsequent investigation into the group had led to a string of arrests and a number of shady businesses being shut down. But the belief was the Night Watchmen were still very much active.

The significant reach of that group had become personal for Joseph when two of their hitmen had targeted a prisoner transfer he and Megan had been escorting. Not only had their prisoner, Daryl Manning, who'd been prepared to give evidence against the group, been killed, but the two police officers driving the van with him in it, PC John Thorpe and PC Paul Burford, had also been shot. Thankfully, both men had made full recoveries, although Paul was still on leave after eventually being brought out of an induced coma.

Joseph was increasingly convinced that it had been Derrick who'd tipped off the crime syndicate about the prisoner transfer so they could intercept it. The only problem was that beyond a hunch, he didn't have any actual evidence so far to prove it. So that was why he'd been running his own clandestine operation for the last month, monitoring Derrick's comings and goings.

Joseph pulled up well away from a streetlight and in, as near as this part of well-lit Oxford allowed, the shadows. He padlocked his mountain bike to a railing just around the corner from the big man's house—the same house that Joseph and his ex-wife, Kate, had once called home.

It ate him to his core that so far, at least, he hadn't dared to share his suspicions with Kate about her husband. But until he had hard proof, he knew just how hollow it would sound if he did try to tell her.

'Yes, Kate, your husband is actually a lying piece of shite. He's also almost certainly on the payroll of the Night Watchmen, the same crime syndicate you were investigating yourself. And no, this has nothing to do with me wanting you to divorce that fecking toerag faster than I can spit.'

Yes, Joseph could easily imagine how that particular conversation would go.

That was the problem right there—he would always be conflicted at a personal level about Derrick marrying his ex-wife—a man whom he'd once, a long time ago, in the ancient dust of time, called a friend. That was, until the now-DSU had delighted in stabbing him in the back to gain a promotion, which by all rights should have been Joseph's. That aside, as far as the DI was concerned, Derrick had never been good enough for Kate.

He pulled the hood up on his waterproof cagoule jacket to hide his face, before setting off on foot. Even though it was only eight p.m. the pavements were deserted. But it was also Sunday night and along this residential area of Oxford, most people would be home, making the most of the last of the weekend before heading back to work the following day. Yes, this was how they liked to rock and roll in this sleepy part of the city. Cowley Road, it wasn't, when it came to a buzzing nightlife.

Just ahead was a detached house with the superintendent's BMW 7 series car squeezed into the narrow driveway. There was a light in the window of an attic that Joseph knew doubled as a home office.

There was no sign of Kate's car parked on the road. Once again, in itself, that wasn't unusual. It seemed Kate spent as much time as she could at work these days. Whether that was down to marital issues, or simply that she had her teeth dug into another major story for the Oxford Chronicle, Joseph wouldn't like to say.

He'd deliberately given her something of a wide berth whilst he investigated what her husband was up to. On the few occasions they had spoken, Kate hadn't dropped a single hint to Joseph that there was anything wrong with their marriage. But even so, he still had his suspicions.

In stark contrast to the warm autumn day, the air was chilling rapidly and Joseph's breath was starting to cloud in front of him. If this had been a proper stakeout, and he actually owned a car, he would be sitting snugly inside it, keeping a beady eye on the big man's home and taking note of any interesting comings and goings.

Unfortunately, a mountain bike was a distant second for any sort of surveillance operation. For one, it would make it bleeding obvious he was watching the house, and two, he would quickly freeze his nads off in the chilly autumn nights. Thankfully,

Joseph had come up with a cunning plan to avoid at least one of those particular pitfalls. He'd go on foot.

On the opposite side of the road, as he drew parallel with his old house, Joseph crouched down, pretending to tie a shoelace. As he did so, he scanned the branches of a dense laurel bush in the front garden of the property across from his old house.

He breathed a sigh of relief when he spotted his hidden wildlife trail camera, still clipped to one of the bush's branches. From there, the camera had a perfect view of Derrick and Kate's front door. The DI had felt a modicum of guilt about spying on them, but he'd had no other choice if he wanted to keep an eye on Derrick's movements outside work hours.

The DI pocketed the trail cam's memory card, swapping it for another. Once he was back safely on his narrowboat, *Tús Nua*, he could afford to take his time to check whatever footage he'd caught this time around. Previous attempts had been abject failures. The only interesting thing had been an urban fox rummaging through a food bin it had managed to unlock with the expertise of a skilled safecracker.

With the memory cards swapped, Joseph stood, about to head back to his bike, when the front door opened and Derrick himself, car keys in his hand, stepped out of the house.

Shite! Joseph thought, as the DSU glanced in his direction. Ducking back down, pretending to tie his shoelace, Joseph tried to formulate a cover story. Something along the lines of a family dinner with Ellie and her boyfriend, PC John Thorpe. One that the DI was there to invite Kate to.

Then Derrick's gaze slid past the DI, as though he wasn't even there, and he climbed into his BMW. Wherever his boss's head was, thankfully, it wasn't focused on his immediate surroundings.

This was new behaviour from the big man. Once Derrick was installed at home, that was usually it for the night, at least according to the camera footage the DI had previously captured. So why this break in his routine? Of course, there could be a million innocent explanations about why the DSU was leaving his home at eight o'clock on a Sunday evening, including getting called into work to deal with some crisis or other. But instinct was already nudging the DI that this might be significant.

Head down, face still hidden by his cagoule's hood, Joseph stood, imaginary loose shoelace tied. He headed away along the pavement, back to where his bike was parked around the corner, mind already made up about what he was going to do next.

The moment Joseph reached his ridiculously expensive mountain bike, he began fumbling with the combination of his heavy-duty lock. He was dealing with the last digit when he heard Derrick's BMW start.

'Will you fecking come on?' he muttered to himself. With a click, the lock finally released. Joseph slung it into his rucksack and leapt onto his bike. He rounded the corner just in time to see the red taillights of Derrick's BMW disappearing down the end of the road.

The DI stood on the pedals as he accelerated hard after it, rocking the bike from side to side. This was one of those rare moments he wished he'd embraced the dark side of electric bikes to give him an added boost.

Giving it everything he had, he tore after the car. Thankfully, this was where his local knowledge of the streets helped. Driving a car through Oxford wasn't necessarily the quickest way to cross the city, where the humble bicycle was still very much treated as King, Queen, and Emperor.

Intending to use that to his advantage, and knowing that Derrick would be forced to double back on a parallel one-way road, Joseph bumped his bike up onto the pavement. Within moments, he was tearing down a brick alleyway between the red-brick houses. He had almost reached the end when he saw Derrick's car head past.

For feck's sake!

Heart racing, Joseph reached the road a split second after the BMW, narrowly missing a dog walker just entering the alley. The man had to dive aside, pulling his yapping terrier with him. The man then let loose with a string of well-deserved expletives at the DI's back.

Joseph ignored all of it, his focus purely on the BMW pulling away ahead of him on the road. He just prayed the superintendent didn't glance in his rearview mirror and spot the maniac cyclist giving it everything he had to try and keep up.

Despite being fit, thanks to all the cycling he did, the DI's heart was well and truly pounding as the car headed towards the junction ahead of him. If this turned out to be a sneaky run for Maccy D's by the big man, Joseph would seriously kick himself.

Blissfully unaware of his pursuer, Derrick paused at the junction. During the day, he would have been stuck there for ages thanks to all the slow-moving traffic snaking its way into Oxford. Unfortunately for Joseph, that wasn't the case at this time of night. Barely hesitating, the BMW pulled straight out onto the main road. But rather than driving out of town, the vehicle headed towards the city centre. That meant Joseph might still have a chance to keep up with him.

But by the time the DI reached the main road, there was no sign of the BMW. Okay, there was a speed camera just a few hundred metres down the road that the DSU would have passed, and no way Derrick would risk racing past it. So that meant...

Joseph swept out onto the road, pedalling hard as he glanced down the side streets he passed, praying he would spot the rear lights of the BMW. But one side street became three as he raced past.

The DI was just starting to lose hope when he spotted the telltale headlight beams crossing the next side road, and he pulled hard on the brakes, bringing his bike to a screeching halt. A car parking in a driveway? *No, not a driveway,* Joseph realised, but the entrance to the car park of the Old Ink Press pub. If that was Derrick, maybe he hadn't gone out for a sneaky burger before Kate got back home, but a quick pint at the nearest drinking hole instead. It was certainly worth checking out since there was no sign of the BMW anywhere else.

The DI turned down the side road, heading towards the pub at a far more sedate pace than a moment ago. Joseph maintained his slower speed as he casually cycled past the car park entrance and glanced over. He saw the BMW parked there with Derrick just getting out of it. A white Mercedes parked opposite flashed its lights once. Then Joseph was past the entrance and had lost sight of what was going on.

Okay, very interesting, he thought.

He pulled up, leaning his bike against the wall next to the entrance of the Old Ink Press pub. Throwing out a prayer to whichever patron saint looked out for unlocked bikes in Oxford, the DI quickly doubled back to the car park.

He peered around the corner just in time to see Derrick getting into the passenger seat of the white Merc. As the interior briefly lit up, he caught sight of a blonde woman sitting in the driving seat, someone he recognised at once. It was none other than Chief Superintendent Amanda Kennan.

What the hell?

The DI quickly pulled his head back before he was spotted and took out his phone instead. He hit the video record button, and extended his hand so only that was showing around the corner as he captured the footage of whatever was about to unfold.

Joseph tried to order his thoughts. Why would Derrick be having a clandestine meeting with the Chief Superintendent? Unless...

The little fecker wouldn't dare, would he? But there were signs that his marriage to Kate might be in trouble. That could certainly explain why his ex-wife was spending so much time away from home. But Derrick having an affair? Seriously?

However, if that was the case, as much as he might love to tell Kate how she couldn't trust her husband, Joseph also knew he needed to steer well clear of this. If Derrick really was straying, this was none of his business, even as much as he might like it to be.

On the phone's screen, Joseph saw the passenger door of the Merc suddenly being thrown open and Derrick getting out, clutching a full-looking envelope in his hand.

'I'm not bloody interested!' he bellowed at Chief Superintendent Kennan, who was looking at him with an amused expression. Derrick threw the envelope at her. It broke open as it struck her arm, scattering fifty-pound notes inside the car like so much oversized confetti.

Derrick slammed the door shut and stalked back towards his car. It was at that moment that Joseph's phone rang. The DSU's gaze snapped towards the car park entrance as the DI quickly ducked back around the corner. He clutched his phone and killed the call, holding his breath. No sound of approaching footsteps met him, just a car door being slammed shut. Joseph seemed to be in the clear.

He quickly headed back to his bike and leapt onto it. His mobile vibrated in his hand again.

Not fecking now! the DI thought. As the BMW roared into life, Joseph killed the call again and quickly pedalled away before he was spotted.

It was only when he had taken several turns he finally dared to stop. Pulling his phone out, he saw Megan's name on the missed calls list. He immediately hit the call-back option.

'Hi, Joseph, a woman's body has been discovered up in Wytham Woods,' Megan said the moment she answered. 'PC John Thorpe was first on-scene, and is still on-site. He sounds totally traumatised. Amy is already on her way, and Chris is pulling together a murder investigation team, including our own good selves.'

'Foul play, then?'

'If you count a crossbow bolt through the eye, then definitely yes.'

'Fecking hell!'

'Oh, I know. Do you want me to swing past your boat to pick you up?' Megan asked.

'I'm already out and about on my bike. I'll see you at the station, and we can head out together from there. Just give me five.'

'Then I'll see you soon.'

But as Joseph rang off, despite the urgency, his mind briefly returned to what he had just witnessed—which was what, exactly? One thing was for sure, whatever that clandestine meeting had been about, it didn't look good at all for either Derrick or Chief Superintendent Kennan. But that would have to wait.

Stowing his phone, he set off at a rapid pace, heading towards St Aldates Police Station in the heart of Oxford.

CHAPTER FOUR

JOSEPH WAS at the wheel of the Volvo V90, with Megan grudgingly riding shotgun in the passenger seat. His rediscovered love of driving was proving to be an itch he needed to scratch whenever he had the opportunity.

Their car's headlights illuminated the small lane they were climbing towards Wytham Woods, where flashing blue lights were lighting up the canopy of trees at the top of the hill.

'It looks like the cavalry has beaten us to it,' Megan said, looking towards the light show.

'You can guarantee Amy is already there with her team,' Joseph replied. 'I swear she makes a point of arriving before us.'

'Knowing how driven she is, she probably has her sights set on getting there before Uniform one day as well,' Megan replied.

Joseph snorted. 'I honestly wouldn't put that past her. But talking of Uniform, you were saying that John sounded a bit shaken up after he discovered the woman's body?'

'Yeah, he definitely didn't sound like himself, almost monosyllabic.'

'Ah, seeing a murder victim can be hard on a young officer.' He raised an eyebrow at Megan.

'Don't worry, I'm not going to forget throwing my guts up when I saw poor Charlie Blackburn's body recovered from the river.'

Sadness filled Joseph at hearing Charlie's name. He'd been a homeless guy who'd been in the wrong place at the wrong time when his life was so needlessly taken by a psychopath, Helen Edwards.

'Chris practically wrote me off there and then, as not being cut out for being on a murder investigation,' Megan continued.

The DI glanced across at his police partner. 'Well, apart from my good self, these days he's probably your other number one fan. You've certainly more than proved yourself since. Besides, as I told you back then, plenty of officers lose their lunch at their first murder scene.'

'What about you?'

'Heck no, but that's only because I hadn't eaten and it was in the middle of the night. Anyway, what else do we know about the victim?'

'Not a lot apart from her name, Gabby Dawson. Apparently, she was a student at the Blavatnik School of Government. Isn't that the same college that Ellie goes to?'

'Indeed, it is.'

Joseph had to suppress an involuntary parental shudder; the murder of any young woman always felt too close to home. And of course, his imagination was already substituting Ellie for this latest victim. Unfortunately, that was an inevitable response for any police officer who was also a parent, attending the murder scene of a younger victim.

'What else do we know?' he asked.

'Apparently, Gabby's body was discovered by one of the foresters who works for Oxford University and helps maintain

Wytham Woods. He was heading to somewhere called the Swiss Chalet where he stays in a flat there.'

'Oh, I know the place. Hopefully, John will have already taken a preliminary statement from the man by the time we get there.'

Megan nodded as they passed through a large gate that had been left open, and into the wood. Joseph spotted a trail cam not unlike his own, mounted on one of the tall posts. If the murderer had come that way, hopefully the device might have picked something up.

A few moments later, they rounded a corner to see an imposing wood and stone three-storey building with a steeply sloped roofline. Two patrol cars were already there, as was Amy's SOC van.

'Bloody hell, that building looks like it's been imported straight out of a Grimm Fairytale,' Megan said.

'Ah, there's a good reason for that,' Joseph replied. 'Dylan told me that back in the nineteenth century a naturalist called Charles Elton built it to do research work. He imported the building from Switzerland. Later, a rich family bought the woods and the chalet, and their daughter used to play in it like an oversized doll's house.'

Megan pulled a sceptical face as Joseph parked. 'You're joking?'

'Apparently not, although admittedly it puts my birthday presents for Ellie back in the day of Lego Harry Potter sets rather to shame.'

'I bet she enjoyed them just as much...' Megan's voice trailed away as she fully took in the tall building before them. 'No, who am I trying to kid? A house totally trumps a Lego set.'

'Aye, that is, unless the Lego house is so big, you could actually move in.'

Megan laughed as they got out of the Volvo. 'Now there's a thought.'

But any amusement dissolved as they spotted John heading towards them, his eyes haunted, face grey.

'Are you okay?' Joseph asked as the PC reached them.

'I've had better days, sir,' John replied, his voice tight.

The DI patted his shoulder. 'I can imagine.' Joseph's gaze travelled past the officer to the cordon tape and the incident tent that had been set up just beyond the building.

'So what exactly did you find when you first arrived, John?' Megan asked gently.

The PC cast a glance towards the SOC incident tent and involuntarily shuddered. 'The victim, Gabby Dawson, had been shot twice with a crossbow. A forester called...' He pulled a notepad out of his pocket and looked at it. 'Lloyd Young discovered her body when he arrived at the chalet where he's been sleeping for the last week.'

'Presumably, he has an alibi?' Megan asked.

John nodded. 'He was actually with his mates at the pub in the two hours before he returned to Wytham.'

'Okay, once we have a time of death from the post-mortem, and as long as his mates confirm his story, that's likely to put him in the clear,' Joseph said.

'Also, raising the alarm isn't the usual behaviour of a murderer,' Megan added.

'No doubt forensics will also confirm that. Let's check in with Amy to see what she's been able to dig up.' But before the detectives headed off, the DI dug into his pocket and took a Silvermint from his pack, before handing one to the young PC. 'I always find these help with the nausea.'

'It's certainly done the trick for me more times than I care to mention,' Megan added.

John nodded and popped the mint into his mouth, taking a deep breath as he sucked on it.

Joseph patted him on the shoulder again, before he and Megan walked off towards the large white tent erected by the SOC team.

Portable floodlights had been set up around the area, casting long, stark shadows from the boughs of the trees into the wood like long pointing fingers. Somehow they only helped intensify the surrounding veil of darkness the light didn't reach.

Part of Joseph's caveman brain half expected to see the light reflected in the eyes of wolves gazing back at him. But then, with the professional part of his brain taking the reins again, he noted that there was plenty of cover for any murderer to melt away into.

Amy was just outside the forensic tent. She spotted them heading over and waved.

'How's it looking?' Megan asked as they reached her.

Amy frowned.

Joseph frowned. 'That bad?'

'Strange, rather than bad,' she replied, her German accent accentuating the word *bad*.

'What do you mean?'

'You need to see for yourself, but in a moment.'

'Okay. I don't suppose you've been able to rule out Lloyd Young yet?'

Much to his surprise, she nodded.

'I don't know if you spotted it on the way up, but there is a security camera near the entrance. One of my team already checked the footage and, according to the timestamp, it confirms Lloyd arrived when he said he did. Based on the victim's body temperature, which had dropped by just under three degrees Celsius, it suggests she's been dead roughly three hours. So within that frame, it puts Lloyd in the clear, unless we turn up something else to directly link him to her murder.'

'I don't suppose there were any other cars, or anyone on foot for that matter, caught by that camera?' Megan asked.

'Unfortunately not, and the forester also told us about the other trail cams at the other gates into Wytham, but we checked and it's the same story. That suggests whoever the murderer is, they probably knew about the cameras. They probably climbed over the high fence bordering the woods, somewhere they couldn't be recorded.'

'Assuming they're not still hiding somewhere here in the woods,' Megan said.

'Exactly, and that's why dog teams are already combing the woods,' Amy replied. 'But there's one piece of curious evidence that's already come to light, which is what I meant by strange, that I'd like your opinions on. But first, if you could do the usual.' The SOCO gestured towards an open crate filled with forensic suits.

A short while later, suitably suited and booted, Joseph and Megan followed Amy into the large forensic tent.

Illuminated by more lights inside was a silver Fiat 500 with scrape marks and a dented wing, suggesting it had been in the wars over the years. Another SOCO with a camera was squatting down on the other side of the vehicle, taking photos of something neither detective could see. They followed Amy to get a look at what it was.

Joseph found himself taking an involuntary breath when he saw the young woman. Her right hand had been pinned to the car's door by a crossbow bolt, leaving her raised arm hanging from it like a broken marionette. But it was where the second bolt had hit that really sent a shudder down the DI's spine.

The projectile was buried almost up to its flight feathers in the woman's eye, smashing the soft tissues into a pulp and shoving her head backwards as it had been propelled into the optical cavity and the brain behind it. A trail of blood had run down over her cheekbone and across her chin while another trail ran towards her hair and down her jaw. From there it had poured over the coat she was wearing, to finally pool beneath her.

'Jesus H. Christ,' Joseph muttered. 'Please tell me that shot killed her instantly?'

'No doubt,' Amy replied. 'However, we're already as certain as we can be that the victim was shot first in the hand and would have been in agony before her assailant finished her off.'

The DI nodded as he slipped a Silvermint beneath his mask into his mouth as nausea threatened to take hold. No wonder John had been so badly traumatised. When he offered a mint to Megan, she shook her head. It seemed his junior colleague was already outgrowing her mentor in at least this respect.

Then Joseph noticed the device mounted on the strap of the rucksack the woman was wearing. 'Is that one of those action cameras?'

'Yes, and before you ask, as soon as we're finished surveying the murder scene, we'll be taking and analysing any footage we find on it.'

'But why would she be wearing one in the first place?' Megan asked.

'No idea yet, but hopefully what's on there might explain that,' Amy replied.

The DC nodded as she squatted next to the woman for a closer look. 'I can tell you one thing for sure, unless her murderer was standing right next to her, whoever fired those crossbow bolts was a crack shot.'

'Maybe that's a clue in itself,' Amy replied. 'Is there an archery club in Oxford?'

'Indeed, there is,' Joseph replied. 'I think they hold regular weekend shoots on the rugby fields in North Hinksey Village.'

'Hopefully when it's not also being used for rugby?' Amy asked with a small smile.

'Yes, that could get very messy quickly, although that could be a new sport in its own right,' Joseph replied. But his sense of humour drained away as he returned his attention to the poor woman sitting dead at his feet.

Megan, without even blinking, leaned in for a closer look at the victim's pinned hand. 'Hang on, that's an odd-looking crossbow bolt.'

Amy gave her an approving look. 'And that's exactly what I wanted your opinions on.'

Joseph cast his eye over the projectile, but it looked entirely normal to him. 'What's wrong with it?'

'If you look closely, you can see the wooden shaft is tapered towards the fletching and the nock at the end,' the DC replied.

'*Nock, fletching,* since when did you become an expert, Megan?' Amy asked.

'Since I used to be in the school archery club. Mind you, I was totally rubbish at it, but I can still find my way around a bow, although less so a crossbow.'

'Just for a minute, I thought I was out of a job,' Amy replied. 'Anyway, this isn't the first time we've had experience dealing with a crossbow wound. Joseph, do you remember that farmer who shot his wife with one whilst she was sleeping in her bed?'

'How could I forget? He was convinced she was having an affair and decided to take matters into his own hands.'

'Well, that's an extreme step by any measure,' Megan said. 'Firing at a target is one thing, but a person...' She looked down at the dead woman and shook her head.

'Quite,' Amy replied. 'But looking at the power of both these shots, I'd say these were fired by a hunting crossbow. And this tapering you noticed on the bolts, Megan, might suggest they're custom-made.'

Intrigued, Joseph also leaned in for a closer look. Then he spotted something gold and glittering on the shaft of the bolt just at the point it had penetrated the woman's hand.

He pointed towards it. 'What's that?'

Amy's forehead creased. 'Hang on.' She waved across at the SOCO with a camera in his hand. 'Can I borrow your camera for a moment for a closeup here?' The man handed over the Canon SLR with a ring flash mounted on its lens.

She lined up the camera, zoomed in on the shaft, and pressed the shutter release. One blinding pop of the flashgun later, the two detectives were looking at the zoomed-in image she'd just taken. Gold lettering spelled out the words 'Winsor and Newton.'

'Is that the name of the bolt manufacturer?' Amy asked.

But Joseph was already shaking his head. 'No, that's the name of an art supplier.'

'And how would you know that gem of information?' Megan asked.

'That would be down to Ellie. She was heavily into art when she was at school. And here's the thing. I actually bought her a decent set of Winsor and Newton sable brushes one Christmas. They cost a small fortune, but I remember they had similar gold lettering on them.'

Amy frowned. 'Hang on, are you seriously suggesting the shaft of these crossbow bolts are adapted from paint brushes?'

Joseph rubbed the back of his neck as he turned the thought over in his mind. 'As unlikely as it is, it would seem so.'

'But why go to all that bother when the murderer could have just bought a crossbow bolt off the shelf?' Megan asked.

Joseph shrugged. 'Maybe it's a play on the idea of the pen being mightier than the sword, albeit in this case, a paintbrush.'

'It certainly points towards an intriguing motivation,' Amy said. 'But there's one other curious thing we found close by and we're fairly certain it's linked to what happened here.' She headed over to a box in the corner and took out an evidence bag. In it, Joseph could see a purple toy gun.

'Why on Earth did she have a Nerf gun on her? Surely she's a bit old for that sort of thing?' Megan asked.

Joseph gave her a straight look. 'Have you ever met an Oxford student, especially during freshers' week?'

'Good point. But why carry one out here in the woods?'

At that moment a female SOCO officer entered the tent, carrying another evidence bag. 'Amy, one of the dog team just turned up something interesting.' She handed the bag to her. 'The dog followed the scent straight from here to the fence and discovered it on the route.'

Amy held up the bag, peering at the blue plastic token with a ripped eyehole inside it. 'There seems to be some sort of markings on it.'

Joseph leaned in for a closer look and took in the design—a hand holding a dagger with a stylised eye engraved into the palm.

'What's that all about?' Megan asked.

'No idea.' Joseph said.

'The fact the dog led its handler straight to it is significant, but there's also this...' Amy leaned down next to the dead woman, hooking a fine silver chain with her gloved finger. She raised it to show a small section of plastic hanging from it, the same colour as the token in the evidence bag. Also, more significantly, it matched the shape of a section that had been torn out of it.

'I think that's pretty conclusive then,' Joseph said.

'So you think the murderer took it as a memento—' Megan started to say, but was cut off by a shout from outside.

That was followed by John's voice. 'I'm sorry, sir, you can't go in there.'

'But Gabby's not been answering her phone. And when I saw all your lights in the wood and then this tent... Please tell me this has nothing to do with her.'

Joseph nodded to Megan, and the two detectives, steeling themselves for whatever this was, headed outside.

John was physically holding back a young man in his early twenties with blond hair and wearing a trench coat.

'What's going on?' Joseph asked as they headed over to assist the constable.

'My girlfriend hasn't been answering my calls. We had an argument at the art studio in the woods where I've been working, and she stormed off. Then I saw you guys, and this set up...' He gestured towards the tent. 'Please tell me Gabby isn't in there. Tell me she didn't do something stupid!'

'What do you mean?' Megan asked.

'Like, I don't know... take her own life or something.'

Joseph exchanged a frown with Megan.

The man noticed and put his hands on his head. 'No, no, no! This is all my fucking fault!' He sank to his knees, tears filling his eyes.

But even as Joseph took in the man's obvious grief, the mention of the Wytham artist's studio had already set his cogs spinning. Unfortunately, that almost certainly meant this lad's night was about to get a lot worse.

CHAPTER FIVE

Through the windows of St Aldates Police Station, a brown smudge was building on the horizon, the first hint of a new sunrise threatening to make an appearance.

Joseph sipped the strong tea Megan had just given him. 'Thanks for this. I seriously need the caffeine hit before we head in to interview Ryan Slattery.'

Megan sipped her own brew and nodded. 'You really think he murdered his girlfriend? The way he broke down outside the forensic tent didn't look put on to me.'

'True, but even that could have been a performance for our benefit. But I'm trying to keep an open mind here, even though the circumstantial evidence is already fairly damning. He also condemned himself, by saying he'd just had an argument with Gabby.'

The DC nodded. 'Not to mention this also falls into the classic territory of the victim knowing their murderer.'

'Aye, right now it isn't looking good for the lad. I mean, just happening to be an artist and the crossbow bolt being made from a converted paintbrush is far too bizarre to just be a coincidence. But even so, we assume nothing heading into the interview, because, for all we know, Amy will uncover some astonishing forensic evidence to clear the lad.'

'You really believe that?'

'Not really, but I'm not going to assume he's guilty yet either, at least not until we've had an opportunity to question him.'

'And right there is why you make such an excellent mentor,' Megan replied.

Joseph made a show of looking over his shoulder and then pointing at himself. 'Who, me? Bad habits and all?'

Megan smiled. 'Bad habits and all.'

The DI smiled back, then glanced at the clock that was crawling towards five-thirty a.m. 'Okay, I think we've probably allowed our suspect to stew sufficiently in his own juices. So far at least, he's waved off asking for a solicitor, because he just thinks he's helping us with our enquiries and nothing more. You never know, we may trip him up and get a full confession before Chris and the others turn up.'

'And then celebrate with a cheeky full English at Wallace's?'

'Now you're talking my language,' Joseph replied, as they headed for the door.

When they entered interview room two, Ryan looked up at them from the table with a hollowed-out expression.

'Do you fancy a tea or coffee?' Joseph asked as they sat down.

'No, water is fine,' Ryan replied with a husky voice, as he reached out for his glass and took a sip.

Joseph didn't need to be a detective to realise the lad had been crying. That was evident by the red rings around his eyes and the pile of discarded tissues in the bin in the corner. Of course, over the years, he'd seen murderers put on some stellar performances worthy of an Oscar. But his instinct was already telling him this was a genuine display of grief. There again, it could equally be the rush of guilt of someone who had just murdered their girlfriend. Either way, hopefully, they were about to get to the bottom of it.

'Before we start, are you absolutely sure you wouldn't like to have a solicitor present?' Megan asked, as she powered up the tablet she'd brought with her.

Joseph suppressed a grimace, even though double-checking was the right thing to do. The truth was, it often made their lives easier the longer a solicitor wasn't present in an interview. However, what was easy for them wasn't always the best approach, and it didn't hurt to be reminded of that occasionally.

Ryan was already shaking his head. 'No, I'm good. Please, let's get this out of the way as quickly as possible. I need to get out of here and let Gabby's family and friends know that she's...' He stared down at his hands clasped together on the table.

'Don't worry about her parents,' Joseph replied. 'Local officers in Nottingham have already been dispatched to let them know in person. Something like this should only be done over the phone as a last resort.'

Ryan nodded as a tremble passed through his body. 'I still can't believe Gabby's gone.'

The way his voice wavered, guilty or not, Joseph felt a lump form in his own throat out of sympathy. Whatever else the DI was, his heart certainly wasn't made of stone, and he was already certain there was nothing fake about Ryan's reaction.

Megan caught Joseph's eye. 'Shall we make a start?'

He nodded, leaned over, and pressed the button on the recorder on the table. A red light blinked on.

'DI Joseph Stone and DC Megan Anderson, commencing the initial interview with Ryan Slattery,' Joseph said. Then he looked at Ryan. 'Let's begin with you telling us about the last time you saw Gabby Dawson?'

'That was yesterday evening. She visited me in the Wytham

Woods studio, where I've been the artist in residence for the last week.'

'And what time was that, exactly?'

'Around seven p.m. She actually arrived to assassinate me.'

'Sorry?' Megan said, staring at Ryan.

He quickly held up his hands. 'Not literally. We're both members of the Oxford Assassins' Syndicate.'

Joseph's eyes widened. 'That doesn't sound much better.'

'I'm not explaining myself well here. It's a student club where the members target each other with Nerf guns. Some even use normal pens as stand-ins for poisoned pens. A successful hit counts as a successful,'—he made air quotes—'*assassination*. You can take out your target anywhere you choose. Mind you, the tutors take rather a dim view if it happens during a lecture.'

'I expect they do,' Joseph said. 'And you're saying that's why Gabby turned up at the art studio yesterday, and why we found one of those Nerf guns on her body?'

'Exactly. We both thought it would be good fun, especially taking part as girlfriend and boyfriend during a game...' The smile that had started to form on his lips gave way to the stark reality of the new world Ryan suddenly found himself plunged into.

'And Gabby turned up to try and shoot you with a Nerf gun. Is that what you're saying?' Megan asked.

'She didn't just try, she succeeded. But out of the two of us, she was way more sneaky, so was always going to win. I didn't stand a chance, really.'

'And does this have anything to do with that?' Megan slipped a photograph of the blue plastic pendant over the desk to Ryan.

He looked at it for a moment, then away. 'I've never seen that before.'

Joseph immediately sensed Ryan was lying. 'Are you absolutely sure about that?'
Ryan met his gaze and rubbed his neck. 'Totally.'
Definitely lying, but why? Joseph thought.
'So then what happened after Gabby shot you?' Megan asked. 'You said something about you both arguing?'
'Yes, and it wasn't pretty. It got totally out of hand and Gabby stormed off.'
'Okay, so what was this argument about exactly?' Joseph asked.
'Just personal stuff.' Ryan squeezed his eyes shut.
'Care to elaborate on that?'
Ryan shook his head. 'Not really.'
'I see,' the DI replied. Why was Ryan being evasive? He sat back in his seat, studying the man before them in an attempt to get the measure of him. 'And what time did Gabby leave you?'
'About five minutes after she arrived.'
'And I assume you didn't accompany her back to her car?'
Ryan's head snapped back up and he glared at Joseph. 'Of course I bloody didn't. This wouldn't have happened if I had. I could kick myself for not insisting on walking her to her car. But the thing is Wytham Woods is basically deserted after it closes to the public at night. How was I meant to know some psychopath was waiting out there in the woods to murder my girlfriend?'
It had been obvious since they'd told him Gabby was dead that Ryan blamed himself for what had happened. Either that, or the art student really was an incredible actor. Then there was the evidence already unearthed, which was pretty damning.
The previous night, Amy's team headed to the art studio to gather any additional evidence they could. One thing that had quickly come to light was something directly linking Ryan to the murder of his partner.

Joseph placed the evidence bag on the table. Amy had made a point of handing it to him in person before she headed off to the lab with the other forensic material they'd recovered from the crime scene.

A confused expression filled Ryan's face as he looked at what was inside it. 'That looks like one of my paint brushes?'

'That's because it is,' Joseph replied.

'And why do you have it exactly?'

'Maybe you can tell us?' Megan said, fixing Ryan with a steady stare.

The art student looked between the detectives. 'I've absolutely no idea what you're talking about.'

'Really?' the DC replied, a hard tone creeping into her voice.

Joseph felt a surge of pride as Megan took over the role of bad cop. Once upon a time, she would have baulked at the idea. But it came naturally to her now when the occasion called for it.

Joseph tapped his finger on the table. 'Oh, come on, Ryan, you'll make life a lot easier for yourself if—'

A knock on the door made her pause mid-sentence. The DI checked the light above the door was illuminated, which would be mirrored by one outside in the corridor to indicate an interview was in progress. That meant, if someone was knocking, it was urgent enough to warrant this interruption. When a second knock came, this time louder, any doubt about its importance was swept away.

Megan looked over at Joseph. 'Shall I deal with it?'

'Please.' Joseph nodded. 'Pausing interview with Ryan Slattery at five forty-five a.m.' He leaned across and hit a button on the recorder as Megan headed out of the door, closing it behind her.

Joseph could just hear Amy talking to Megan in hushed

tones. That immediately raised his interest. That meant the SOC officer had rushed straight back from the lab.

Whilst they waited, Ryan stared at the wall with the zoned-out expression of someone in shock. The DI had certainly seen that expression plenty of times on the faces of relatives when he'd had to break the news to them that a loved one had been killed. It was always either shocked silence, or they'd break down then and there. Much like Ryan had at the crime scene.

'Are you sure I can't get you anything?' Joseph asked gently. 'The coffee is shite, but I could rustle up a decent cup of tea for you.'

That didn't raise so much as a smile from Ryan, who blinked and slowly shook his head.

The more that Joseph studied him, the more his instinct said the lad might actually be innocent.

The door opened and Megan entered the room again. Joseph briefly caught Amy looking in. She gave him a thumbs up before she was lost from view as the door was closed again. Then he spotted the new evidence bag that the DC was carrying as she placed it on the desk.

Both his and Ryan's eyes immediately shot to it. It contained a crossbow bolt with a barbed hunting tip soaked with blood. That suggested Amy had brought it directly to them from the pathology lab, meaning that it was something significant and urgent.

He glanced at Megan with a questioning look. She widened her eyes at him briefly as she leaned across and pressed the recorder button again. As the red light blinked on, she turned towards Ryan, who was staring at the crossbow bolt with considerable confusion.

'Recommencing interview at five forty-seven am,' Joseph said, for the benefit of the recorder.

Megan quickly wrote on the tablet, before showing it to the DI. *'Can you let me lead the interview for a bit?'*

Joseph nodded, immediately intrigued about what Amy had been able to dig up.

Megan leaned forward, elbows on the table, expression stern. 'Can you tell us what's in this evidence bag I've just placed on the table, Ryan?'

'Yes, it looks like some sort of short arrow...' His gaze snapped back to Megan's. 'Is this connected to Gabby's death?'

'Why don't you tell us?'

His eyes widened. 'You're saying you think I had something to do with Gaby's murder?'

'Come on, cut the act.' Megan pointed towards the crossbow bolt. 'Go on, take a closer look at that and tell me what you see?'

Ryan gave her a confused look, before leaning in to study the bolt. He shuddered when he spotted the lethal blood-covered tip. But then his expression widened when he noticed the writing on the shaft. Then he glanced back to the first evidence bag with one of his paintbrushes in it.

'Hang on, that arrow looks like it's been made from the same type of sable paint brushes I use.'

Megan crossed her arms. 'Like, or exactly the same?'

'What are you driving at?' Ryan replied, his expression growing wary.

Joseph noticed the black residue of the powder used to take a fingerprint on the side of the shaft of the crossbow bolt, and he knew exactly why Amy had rushed over, presumably receiving the bolt back from Doctor Reynolds once the autopsy had been finished. He sat back in his chair, waiting for Megan to hit Ryan with the evidence discovered by the SOC team.

'When this bolt was checked for prints, guess whose they found on it?' Megan said.

Ryan blinked several times. 'You can't be serious?'

'Oh, I'm afraid I am. Several prints from your fingers and thumb on your right hand were lifted from the shaft, indicating you handled it. Look, if you just confess now, it will make all our lives easier, especially yours.'

'I don't understand. This is the first time I've seen that arrow, let alone touched it.'

'So how do you explain your prints being present on the crossbow bolt that killed Gabby?' Megan asked.

Ryan's shoulders dropped as he gave the DI a hopeless look. 'I honestly don't know.'

'I see. In that case...' Joseph nodded to Megan. 'You best do the honours.'

The DC sat up straighter, looking the suspect directly in the eyes. 'Ryan Slattery, I'm going to caution you. You do not have to say anything. But it may harm your defence if you do not mention when questioned something which you later rely on in court. Anything you do say may be given in evidence.'

Ryan's head jerked back like they'd physically struck him across the face. Then he put his hands on his head. 'This just can't be happening.'

'I'm afraid it is, son,' Joseph said. 'I know you decided to waive a solicitor at the start, but I strongly advise you to get yourself one now.'

'I can't afford that. I'm a student. I've barely enough money to pay my rent as it is.'

'Then we call in a duty solicitor who will be able to give you free legal advice.'

'Yes, okay, I'll do that.'

'Okay, then I'm terminating the interview at five-fifty a.m.,' Joseph said. He reached across and turned the recorder off. 'Now what do you say to that cup of tea, Ryan?'

The lad managed a vague nod.

'I'll rustle one up for you, pronto. Another officer will be along in a minute to escort you back to your cell. Meanwhile, we'll get straight on sorting out that solicitor for you.'

'Thank you,' Ryan replied, in a small voice.

The moment the two detectives headed out of the interview room, Amy emerged from the viewing room on the other side of the one-way mirror, where she must have been watching.

'So it looks like that fingerprint is going to be the clincher for the prosecution,' she said.

'I'm not so sure,' Joseph replied. 'Something still feels seriously off here.'

To the DI's surprise, Megan nodded. 'I agree. This was almost too easy.'

'What is that English expression you like to use?' Amy said, looking between them. 'Oh yes, don't look a gift horse in the mouth.'

'Maybe, but even if Ryan's prints were found on that crossbow bolt, let alone using one of his own brushes, it really doesn't make any sense,' Joseph said. 'Surely to turn a paintbrush into an arrow would take a lot of planning, so why not wear gloves? Not to mention he used one of his own bloody paintbrushes that could easily be linked back to him.'

'Yes, and why go to all that trouble and not buy an off-the-shelf crossbow bolt, anyway?' Megan added.

'Maybe there was some personal significance between Ryan and Gabby for him doing that,' Amy suggested. 'Mind you, we also haven't found any sign of the crossbow yet, which would be the clincher if we found Ryan's prints on that as well.'

Joseph nodded. 'That's the thing, even with the prints, I'm not sure we're anywhere near a watertight case yet. I can already see the defence having a field day with that if CPS allows this to go ahead to trial as things stand.'

'But you just read him the riot act,' Amy said.

'Aye, I did. And it won't hurt to keep him in custody a while longer to double check we really have our man, or perhaps confirm we haven't.'

Amy looked at the two detectives and slowly nodded. 'Then I will make it my team's mission to discover what evidence we can to prove Ryan's innocence or guilt.'

'We can always rely on you for that,' Megan said.

Joseph nodded, his gaze lingering on Amy, the woman who had come to mean so much to him. 'Okay, I have a cup of tea to make for Ryan. Who else also fancies a cuppa?'

'Count me in,' Megan said. 'I don't know what it is. You use the same teabags as the rest of us, but your brews are always some of the best.'

'That will be down to the Gaelic charm I use on the teabags to extract the best possible flavour. That, or the Irish mist I use instead of water.'

Amy laughed. 'Right.'

'Did someone say tea?' Chris asked from behind them.

'I'll add you to the list,' Joseph replied. 'Anyway, I'm glad you're here, Boss. We have someone we've been interviewing in connection to the murder of that woman last night in the woods.'

Chris gave him an impressed look. 'You already have someone in custody?'

'Yes, but even though we've formally cautioned him, we still need to kick the tyres a bit more.'

'In that case, when you've made that tea, you'd better get me up to speed,' Chris replied. 'Apparently, for my sins, Derrick wants me to be the SIO on this investigation.'

'Good, because something is telling me that this case isn't going to be straightforward,' Joseph replied, as they heard sobbing coming from the other side of the interview door.

The DI exchanged a look with the others, before heading to the kitchen. Maybe he would give the lad one of the biscuits from his personal supply as well.

CHAPTER SIX

Chris looked across his desk at Joseph, Megan, and Amy. 'From everything you've told me so far about Ryan Slattery, it sounds like you've already found our man.'

'Yes, I know it certainly looks that way on the surface, and he was definitely lying about not recognising the cheap plastic pendant that turned up at the scene,' Joseph replied.

'What's the significance of that?' Chris asked.

'We're still trying to work it out, but it looks like it was torn from a silver chain Gabby was wearing. Presumably dropped by the murderer as they fled the scene, which may or may not be Ryan. Here's the thing. Despite how it's looking for the lad, I get the impression he may actually be innocent. There are some things that don't quite stack up here. If Ryan really did kill Gabby Dawson, doesn't it strike you that he's highly incompetent as a murderer? After all, why go to all the trouble of creating a unique bolt made from his own paintbrush?'

Megan nodded. 'Yes, if Ryan had confessed to Gabby's murder straight away, then it might make sense. But why leave such an obvious clue linking him to her murder, especially if he was going to attempt to get away with it?'

'But what about Ryan's print your team found on the arrow, Amy?' Chris asked.

'It's a definite match,' the SOCO replied. 'However...'

Then Joseph knew exactly what Amy was about to suggest. 'Oh, you absolute genius.'

'Sorry, I haven't actually said anything yet, although I'm happy to take the compliment.'

'But I know the way your brain works. You were about to say that's why they used one of Ryan's paint brushes. It would have been covered with his fingerprints. What better way to frame the lad than by stealing the paintbrush from the cabin where he was working, carefully converting it to a crossbow bolt to preserve the prints, and then using it to shoot Gabby.'

'Okay, maybe you do know the way I think,' Amy said, giving Joseph a small smile.

Chris looked between them as their gazes lingered on one another a moment longer than was professionally necessary. Joseph caught the brief grin on his boss's face as he tore his gaze away from the SOCO.

Megan, also fully aware of the DI's relationship with Amy, quickly dived in to keep the conversation on track. 'So you're saying that Ryan could have been framed?'

'I certainly don't think we can rule it out at this stage,' Joseph replied. 'Also, going to the trouble of converting a paintbrush in the first place, suggests the murderer had some kind of strange motivation.'

'Such as?' Chris asked.

Megan looked off into the middle distance. 'It almost has a theatrical flair to it, like...' Her eyes widened. 'Like maybe another member of the Assassins' Syndicate who wanted to show off.'

'You're suggesting someone has literally turned murdering someone into part of a game?' Amy asked.

'Possibly. I certainly think it's worth taking a closer look at the other members of this Assassins' Syndicate.'

'You do realise that still includes Ryan?'

'Maybe it does, but it also widens the scope of our investigation.'

Chris sucked his cheeks in. 'What about this forester who was first at the scene of the crime?'

'Everything has checked out with his story so far,' Megan said.

'We should still pull Lloyd in for questioning, just to be sure. I don't suppose you managed to recover any boot or shoe prints near the murder site, Amy? Just in case they're a match.'

'If only our life would have been made so easy. Unfortunately, with the lack of rain recently, the ground was bone dry, so we had no joy there. All we can hope is that maybe Gabby struggled with her attacker and when Rob does the autopsy, he manages to recover some of the murderer's DNA on her body.'

Chris nodded. 'Okay, from what I'm hearing, it doesn't sound like this is the open and shut case it first looked like. Apart from anything else, I can already hear the CPS saying it would be a major punt trying to secure a prosecution based on the existing evidence alone. Ryan's print on the arrow might be enough, but to be certain, we need more than that, especially if someone really is trying to frame him. You can be sure that's exactly the line his defence will take in court.'

'The Digital Forensic Unit will obviously run a full technical forensic sweep, looking at both Gabby's and Ryan's phones and computers to see if they can dig up any more evidence,' Amy said.

'Especially anything that could be seen as an actual motive for Ryan murdering his girlfriend,' Joseph replied. 'We do know they argued, although Ryan is being cagey about what exactly.

We also need to try and draw up a list of who might have had access to a crossbow.'

Chris pulled a face. 'That's not exactly easy when a crossbow doesn't have to be registered in this country.'

'Aye, but we can talk to the archery club to see if they might have any ideas, or at least suggest local suppliers where the murderer might have picked up the weapon.'

'Good idea. In the meantime, we will hold Ryan for the maximum thirty-six hours. Whether we can move ahead with a formal charge of murder will be down to whatever you can collectively dig up within that time frame.'

'Then what sort of manpower can you assign to help us?' Joseph asked.

Chris grimaced. 'I'm afraid not a lot for now, at least until you can dig up something more solid. For the time being, it will just be you and Megan. Although I'm already working on Derrick to make Ian and Sue available as well.'

Joseph sighed and nodded, understanding the real reason why.

Most of the team wasn't available thanks to a recent spate of bank robberies. They'd become something of a pet project for Derrick, who'd assigned nearly everyone to surveillance operations of any bank likely to be targeted. In Joseph's opinion, throwing people at the case without any real intelligence to direct their efforts didn't make a lot of sense, especially from a budgetary point of view. That was what usually dictated the superintendent's approach to any case. But at least that suggested the bank robberies had nothing to do with the Night Watchmen. Joseph suspected if they had been, and his instinct about Derrick was right, the DSU would be doing everything in his power to limit the scope of any investigation.

One thing was for certain, if the big man really was guilty, the sooner that gobshite was removed from active service, the better it would be for everyone working at St Aldates. And if Chris decided to go for his job, he would certainly have Joseph's support. But right now, he also had a murder investigation to deal with.

'We better get to it,' Joseph said as he stood.

But Chris was already holding up his hand. 'Just how much sleep have you and Megan had since last night?'

Joseph shrugged. 'Basically zero.'

Megan nodded.

'Then I need you at your sharpest. I want you both to head home, get at least a few hours' sleep, freshen up, and then come back in for ten a.m.'

'But you've already reminded us that the clock is running,' Megan said.

'And that's why I will hold the fort here, doing some initial digging into Ryan and Gabby's backgrounds, whilst you both catch some shuteye.'

'And what about me?' Amy asked, giving him a hard blue-eyed stare.

'Well, as you aren't under my command, if I suggested you get some sleep as well, would you actually listen?'

'Of course not,' she replied. 'That's what coffee's for.' With an amused expression, she followed Joseph and Megan out of Chris's office.

Megan headed over to her desk to grab her bag. As Joseph did the same, Amy reached out and held his arm, leaning her head in towards his.

'Of course, I'm obviously tempted to come back to yours, but I'm not sure how much sleep either of us would get.'

'You're telling me,' he replied, grinning. Then he made a shooing gesture. 'Away with you, temptress, and see what else you can dig up for us once you're fuelled up with caffeine.'

Amy smiled at him, squeezing his hand, before heading

away. She gave him a backward wave over her shoulder, with an extra hip swing thrown in, no doubt for his benefit.

That woman, Joseph thought to himself, his smile growing wider as he watched her disappear out of the door.

Despite Joseph's reservations a few months earlier, even if they did continue to lead very separate lives because of work, things were definitely good between them.

Megan was stifling a yawn as she materialised next to him. 'I can drop you and your bike off on my way back home if you like?'

'That would be grand,' Joseph said, gathering up his things.

CHAPTER SEVEN

A PING ROUSED Joseph from his sleep. He closed his mouth, which had been open, dribble leaking from the corner, just to add to his *old man waking from the land of nod* look.

Tux, the black and white cat he'd inherited during the Burning Man case, roused himself from his favourite sleeping spot at the foot of Joseph's bed. He stretched his front legs out, before padding over to mew directly in Joseph's face, obviously believing a second breakfast was in the offing.

The DI, trying to ignore the insistent head bumps the cat was now giving him, looked at his phone's screen to see it had been a text from Amy that had woken him.

'When you're awake, you may find this of interest...'

He really needed to learn to put his phone on mute when he was trying to catch up on sleep. The DI scanned down the rest of the message.

'When Jacobs was doing the autopsy on Gabby, he found nothing we wouldn't have expected. And as regards the plastic pendant, at first, I thought it might be 3D printed, but it doesn't appear to be. There is a seam round the edge, suggesting it was cast and probably mass-produced. Unfortunately, there's no

match for it on the database. But I'm attaching a photo, just in case it's some sort of occult symbol. Knowing Dylan has helped out before, I thought you might want to run it past him for his professional opinion, as he's something of an expert in that area.'

Tux sat on Joseph's chest and gave him an indignant look because his breakfast needs hadn't been immediately attended to. The DI, blurry-eyed, doing his best to ignore the cat's gimlet stare, opened the photo Amy had sent.

To his eyes at least, it looked more like a toy you might pull out of a Christmas cracker rather than a piece of jewellery someone studying a degree at the Blavatnik School of Government might wear. A heart maybe, even a carpe diem motto for a woman at Oxford, but this?

Then he spotted the second message that Amy had sent. 'We also retrieved the footage from the action camera Gabby was wearing. The only thing recorded on it showed her shooting Ryan with the Nerf gun from a tree she climbed earlier that night, which corroborates his version of events. She and Ryan also mentioned something about freerunning and climbing, before she turned the camera off.'

That last sentence rang a bell. Something about people who saw themselves as athletes and set up crazy courses through cities. The previous year, there'd been a flood of reports from the public about seeing people running over the roofs of some of the colleges. No one had been arrested for it because by the time the police turned up, the suspects had been long gone.

Joseph glanced at the clock to see it was six a.m. Now, thanks to Amy's message, he was wide awake. However, that wasn't the only reason he wasn't going to get back to sleep anytime soon. His brain was already fixating on the subject of his other investigation.

The DI pulled up his phone's photo library and selected the video he had taken of Derrick in the car park the night before with Chief Superintendent Kennan. He watched it for what had to be the twentieth time, pausing on the frame when Derrick had thrown the envelope of money back at her. He took a screenshot of the still frame, clearly showing the two serving officers, then sent it to the Wi-Fi printer Ellie and John had helped him set up on his boat. A moment later, he had a hard copy of the photo in his hand.

Joseph turned over the pinboard on the boat's cabin wall to reveal his very own secret evidence board mounted on the other side. It was filled with everything he'd uncovered during his investigation into Derrick and his possible involvement with the Night Watchmen. Other than his instinct that something was seriously off with his commanding officer, he hadn't found any real evidence. But thanks to the photo in his hand, that had now changed.

As he took a step back to consider the board, he almost tripped over Tux, who had taken up position standing right behind him. When the cat gave him an indignant miaow, in the way of an apology, Joseph finally filled up the cat's bowl. That job done, he then set to work on what the human on the boat now desperately needed—coffee. With the kettle on the stove, and with a certain amount of satisfaction, Joseph added the photo of Derrick and Chief Superintendent Kennan to the board.

The DI looked at the newspaper clippings about the ambush that had left two officers badly injured and their prisoner killed. He was certain to the depth of his bones that someone had tipped off the Night Watchmen about the witness who was being transferred. At the time, the finger had been pointed at a dodgy solicitor tipping the syndicate off, but Joseph wasn't so sure. His instinct, then and now, was that Derrick had something to do with it.

He focused his attention on the new photo of the DSU

throwing the money back at the chief. Although it wasn't damning proof, at least on first impression, it wasn't a good look either. If there was an innocent explanation for a clandestine meeting in a pub car park involving the handing over of a large amount of cash, the DI certainly couldn't wait to hear it.

Guilty is as guilty does, he thought to himself as the kettle whistled on the stove.

Joseph got to work grinding some Brazilian Santos beans from Taylors in the Covered Market in Oxford. It was a roast that managed to hit all the right notes to his discerning coffee aficionado palette. He was just filling his cafetière with this elixir of life, when Tux stopped eating from his bowl and his ears pricked up. A moment later, a knock came from the cabin door.

'I do believe I heard the jaunty whistle of your kettle a moment ago,' Professor Dylan Shaw's voice called out. 'Making coffee, by any chance?'

'How did you guess?' Joseph said, opening the door to his friend and neighbour who lived on his own boat, *Avalon*, next door.

The grey-bearded face of the retired professor appeared, looking in at him from the cabin of the narrowboat. Behind him, sitting on the towpath, looking expectantly at the DI, were White Fang and Max, the terrier and beagle who belonged to the professor.

Dylan nodded towards his dogs. 'Permission for us all to come aboard? I come bearing gifts.' He nodded down at the tray covered with a tea towel in his hands.

Joseph was instantly intrigued. 'What have you got there?'

'All in good time, my friend.'

'Oh, the suspense is already killing me. Anyway...' With a slight bow and a flourish of his hand, he directed the man and his dogs to enter.

White Fang and Max immediately shot past the professor into the cabin to greet Tux. Thankfully, the dogs and cat had got on famously with each other from the first day they'd met. Tux rubbed along the flanks of both dogs as they both tried to smell his bum. Such is the strange world of the animal kingdom.

'I can see that your cat has really settled in now,' Dylan said. 'Mind you, he treats my boat as an extension of his new home here.'

'That's the life of a cat for you,' Joseph replied with a shrug. 'I still can't believe Norman and Clare Robinson somehow manipulated me into adopting him when they moved into that retirement village after their house burned down.'

'I'm not so sure *manipulated* is quite the right word. If I recall correctly, I'm pretty certain it was your good self who suggested the idea of you adopting Tux. Anyone would've thought the very idea of you losing your new housemate would have broken your heart.'

'I'm not admitting anything unless you drag me into a court of law,' Joseph said, reaching down and scratching Tux behind the ear, who leaned into the sign of affection from his *member of staff*.

Dylan chuckled. 'Talking about the Robinsons, how are they doing?'

'I spoke to Norman recently. Although they both miss their old home, they've settled into the retirement place really well. Apparently, Clare has started up a poker club and has been fleecing the other tenants.'

The professor snorted. 'We all need our hobbies in later life.' Then his nose twitched. 'Ah, Santos beans, I do believe, one of my favourites.'

'Good grief, are your nostrils that finely tuned?'

But a grin was filling the professor's face. 'Actually, I just read it on the side of the bag you left on the worktop.

Anyway, I think my gifts will go well with a cup of your excellent coffee.' With a flourish, he whipped the tea towel off the tray to reveal fragrant steam rising from a pile of Indian samosas.

'Wow, those smell fantastic. Your own creations?'

'Indeed they are, and even the pastry is homemade. I think I've nailed both the chicken and the veggie versions, but I need your verdict to be sure.'

'Then I'm honoured as always to be your guinea pig.'

'Good. Now try one of the chicken ones and let me know what you think.' The professor indicated the samosas nearest to the DI.

Joseph, who hadn't had breakfast yet, didn't need to be told twice. The moment he took his first bite, his mouth was flooded with an incredible mix of perfectly balanced spices woven into the potato and chicken filling.

His eyes widened as the full taste sensation hit him.

'Okay, you've done it again. I swear those are the best samosas I've had in my life, and I say that as a man who's had quite a few over the years.'

The professor beamed at him. 'Wonderful to hear. It's actually based on a family recipe one of my Indian students gave me. She made a large batch at the end of the final year as a thank you to her tutors. They were demolished within seconds of being left in the staff room.'

'I can see why,' Joseph said, as he took a second mouthful, which was just as delicious as the first.

Once the coffee was served and the two friends settled in for their alternative breakfast, something over Joseph's shoulder caught Dylan's attention.

'What's that now?' Dylan said.

When the DI glanced behind him, he realised his mistake—his homemade evidence board was still very much on display.

He quickly jumped up and turned it back around before the professor spotted Derrick's photo on it.

'Oh nothing, just something connected to a case I'm working on,' Joseph said.

The professor immediately narrowed his eyes at his friend. 'It's not like you not to share the details of a new case with me.'

Joseph's mind raced as he tried to come up with a plausible explanation. 'I'm still trying to get things straight in my mind before I'm ready to talk it through with you.'

But Dylan's eyes only narrowed further.

Joseph realised he needed to distract the professor before the man guessed he was deliberately keeping something from him. He really wasn't ready to talk about what he'd dug up on Derrick just yet. Thankfully, there was something that he did need to pick his friend's brain about and would be the perfect way to steer the subject to safer waters.

'Okay, if you insist.' Joseph quickly pulled up Amy's photo of the pendant and handed it to the professor.

'What have we got here?' Dylan asked, looking down at the screen through his half-moon specs.

'It was a plastic pendant discovered near the body of a woman who was found shot with a crossbow up in Wytham Woods.'

'Flipping Nora, the poor woman. And what, may I ask, is your current state of play with the investigation?'

'It's the usual merry-go-round. All the current evidence points towards her boyfriend murdering her, and that may be the end of it. But something isn't stacking up here. Amy just sent me this photo through and she was wondering if there was any possible occult connection with the knife and hand symbol on it?'

Dylan peered at the photo. 'The eye symbol in the hilt of the dagger is certainly very interesting.'

Joseph sat forward. 'You recognise it then?'

'The hand and eye symbol does remind me of the Hamsa symbol that's often seen in the Middle East and also in Africa. The idea is that it wards off evil.'

'And the dagger motif?'

'Well, daggers are certainly used in occult ceremonies, especially for sacrifices. However, that doesn't seem quite right in this context. Is there anything more you can tell me about the victim?'

'Well, she was a student at the Blavatnik School of Government.'

'Just like Ellie.'

'Indeed, and because of that, a bit uncomfortably close to home.'

'Of course, especially after the Midwinter Butcher case. Anyway, does Ellie know the victim?'

'I don't know yet, but I thoroughly intend to pick her brain about it later today.'

'So what about the victim's boyfriend? If you have your reservations, let's start with the evidence stacked against him.'

'That has to do with the murder weapon, a crossbow with two bolts made from converted paintbrushes. You see, Ryan Slattery is an art student, and was using that small studio they have in the middle of Wytham Woods during an artist-in-residence week. The victim, Gabby Dawson, was visiting him there. And this is where it gets interesting. It turns out the reason that she was there was to *assassinate* Ryan.'

'Good grief!'

Joseph quickly held up his hands. 'Not literally. They're actually members of something called the Assassins' Syndicate. It's some sort of Oxford college club where students try to take each other out with Nerf guns.'

A look of comprehension had already filled the professor's

face. 'Yes, I know all about them. That club has been running for years. However, it's not just students, but former alumni as well. I've even known professors to take part.'

'Oh, now that is interesting.'

'What, you think there might be some connection between this group and Gabby's murder, then?'

'Well, it does seem to be one hell of a coincidence that she had just carried out a successful hit against her boyfriend, then she ended up shot to death with a crossbow.'

Dylan nodded and took a thoughtful sip of his coffee. 'It seems like exactly the sort of thing that an assassin might use to kill someone.'

'It does, especially if that person was a bad loser.'

'That sounds like you've already made up your mind about Ryan?'

'I'm trying not to rush to conclusions here, especially if someone is going out of their way to frame him.'

Dylan's eyes had narrowed as he became lost in his thoughts.

'What are you thinking?' Joseph asked.

'What if this pendant is some sort of membership badge? The knife could represent the *raison d'être* of the Assassins' Syndicate.'

'That makes a lot of sense. The only problem with that is Ryan denied ever seeing it before. Mind you, I definitely got the feeling he was lying about that, which is interesting in itself. Anyway, that brings us to our other theory that maybe a member might have been playing this game for real.'

'Like Ryan, you mean?'

'Or someone else who wanted to frame him. That would certainly explain why the clues we've found are so clear-cut and incriminating towards Ryan's involvement.'

'It almost sounds like someone is turning this whole thing

into a game, having planted false clues and the rest,' Dylan replied.

'It does, doesn't it? And that's certainly an idea worth pursuing. Like always, just talking to you helps me see the wood for the trees.'

'Which is rather an apt saying when you're talking about a murder in Wytham Woods.'

Joseph chuckled. 'Yes, I suppose it is.'

CHAPTER EIGHT

Joseph pushed open the door with his foot as he carried in the sealed plastic box filled with what was left of Dylan's samosas. He headed into the relatively tiny incident room with a grand total of five desks that had been set aside for the investigation of Gabby Dawson's murder.

Megan was already there and dipped her chin in greeting. Then, like a heat-seeking missile sensing its target, her eyes locked onto the plastic container of food.

'What have you got there?' she asked, as Joseph headed to his desk.

'Jesus, you really are psychic when it comes to food,' he replied.

She grinned at him as he set the box down on his temporary desk. As Joseph slipped off his coat, his gaze travelled automatically to the incident board.

A dozen photos of the crime scene taken in Wytham Woods by the SOC team, were already on it. Among them was a close-up image of one of Ryan's paintbrushes recovered from the studio. It matched one of the converted bolts used to shoot Gabby. Under a photo of Ryan, *Chief Suspect*, had been written in Chris's writing. There was also a close-up of the blue plastic token with *Significance?* written below that. The final thing the SIO had written on the board was *Possible Motive?* The only item written under that was, *An act of passion?* That was followed by, *Game played real?* A line from both were linked to Ryan's photo. That said everything about the current state of their investigation.

Megan followed his gaze and frowned.

'What's with the expression?' Joseph asked, opening the pastry box.

'Chris discovered next to nothing unusual in Ryan's background. Certainly nothing to suggest he's capable of murder. But the more I've thought about the case, the more something seems off here about Ryan killing his girlfriend.'

Joseph nodded. 'I agree. Maybe Ryan isn't the sharpest knife in the box when it comes to killing someone and went a bit too poetic by using a converted paintbrush. But even so, as the evidence board tells us, we're very much still missing a real motive here, other than knowing he argued with Gabby about something.'

Just then Chris entered the room, carrying a tray with three cups with the mobile coffee van Steaming Cup's logo of a roasted bean on their sides.

'I come bearing gifts,' he said, handing the two detectives a cup each, before taking one for himself.

'Thanks, and I've just the thing to go with that,' Joseph said, proffering the box of samosas to the others.

Chris took one and Megan gave the DI an approving nod as she took two.

The DCI's eyes widened after his first bite. 'This is fantastic. Where did you get these?'

'From my scholastic neighbour, Dylan,' Joseph replied. 'He's something of a dab hand in the kitchen.'

'I can tell that,' Chris said, taking another appreciative bite. As he munched on it, his attention fell on the sparse forensic board before them. 'So, having had some time to catch up on your beauty sleep, what are your thoughts about the lack of any real evidence so far?'

'It's obviously still early days in our investigation, but if Ryan Slattery really is our man, we need to do a lot more digging. I'm intrigued by the mention of freerunning and climbing on the video that Gabby took before she was killed. Although, as she wasn't murdered on the rooftops of Oxford, it remains to be seen if that has any relevance to this case.'

'Well, we have discovered one thing at least. Amy and her team confirmed that the blue token definitely belonged to Gabby Dawson.'

'Did they find her DNA on it then?' Joseph asked.

'They did, but unfortunately, only hers, even though it was obviously torn from her neck and found some way from her body,' Chris replied. 'That suggests it was dropped by the murderer as they fled the scene, and they were wearing gloves.'

'Which, after Ryan's fingerprints on the crossbow bolts, seems strange.'

'Exactly.'

'Maybe whoever it was, took it as a memento, then?' Megan said.

Chris nodded. 'That's certainly a possibility—'

'And how are you getting on in here?' Derrick's voice said from behind them, interrupting the DSI.

They turned to see the superintendent leaning against the doorframe.

Joseph couldn't but help feel a physical repulsion as he looked at his commanding officer. But this was work and, for now at least, he needed to keep it together when it came to the gobshite.

'It's still early days,' Chris replied.

'Well, as I've already told you, I want this case wrapped up double-quick and to be in a position to formally charge Mr Slattery before the statutory thirty-six hours is up,' Derrick replied. 'We'll hold off letting the press know about it for now. Something along the usual lines of preserving the integrity of the investigation until we're ready to go public with it. That will hopefully give you all a clear run at this without the press sticking their noses in.'

Joseph gestured towards the nearly empty evidence board. 'We're going to need a lot more time than thirty-six hours, if you want a watertight case for the CPS.'

A hardness crept into Derrick's eyes. 'Only if you're slack in the investigation. I want results, and I want them now. Do you understand me?'

Although there were three other officers in the room, the way Derrick's eyes bore into Joseph's left him with no doubt that it would be his neck on the line yet again. But, whatever Joseph actually thought of the arse-wipe, he also wasn't going to go out of his way to alienate him while he was actively trying to investigate him.

So, even as he seethed, Joseph sucked it up and nodded. The sooner he had the hard evidence he needed on the DSU, the sooner he'd be able to act.

Then, just to make sure that he added insult to injury, Derrick's gaze alighted on the open box of samosas. Without even pausing to ask, he walked into the room and helped himself to one.

'Don't mind if I do,' Derrick said. 'Thanks to whoever brought these in.' He turned on his heel and headed back out of the room.

'I'll give you *don't mind if you fecking do*,' Joseph muttered under his breath, but still loud enough for Chris, who was standing nearby, to frown. The DCI gestured with his chin a fraction towards Megan who was sitting close by. The DI knew sounding off about Derrick in front of a more junior officer was something Chris didn't condone. He'd more than once bent the DI's ear about it. But sometimes it was impossible to adhere to the rules of office politics, especially when you had some serious dirt on your superintendent.

But Megan was already shaking her head as Derrick's footsteps receded down the corridor.

'How on Earth are we meant to wrap everything up in that time frame?' she said.

Joseph scraped his hand through his hair. 'It's certainly a big ask.'

'It is, and that's why I'm going straight after Derrick. Convince him to do whatever it takes to have Ian and Sue put on the case as soon as possible,' Chris said.

'Good luck with that,' Joseph replied. 'If the big man is serious about this deadline, maybe he'll actually listen to you. We certainly need as much help as possible.'

Chris nodded. 'Megan, can you pull up the details of where Gabby lived so you and Joseph can start there? Then I suggest you head to the Blavatnik School of Government to start interviewing her fellow students and friends.'

Megan nodded as she tapped at her keyboard.

'We should also seriously look into the archery club and any suppliers who sell crossbows, as well,' Joseph said.

'Good idea,' Chris replied. 'I'll get Ian and Sue to cover that, along with checking out Ryan's home for any incriminating evidence. Then, like you with Gabby, I'll get them to talk to Ryan's friends and tutors at the art college. Maybe if someone is trying to frame him, it's another artist, hence the paintbrush arrows.'

'Certainly worth a punt. That will also free me and Megan

to find out what we can about this Assassins' Syndicate and its relevance to the case.'

'I know it's meant to be a game, but the way Gabby was shot feels uncomfortably close to what they get up to,' Megan added.

Chris looked at the photo of one of the bolts and nodded. 'I agree, and that's certainly an angle that's worth pursuing. I've also got Gabby's parents coming in for an interview. They should arrive in Oxford around lunchtime. If there were some serious problems between Gabby and Ryan, perhaps she confided in them.'

'That question aside, that's going to be a difficult meeting,' Joseph replied.

Chris frowned. 'Don't I know it.'

The two detectives exchanged a knowing look. Dealing with a grieving parent was always one of the worst aspects of the job. Joseph certainly respected the DCI for not farming that job out to someone else to deal with.

Megan looked away from her screen as she jotted down a note. 'Okay, I have Gabby's address. She lived in one of the flats owned by, and right next door to, the Blavatnik School of Government.'

'I'll try to expedite a search warrant by the time you get there,' Chris replied.

'That would be a great help, you know what a stickler for the rules college porters can be,' Joseph replied, as he and Megan stood.

Joseph and Megan exited the elevator on the third floor and headed along a wood-panelled corridor, following the porter who was leading the way to Gabby's room.

'Are you sure this is student accommodation? It feels more like quite a plush hotel to me?' Megan asked their guide.

'The Oxford colleges certainly like to make sure that their students are well looked after,' the porter replied with a slightly sniffy tone, as though the DC was directly criticising the college.

'Student digs have certainly come a long way since my day,' Joseph said.

Megan raised her eyebrows at him. 'You make it sound like you lived in a Victorian hovel when you were a police cadet.'

'Not quite, although mould on the bathroom wall was almost bad enough to have mushrooms growing on it.'

The DC gave him an appalled look as the porter stopped at a door and unlocked it with a keycard.

'Here we go,' the man said.

The two detectives followed the porter into a room that was the very definition of chaos. Clothes were piled up on every available surface. The double bed was a knot of sheets and duvet, with no sign of pillows anywhere.

Joseph noticed photo-booth images of Gabby and Ryan had been stuck on a notice board and went in for a closer look. Both students were doing the classic pose, namely pulling faces at the camera as they made bunny ears behind each other's heads. But the thing that really struck the DI was that if he was any sort of judge, they looked very much in love, particularly in one photo where they were gazing into each other's eyes. Beneath the notice board was a pile of paperwork and an empty Pot Noodle carton perched on top of a closed laptop.

The porter pulled a face at the contents of the room. 'Unfortunately, as you can see, Miss Dawson wasn't always the tidiest of students.'

'Oh, trust me, we've seen much worse,' Joseph replied, as he slipped on a pair of latex gloves and Megan did the same.

The porter's mouth turned downwards. 'I can't believe that

Miss Dawson has been murdered. She was always such a sunny student.'

'This sort of thing is always a shock, especially when it happens to someone so young,' Joseph replied, trying not to think of Ellie. 'I don't suppose you can think of anyone who might have wished Gabby harm?'

The man's brows drew together. 'No one. As far as I know, she was well-liked by everyone, and was especially popular with the porter team here.'

'And what about her boyfriend, Ryan?' Megan asked.

'He always seemed polite enough when he stayed over. Beyond that, there's not a lot I can tell you.'

'So you never heard them argue?' Joseph said.

A troubled look filled the porter's face. 'Just once, as they passed the front desk. Some disagreement over money.'

'Any specifics?'

'I'm afraid not, although Gabby seemed very cross with Ryan about whatever it was. But that was a one-off though, and otherwise, they seemed very happy together. Anyway, I'd better leave you to it. Let me know when you've finished in here. I need to collect Gabby's things for her parents, who are arriving later today.'

'We will, and thank you,' Megan replied.

The porter smiled and headed out of the door.

Before he'd even closed it quietly behind him, Megan turned to Joseph. 'So arguments about money, hey?'

'If it were serious enough, I suppose it might be a motive. We better see if we can find something to support that theory.'

Megan nodded as she picked up the Pot Noodle and gave it an approving nod. 'Ah, Chinese Chow Mein, a classic.'

Joseph gave her an appalled look. 'You actually eat that stuff?'

'I used to live on it back in the day. Less so now, but the

craving still hits me occasionally when the midnight munchies strike.'

'Don't let Dylan hear you say that or he'll run you out of the city.'

'Then it will just have to be our dirty little snack secret.'

Joseph hitched an eyebrow at the DC as she opened the laptop. A password box immediately popped up on the screen.

'I'll check to see whether Gabby has written her password down anywhere in here, not that I'm holding out much hope,' Megan said.

'If not, do the usual and bag it up so the TFU can have a crack at it,' Joseph replied, thumbing through the pile of papers piled high next to the computer.

Most of it seemed to be connected to research work for Gabby's Master of Public Policy degree. However, of immediate interest was a bank statement. It showed Gabby's account was seriously in the red. Several credit card statements were in even worse shape.

'Okay, this could be linked to the argument the porter heard them having,' Joseph said, holding the statements up for Megan to see. 'It looks like Gabby was badly in debt to the tune of...'—he did a quick mental calculation—'all told, around thirty thousand.'

Megan whistled. 'That's going to hurt, especially when you add in the student debt on top of that. But the porter said she was cross with Ryan rather than the other way round.'

'So maybe he was giving her a lecture about money?'

'In which case, she might have asked her parents for money, maybe even Ryan as well?'

Joseph pulled a sceptical face at his colleague. 'What I know about most artists is that they tend to live on the poverty line unless they have a second income. Because of that, I strongly suspect Ryan wouldn't have been in a position to lend her money, even if he'd wanted to. Anyway, we should let Chris know so he can ask her parents if they know anything about it.'

'Not to mention Ryan as well, when we interview him next time round.'

'Aye, at least it's a solid lead to follow up on. Let's see what else we can discover here.'

Megan nodded and set to work on a chest of drawers next to the bed.

Joseph paused for a moment, taking in the pile of Gabby's clothes that hadn't quite made it to the open laundry bin. He felt an ache of sadness for the young woman who'd lost her life in such a terrible way. No one deserved to die like that.

CHAPTER NINE

When people think of Oxford, the dreaming spires are usually one of the first things that come to mind. Certainly, there's an abundance of beautiful stone colleges spread throughout the city. However, as anyone who actually lived there knows, the university isn't resting on its historical laurels and had continued to evolve as the years rolled past. The Blavatnik School of Government was one of the latest examples of that constant movement forward into the twenty-first century.

The purpose-built building Joseph and Megan were heading towards through a thin mizzle of rain, consisted of a series of circular upper floors standing on top of a square ground floor base section. It was certainly a striking example of architecture. But what elevated it to a higher level were the mirrored windows across the curved surfaces that perfectly reflected the sky overhead. The overall effect, despite the mass of the structure, was that the building seemed to float, defying gravity.

'That really is stunning,' Megan said as they neared the building.

'It's grand by any measure, and it's almost as impressive on the inside,' Joseph replied. 'Anyway, there is already one bit of good news for our investigation—no sign of a pack of reporters camped outside on their doorstep, trying to grab students for a comment.'

'Surely, whatever Derrick says, it's just a matter of time before the press gets hold of this?'

'You can guarantee it, especially in the case of the tabloids where making money from other people's misery is at the centre of their business model.'

'That sounds like the bitter voice of experience.'

'You better believe it,' Joseph replied as they headed through the doors into the college. The detectives held up their lanyards to the woman seated at a reception desk.

'We have an appointment with Dean Ragnar Higginson,' Joseph said.

The woman's gaze skimmed over her computer screen and she nodded. 'I'll let him know you're here. The dean should be right down in a moment. Please take a seat, and I'll send him over when he gets here. In the meantime, can I get you both a drink?'

With their coffee orders sorted, the two detectives headed into the middle of the college and grabbed a couple of seats.

Megan immediately craned her neck up to look at the spectacular central circular atrium. The space was dominated by a broad, spiral staircase, gracefully winding its way up and linking the various levels together. But the thing that really struck Joseph was, despite the grey day outside, how much bright natural daylight flooded this internal space. The white walls positively glowed despite the gloomy day outside.

'You really weren't kidding; the inside of this place really is spectacular,' Megan said. 'It must have cost a fortune to build.'

'Ellie was telling me it was about fifty-five million, which for once I think was money well spent when you get something this impressive out of it. And talking of my precious daughter, we should check in with her to see if she knew Gabby.'

'And maybe what gossip she knows about her, that maybe the other students might be more reluctant to voice to us.'

Joseph nodded as a man with a sweep of grey hair, which wouldn't have looked out of place on a man conducting an orchestra, appeared before them.

'Detectives Stone and Anderson?' the man said.

'Indeed, and I take it you're Dean Higginson?' Joseph replied.

'In the flesh, although please call me Ragnar,' he said, shaking both the detectives' hands.

'Is that a Swedish accent I'm picking up on?' Megan asked.

'Close, but no cigar,' Ragnar replied with a smile. 'I'm actually Icelandic.'

'Oh, that's a stunning country,' Megan said. 'I went there once to try and see the Northern Lights, but no joy because of the weather.'

'I'm afraid that's not unusual for visitors. You really need to live there for it to be guaranteed. Anyway, you're not here to discuss the merits of my home country.'

'No, sadly we're not,' Joseph replied. 'Is there somewhere we can talk to you in private about Gabby Dawson?'

'Of course. We should continue this discussion in my office.'

The detectives followed the dean as he led the way up the curving staircase to the first-floor level.

As Joseph glanced down into the atrium, another group of students walked across the round floor beneath them. He was struck by the similarities to a traditional college quad, albeit a very comfortable one that was also protected from the elements.

Ragnar headed towards one of the wooden doors radiating out around the edges of the open space. He ushered his visitors into his very comfortable office with a view of the stone entrance of the Oxford University Press building across the road.

Joseph wasn't at all surprised to see leather and chrome designer seats waiting for them. They were arranged around a coffee table made from some sort of polished stone. It all looked very expensive and straight out of a high-end designer shop.

'So, obviously, my team here at Blavatnik are keen to help your investigation in any way we can,' Ragnar said. 'Whatever you need, you just need to ask.'

'Thank you, and we'll definitely be taking you up on that,' Joseph said. 'But to get us started, we're currently trying to build a fuller profile of who Gabby was. What can you tell us about her?'

Ragnar sat back in his chair. 'The first thing is, and if you pardon the cliché in the awful light of her murder, she really did have her whole life to look forward to. She excelled in all her exams and was even in line to take on a job in parliament as a research assistant when she graduated next summer.'

'So she was a high flyer, then?' Megan asked as she took notes.

'Definitely and very much destined for great things,' Ragnar replied.

'Was she well-liked by her peers?' Joseph asked.

'Extremely, both with her fellow students and her tutors, as well. That's the thing, I've been racking my brain about this, I honestly can't think of anyone with a motive to kill her.'

'In that case, what about someone who might have been jealous of her success at college?' Megan asked.

'Well, I'm not going to deny it's a highly competitive environment here at Blavatnik. However, with the areas the students are likely to work in eventually, you would expect that. Our college endeavours to help prepare them for the often challenging careers they'll be embarking on. But for someone to be jealous enough of Gabby to murder her—sorry, I find that hard to believe.'

'I'm afraid that's often the way of these things until they happen,' Joseph replied. 'But there is another thing. Are you aware that Gabby was a member of a club called the Assassins' Syndicate?'

Ragnar scowled. 'Really? That's news to me.'

'But you know about the group itself?' Megan asked.

'Yes. Let's just say that sometimes their antics have become a bit disruptive. They actually ambushed other club members while in classes. I had to really put my foot down when they started trying to assassinate each other during lectures, obviously meaning that word figuratively in this context...' His as his eyes widened. 'You don't mean to say that you think Gabby was murdered by another member of the club?'

'We're not ruling anything out at this stage,' Joseph said.

Ragnar wrung his hands together. 'But that's beyond belief. It's just a game.'

'Meant to be a game, but perhaps someone got carried away. There is one other thing you might be able to enlighten us about. Did Gabby ever mention anything about her financial situation to anyone here?'

'For that, I'll need to check with the bursar to see if she ever applied for any form of support. However, unless Gabby came from a very low-income family, we're only talking a few thousand pounds at most per year, and that doesn't go far when living in Oxford.'

'You're telling me,' Joseph replied.

Ragnar nodded. 'I'm afraid debt can be an ongoing problem for students and can even cause some to drop out if they can't find a part-time job to help ease their finances. In Gabby's case, I'll check to see if she applied for any financial help.'

'If you could, we'd certainly appreciate it.'

'Of course...' Ragnar gave them a thoughtful look. 'I really don't want to pry into your investigation, but do you think that could be related to her murder?'

'I'm afraid we can't talk about that. But we need to talk to Gabby's classmates as a matter of urgency. Would it be possible to arrange for us to use a room in the college to interview them?'

'Of course. I'll also talk to Gabby's tutors to ask anyone who knows her to come along and talk to you. I'm afraid it will take about thirty minutes to get everything set up. Is that alright?'

'No problem. I need to find my daughter, Ellie Stone, who's also studying here. We'll whisk her away for a quick chat.'

A look of surprise crossed the dean's face. 'Well, I'm delighted to say Ellie is another star student in the ascendant. Her tutors have nothing but glowing things to say about her.'

'Why am I not surprised?' Megan said, smiling at the DI.

'Well, it's news to me,' Joseph replied. 'She doesn't really say much about the course, even when I ask her about it directly.'

'Then she's being far too modest, and you have every right to feel very proud of your daughter,' Ragnar replied.

Joseph felt a glow build in his chest. 'That's grand to hear, and I'll be sure to let her mother know.'

The dean nodded. 'Anyway, just let me check to see whether she's on campus today.' He crossed to his desk and powered up his desktop computer. He scanned down the screen and nodded.

'Yes, Ellie's in a Social and Environmental Policy lecture currently. If we head over right now, we should just be in time to catch her as the lecture ends.'

'That would be perfect, thank you.'

A short while later, they were all heading towards the doors of a lecture theatre. Through the large window, Joseph could see the screen behind the tutor had a series of charts on it. All the students had their heads down, their faces lit by the glow from their laptops.

'Good, we're just in time,' Ragnar said. 'I'll leave you here. I'll call you when we have a room sorted out.'

'We'll be in the Jericho Café, waiting for your call,' Joseph replied.

'Ah yes, a splendid establishment, and I can personally vouch for their carrot cake.'

'Oh, I know—some of the best in Oxford.'

'I couldn't agree more.' Ragnar smiled, then headed back to his office.

Joseph looked in through the window at the students, trying to locate Ellie.

A woman's hand shot up near the front, and the lecturer nodded. Even though the DI couldn't hear what was being said, the way the tutor was smiling and nodding as she listened, told him the question was well received. But it was only as the student turned her head slightly he realised it was actually Ellie.

That's my girl, he thought to himself.

'Ellie certainly looks at home in there,' Megan said, also spotting her.

'She does, doesn't she?' Joseph replied, his sense of parental pride swelling even more.

The tutor, having answered Ellie's question, flicked a switch on the lectern. A moment later, the lights came up in the lecture theatre. Immediately, the students began closing their laptops and filing out of the room.

Ellie, who'd grabbed the opportunity to talk to the lecturer again, ended up being the last to leave. But the moment she spotted her dad and Megan in the doorway, her eyes widened.

She walked straight up to them 'You're here because of what happened to Gabby, aren't you?'

'You already heard about that?' Joseph asked.

'A student who knows Gabby's parents found out. I'm afraid the news has spread like wildfire throughout the college.'

'Ah, well, at least that means we won't be breaking the news to her friends when we interview them. Talking of which, have you got time to grab some cake and coffee down at Jericho Café?'

'I always have time for cake and coffee. Just let me get my things, and we can head straight out.'

Despite it barely being ten thirty in the morning, Jericho Café was already packed with people, testimony to just how many people in Oxford held this particular eating establishment in such high esteem.

'God, that is seriously good,' Megan mumbled through the mouthful of carrot cake she was currently devouring.

'Isn't it just,' Ellie said, licking the buttercream topping from the tips of her fingers.

'And the coffee is excellent, too,' Joseph added, taking a sip of the superior house blend. 'Anyway, down to business. Ellie, what can you tell us about Gabby?'

His daughter sat back. 'First of all, she's not a direct friend of mine, just an acquaintance. I know of her more by reputation than anything else.'

Joseph tipped his head to one side. '*Reputation?*'

'This is only what I've heard, but by all accounts, she was something of a party girl. She had half the male students and a few women, too, lusting after her. Some of them even tried their luck, even though she was involved in a serious relationship with an art student.'

'Ryan Slattery?' Megan asked.

'Yes, that's him. Apparently, Gabby absolutely worshipped

the ground he walked on. She certainly didn't have an eye for anyone else, even if some of the men didn't always get the memo.'

'So, did Ryan know about any of this unwanted attention?' Joseph asked.

'Oh, most definitely.'

Joseph's interest sharpened. This sounded like a highly promising line of enquiry. Jealousy as a motive for murder was as old as the hills. 'Any names you can give us for any of her admirers?'

'A few spring to mind. I can give you a list.'

'That would be a great help.' Then Joseph gave his daughter a thoughtful look. 'Do you happen to know about the Assassins' Syndicate club Gabby and Ryan were members of?'

'Oh that lot. If you ask me, they're a bunch of big kids who love running round Oxford with Nerf guns, but you probably know that already.'

Joseph and Megan both nodded.

'Okay, but you might not know this yet.' Ellie leaned in conspiratorially. 'There was an incident a few months ago during one of the Assassins' games. Apparently, Ryan's target was a woman called Anita Steadman. By all accounts, Ryan got a bit carried away and she ended up with a minor wound on her throat when he was pretending to slit it. Although Anita was fine and laughed the whole thing off, Ryan still got thrown out of the club for that little stunt, and Gabby resigned in protest.'

'So you're saying neither of them are current members?' Joseph asked.

'That's my understanding.'

'Interesting. So if they weren't playing an Assassins' Syndicate's game, what were they playing?' Joseph asked.

'Sorry?' Ellie replied.

'Don't worry. Anyway, does this Anita Steadman study at Blavatnik? We'll need to make a point of talking to her.'

'No, she's actually over at Magdalen College.' Ellie studied their faces. 'So do you have a suspect?'

Joseph just raised his eyebrows at his daughter.

'Yes, I know. You can't talk about an active case. So how's Ryan doing?'

Even though it was the barest look Megan exchanged with Joseph, Ellie still caught it.

'Hang on, you've already got Ryan in custody, haven't you?' she asked.

Joseph sighed.

Ellie raised her eyebrows at him. 'I'll take that as a *yes,* then.'

Joseph spotted Megan trying to suppress a smile as he gave his daughter a straight look. 'And I'm sure a certain boyfriend didn't tell you anything about this case, either?'

'I haven't seen John yet today. He was working late, if that's what you mean?' Ellie replied. 'Why, is he involved in this case as well?'

'He was the first officer on the scene,' Megan said.

'Oh, bloody hell.'

'Exactly. It's never easy witnessing a murder victim early on in your career,' Joseph replied.

Ellie looked out of the rain-streaked window and nodded. 'Of course not...'

The DI's heart went out to his daughter. This was the stark reality of dating a serving police officer—there was always something to worry about, lurking just beneath the surface.

He reached over and squeezed her shoulder. 'Maybe I should grab a quick pint with him to see how he's doing?'

She looked from the window and met his gaze. 'I'd really appreciate that, Dad.'

'Then consider it done. Anyway, is there anything else you think we should know that might be useful?'

'Nothing off the top of my head, but if I think of anything else, I'll let you know.'

'Well, you've already been a huge help,' Megan said.

Joseph nodded as his phone warbled. He took the call.

'We're ready for you now, and the students are already gathering,' Ragnar said at the other end of the line.

'Good, we'll be there in five.'

Megan was already slipping her coat on, but as Ellie started to get up, Joseph shook his head.

'Why don't you take a moment and finish your cake,' he said. 'If I run into John at work, I'll make sure he gives you a quick ring as well.'

'Please do,' his daughter replied with a small smile.

But as Joseph headed out of the door with Megan, he noticed a faraway look had already descended on Ellie's face as she gazed out of the window, lost in her thoughts about her boyfriend. It was the same look he'd seen on Kate's face far too many times back in the day.

CHAPTER TEN

MUCH LATER THAT DAY, Joseph and Megan were sitting in their broom cupboard of an investigation room, comparing notes, when Ian and Sue walked in with Chris.

Ian made an expansive gesture. 'It's alright, you can both relax, the cavalry is here.'

'You've finally been assigned to the case, then?' Megan asked.

'Yes, and you'll be relieved to hear, we're already on the clock,' Sue replied. 'We've just been through Ryan's flat and visited his college.'

'Not to mention the archery club and every crossbow stockist between here and Gloucester,' Ian added.

'That's why I wanted to get you all together so everyone could compare notes,' Chris said. He gave Joseph and Megan an expectant look. 'How did you get on at Blavatnik?'

'We spent most of the afternoon talking to Gabby's friends and fellow students,' Joseph said. 'The bottom line is Gabby was well-loved by everyone, especially the lads, so we're going to look into that. But to a person, they said how besotted Gabby was with Ryan and would have done anything for him. Based on what we were told, she didn't have an enemy in the world. But the one promising lead, as I told you when we rang in this morning, Chris, is the serious money problems Gabby was having.'

The SIO nodded. 'Yes, after your phone call, I briefed Ian and Sue about it and I made a point of bringing that up with her parents when I spoke to them. They were shocked. She never asked them for any help financially. Also, Gabby apparently inherited thirty grand from a great aunt and had been using that to help finance her education.'

'So, the question is, where did that money go and could it be linked to her murder somehow?' Megan said.

Ian sat back in his chair, hands behind his head, giving off the air of someone who'd already solved the case. 'Now, we may have a little theory about that.'

'You found out something interesting at Ryan's flat?' Chris asked.

Ian sat forward. 'Very *interesting*, Boss. You see, according to Ryan's friends at the Ruskin School of Art, our little chum currently tucked up in the cell, had something of a crypto investing habit that had gone really badly. His tutor even told us that Ryan was on the verge of dropping out of college because of a lack of cash.'

'So you're suggesting this could have been Ryan's motive—to get his hands on the inheritance that she didn't actually have any more?' Joseph asked.

Ian shrugged. 'For all we know, Gabby might have used that thirty thousand to fund Ryan until he ran out of money. Perhaps that's what they argued about. Then, in a fit of anger, Ryan shot her.'

'But even so, would he really have been prepared to do that to someone he was meant to be deeply in love with, especially when it's not exactly a life-changing amount of money?' Megan suggested. 'It's what? A single semester at Blavatnik?'

Joseph glanced at her. 'But don't forget the porter at her student accommodation, did report hearing them arguing about money on one occasion.'

'There you go, then. Ryan soaked up all the money Gabby could give him, then when there was nothing left in the kitty...' Ian shrugged.

Chris frowned as he wrote the information on the board. 'Okay, Ian, I'll give you that it's a possibility, but we need harder evidence than just idle speculation for the CPS to be convinced.'

Joseph turned the thought over in his head. 'It sounds to me like we need to get a forensic accountant to go through all of Ryan's and Gabby's finances. Let's see if there's any clues as to where her inheritance actually went. Follow the money and maybe everything else will begin to fall into place.'

'Shouldn't we interview Ryan again since we're up against the clock on this?' Sue suggested.

Chris shook his head. 'I think it's better not to show our hand too early, especially as next time he'll almost certainly have a solicitor in tow. We need to make sure we have all our ducks in a row, first.'

'So are these detective ducks we're talking about here?' Sue asked, almost holding a straight face.

Ian smirked. 'They'd certainly be great for policing the waterways of Oxford.'

Sue laughed. 'All wearing little deerstalkers.'

The DCI shook his head. 'Thank you for the comedy double act, you two.'

'Anytime,' Ian replied, grinning.

Joseph rolled his eyes at the two of them. 'Ignoring that particular contribution from our colleagues, I think it's the right call to hold off with Ryan for now. We have snippets of information, but not enough to prove Ryan's guilt or innocence either way. However, there is one lead I would like to follow up on. Ellie told us that there was a rumour going round Blavatnik that Ryan got carried away in this Assassins' Syndicate game and ended up actually injuring another student called Anita Steadman.'

'You're saying Ryan might have a previous form for hurting someone and actually got a taste for it?' Sue asked.

'An accident with a player, to Ryan actually murdering his girlfriend, is a huge leap,' Megan said. 'However, if there was the added incentive of money involved, who knows?'

'Okay, then it definitely sounds like it's worth talking to Anita to see what she can tell us,' Chris said, adding her name to the board.

'Leave it with us, Boss,' Joseph said.

The SIO nodded. 'Okay, let's try and summarise where we're up to. There was a possible financial incentive for Ryan to murder Gabby. Alternatively, maybe he developed a taste for hurting people after the incident with Anita. Of course, it could have been a combination of the two that set Ryan on the path to murder. Can anyone think of any other reason he might have had for doing this to someone he claimed to love?'

Megan nodded. 'As Joseph said, there were plenty of male students who had an eye for Gabby. Maybe Ryan got jealous, and if he thought she was encouraging anyone in any way, he took matters into his own hands.'

Chris gave her a thoughtful look. 'Yes, if he really believed Gabby was being unfaithful, that could be a possible motive for murder.'

'It certainly adds to the toxic profile we're building up about Ryan in the guilty column,' Sue added.

Joseph grimaced. 'Yes, but we also need to look at why and how he may be innocent. Apart from anything else, if he is, that means we still have a psychopath out there running around Oxford.'

'Someone who framed Ryan, you mean?' Chris replied.

'Exactly. Why leave us a massive clue in the form of one of his paintbrushes converted into a crossbow bolt?'

'Yes, I have to admit that isn't sitting comfortably with me either,' Chris said. 'The question then is, if someone really is trying to frame him, why?'

'Someone with a grudge like a love rival?' Megan suggested.

'And have you got any names yet?'

'A few from my daughter who goes to that college too,' Joseph replied. 'But before you get too excited, we've already spoken to them and their alibis check out for the time of Gabby's murder.'

'Right. In that case, any thoughts about next steps whilst we still have time before the deadline to charge Ryan expires tomorrow?'

'What about doing the usual and checking doorbell and dash cams in case they spotted anyone else heading up to Wytham Woods on the night of the murder?' Sue suggested.

'Yes, even though that's a major time sink and there aren't a lot of us assigned to the case, it's still worth doing,' Chris replied. 'The problem is, I doubt I can persuade Derrick to free up enough Uniforms to cover that task.'

'We don't mind covering that duty,' Ian said, and Sue nodded.

'Thank you, then Joseph and Megan, you should pursue this Anita Steadman lead. If nothing else, that could help give us an insight into Ryan's character.'

They both nodded.

The SIO glanced at his watch. 'Okay, as time's getting on, let's park this for now. Everyone get some beauty sleep, so we can crack on first thing in the morning with clear heads.'

As everyone started to gather up their things, Joseph noticed that it had just passed eight on the wall clock. This time last night, Derrick had been headed out for his clandestine meeting. Just for a moment, he seriously considered hanging back and telling Chris about what he'd discovered. But just like with the investigation into Ryan, right now knew he didn't have anything like enough hard evidence.

Chris caught Joseph looking absent-mindedly at him. 'Is there something else you wanted to say?'

'No, I'm grand,' Joseph replied, closing his bag.

The DI knew it was best to keep this all to himself for now. At least until he had the headspace to work out what to do next. Also, tonight he had a promise to keep to his daughter, and that involved PC John Thorpe.

Joseph set down a pint of Flowers real ale before John as he joined the constable at the corner table in Scholar's Retreat pub. Ian was currently at the bar with Sue, having a fierce debate over whether pork scratchings actually counted as a food source, or something you just scraped from the bottom of an oven.

'So how are you doing, John?' Joseph asked, as he settled into the seat next to him and took a sip from his pint of Guinness.

'I've had better days,' the young officer said, lines radiating out from the corners of his eyes.

'I'm guessing this has to do with Gabby Dawson's murder?'

John frowned. 'It's everything to do with it, Joseph. I just can't get the mental image of that poor woman out of my head.'

'Aye, and you probably never will. Not the first, at least. After that, sadly, and partly as a way to survive in the job, you start to develop emotional armour.'

'I'm not sure it will ever be thick enough for me to cope,' John said.

Joseph met the man's eye and shook his head. 'Don't be so sure. Plenty have said the same ahead of you and now have no problem. I'm sure Megan won't mind me telling you that she really struggled with it at first, but you should see her during an autopsy now, barely batting an eyelid over what goes on there. She doesn't even really need a Silvermint anymore to help with the nausea like I do.'

'You do?' John said, giving the DI a surprised look.

'God, yes. But the thing is, I've learned to cope with it—not least because what focuses me more than anything else, is a real determination to bring to justice the feckers who would do something like that to another human being.'

John slowly nodded. 'Maybe I need to invest in buying a pack of these famous Silvermints you always seem to have on you. That one you gave me last night at the crime scene certainly helped.'

Joseph smiled, and took a pack from his pocket and handed it over. 'That should keep you going for a while. Let me know if you need more. I buy them in bulk from an online supplier who ships them over from Ireland.'

'Thank you, but hopefully I won't have too many occasions to need them in future.'

'Then let's drink to that,' Joseph said, raising his Guinness to John's beer and clinking the two glasses together.

Megan entered the pub and, spotting them, headed over. 'Here you are.' She spotted the pack of Silvermints in John's hand. 'Ah, has our DI been giving you the talk about how to cope with a murder scene?'

'Yes, and he used you as an example of how well you cope now,' John replied.

'Did he now?' Megan said, giving Joseph an amused look.

'Did he also tell you that the first time we met, I was throwing up the remains of my dinner after seeing a decapitated goat?'

'No, he spared me that juicy detail.'

'There you go, saving my blushes. A pure gentleman, as always.'

'I try my best,' Joseph said with a small smile. 'Anyway, how did you get on tracking down Anita Steadman, Megan?'

'Set up a meeting with her at Magdalen College first thing in the morning. She was fairly cagey when I said we wanted to talk to her about Ryan.'

'Interesting. Maybe she doesn't want to get him into trouble for what he did to her?'

'Guess we'll find out when we speak to her.'

'I just hope you catch whoever is behind Gabby's murder,' John said.

'That's certainly the plan,' Joseph said. But as he took another sip of his Guinness, his thoughts briefly returned to all the victims he'd seen during his time as an officer. Not all of those cases had been solved. Those were always the worst, and they still haunted him.

He just prayed that Gabby's wasn't going to be added to the cavalcade that filled his darkest memories.

CHAPTER ELEVEN

A CHILL AUTUMN fog was rolling over Magdalen College's grounds the following morning, transforming the green grasses of the Water Meadow into a hazy grey watercolour. The neoclassical and Victorian buildings of Magdalen College had already been reduced to faint silhouettes in the mist as the detectives walked away from them.

Joseph buried his cold-numbed hands deeper into the pockets of his Barbour jacket.

'Where is it you said Anita Steadman wanted to meet us?' he asked, as they began skirting the field next to the River Cherwell, a tributary of the Isis, otherwise known as the Thames beyond the boundaries of the city.

'Apparently, there's a bench along here she likes to use,' Megan replied.

'What, especially set aside for her clandestine meetings with the police?'

Megan chuckled. 'Not quite. Anita is a keen amateur wildlife photographer. It turns out this is one of her favourite spots to take photos of the roe deer that graze in the park.'

'And that couldn't wait for later in the day, so we could meet somewhere more civilised like a nice warm coffee shop?'

'That's exactly what I suggested, but Anita is desperate to get a good enough shot for a college nature photo competition. Apparently, she's after, and I'm quoting here, *a mysterious photo of a deer in the fog.*'

'How very Scottish Glens of her.'

'Oh, I know...' Megan's words trailed away as a large shape emerged from the mist less than ten metres away towards their left. A magnificent stag stood there looking at them, its ears erect, its magnificent four-point antlers perfectly framing its head.

'Don't move a muscle,' a woman's voice said softly from behind them.

Both detectives glanced around to see a young woman with long brunette hair, wearing a puffer jacket, crouched on the embankment behind them. Of immediate interest was the camera she was holding. A very large white lens had been mounted on it, and she was pointing it at the stag. A quiet whir came from it as the woman pressed the shutter release button. Even though it was the faintest sound, the deer's ears pricked forward. Then it turned away and silently melted away back into the mist like some sort of spectre.

Ignoring the two detectives, the woman was examining the back of the camera. She then punched the air. 'At last.'

'Anita Steadman?' Megan asked.

'Ah, you must be the detectives who wanted to ask me some questions?'

Joseph nodded, showing Anita his warrant card, as Megan did the same. 'So, did you get it?'

The woman gave him a confused expression. 'Get what?'

The DI gestured to her camera. 'Your competition-winning photo of that deer just now?'

A smile filled Anita's face, and she turned the camera around so the detectives could see its rear screen. 'What do you think?'

Joseph took in incredible detail in the extraordinary photo of the stag. Every single hair had been picked out by the camera and was glistening with beads of mist. A curling breath wreathed the deer's head like tendrils of smoke. But more striking than any of that was that the magnificent creature seemed to look directly into the lens, its body rimmed by diffused sunlight.

Megan shook her head with wonder as she stared at the photo. 'Wow. If that doesn't win the competition, I don't know what will.'

'Fingers crossed,' Anita replied, beaming at them. 'Anyway, if we head a bit further along the path, there's a bench where I left my things, and we can talk.'

'Lead the way,' Joseph replied, seriously starting to wish he'd brought a flask of coffee to stop him from freezing to death.

Anita set off at a brisk walk, constantly scanning the meadow, camera clutched in her hand, at the ready to pounce on any wildlife subject that might stray across her path.

Thirty metres along, a bench came into view with a large camera bag on it and a tripod leaning against an arm.

Anita immediately settled herself down. As she started detaching the lens, she gave the detectives an expectant look. 'So what is it you wanted to know about Ryan and why ask me specifically?'

'You obviously haven't heard the news yet, then?' Joseph said.

Anita stopped what she was doing and looked at him. 'Why, has something happened?'

'I'm afraid Gabby Dawson was found dead in Wytham Woods on Sunday night.'

Anita's pupils dilated. 'Gabby... I didn't know...' She almost dropped the lens she'd been about to put back into the bag. The student blinked rapidly. 'How?'

'I'm afraid we're not at liberty to discuss that,' Joseph said.

She stared at them. 'Is this why you wanted to talk to me about Ryan, because you think he has something to do with it?'

'We're not ruling anything out at this stage of our enquiries.'

Anita shook her head. 'Look, I can already tell you for a fact you're totally barking up the wrong tree. Ryan would never, ever, do anything like that. He's just not that man.'

'You sound very sure about that,' Megan said.

'That's because I am. You don't know him like I do.'

To Joseph's ears, she certainly sounded sincere. 'Okay, but what about what Ryan did to you during an Assassins' Syndicate game?'

The student looked between them, eyes narrowing. 'Don't tell me, someone's been gossiping. It was an accident.'

'We'd like to hear your version of events,' Joseph said.

Anita scraped her hair back to show the faintest mark on her neck. 'You see that? It was barely a nick. That's all that Ryan did to me when he was pretending to slit my throat.' She quickly held up her hands. 'And before you say anything, that's nowhere near as bad as it sounds. He was using a plastic knife and had snuck up behind me in the Westgate Shopping Centre. But at the last moment, he tripped and just managed to nick my skin with the serrated edge as he tried to steady himself.' She shrugged. 'No biggy.'

'You don't sound upset about it,' Joseph said.

'Why should I be? Ryan completely caught me by surprise and it was almost a great hit. But then Geoff completely overacted and permanently banned him from the game. But I guess he was just being overprotective of the other members and his precious game.'

'Geoff?' Joseph asked.

'Yes, Geoff Goldsmith is the Guildmaster of the Assassins' Syndicate. He gave Ryan a really hard time over what happened, reading him the riot act and slinging him out.'

'But you don't believe Ryan intended to actually hurt you?'

'Of course he didn't. If he had, he would have used a real knife, wouldn't he?'

'Aye, I suppose he would.'

Anita's mouth thinned. 'Look, whatever else it is you believe Ryan is, I can tell you he's certainly not the psychopath you seem to have him pegged as.'

'That's good to know.'

Megan nodded her agreement. 'In that case, is there anyone you can think of who could have wished Gabby harm?'

'Well...' Anita gave a small head shake. 'No that doesn't make sense.'

'Look, even if you have the vaguest suspicion, you need to tell us, especially for Ryan's sake.'

'Okay, but I think it'd take a huge leap for this guy to actually want to take it as far as murdering her. It's just that Geoff was really furious with Ryan about what happened, and was worried it would damage the reputation of the club. Then when Gabby resigned, he became incandescent.'

'You're telling us he might have a big enough grudge to take it out on her?'

She raised her shoulders. 'Look, if you're already grasping at straws with Ryan, you might as well look at Geoff, too. I know how lame it sounded the moment I even suggested it.'

'Okay, we'll talk to him,' Joseph said. 'Any lead, however vague, is worth pursuing at this stage.'

Anita nodded. 'Just please don't say I mentioned his name.'

'Don't worry, we won't. We need to talk to him about the Assassins' Syndicate anyway.'

Megan looked up from the notes she'd been taking. 'I don't suppose you happen to have Geoff's contact details?'

'Actually, I do via the WhatsApp group.' Anita took out her phone and turned it to show the DC the number. Megan scribbled it down.

'When Geoff isn't at a lecture at Mansfield College, or down at that board game cafe in town, which is a real passion for him, most Tuesday mornings you'll find him in the college library,' Anita explained. 'He's researching old and early Middle English, when he's not studying for his sociology degree. Between us, I think he fancies himself as another Tolkien.'

'What, he wants to be a fantasy writer?' Joseph asked, confused.

'Well, Geoff definitely loves Lord of the Rings. Don't we all? Whether he wants to be a writer, I've no idea.'

'Right...' Joseph now had a mental picture of Geoff as someone with a corduroy jacket, leather arm patches, who occasionally smoked a pipe. Maybe he was even part Hobbit.

'We better get going then,' the DI said. 'Thank you for your help and the best of luck in the competition.'

'Fingers crossed.' Anita held up her hands and did exactly that. 'But if you see Ryan, please send him my condolences and love. He must be heartbroken.'

'We will,' Joseph said, making sure he kept his face as neutral as possible.

As they turned to go, the DI caught sight of a man who appeared to have been watching them from further down the pathway. He had a baseball cap pulled down low over his forehead. The guy couldn't have looked more furtive if he tried. That was more than underlined when he suddenly turned and began walking rapidly away.

'Was he just watching us?' Megan asked, also spotting him.

'Or maybe Anita,' Joseph replied. He cupped his hands around his mouth. 'Hey you, hang on a moment, we'd like a quick word.'

But far from stopping, the man actually increased his pace and then took a sharp left off the footpath, sprinting away into the fog and towards the river.

The detectives exchanged a glance and immediately set off after him. His faint silhouette veered towards a fence bordering the River Cherwell and the college grounds.

Joseph had a turn of speed to him, but Megan was even faster.

'Hey, you! Police! Will you bloody stop already!' she bellowed, as she kept pace with the man. But he didn't so much as turn as he reached a high fence.

Joseph already had his phone out and was taking video just in case their fugitive managed to get away by diving into the river. Otherwise, they had him cornered. But what the DI hadn't been expecting was for the guy to somehow scramble up the iron bars and vault over the top in a move that would have put a monkey to shame. Then he was swallowed by the fog and the detectives lost sight of him.

Megan reached the fence, looked up at it, shook her head, and turned back to Joseph.

'Sorry, no way I can get over that like he just managed to,' the DC said, as Joseph reached her.

'Don't worry about it. What he just did bordered on the superhuman,' Joseph said, as he sucked in a lungful of air.

'Actually, isn't that exactly the sort of stunt a freerunner could pull off?'

'Christ on a bike, you're right. So maybe someone with a connection to Gabby then?'

'And now Anita, it would seem. Whoever it was, they were

obviously interested in her, too,' Megan replied. She peered into the fog that was starting finally to burn off as the sun grew stronger. 'Should I raise an alert for everyone to keep an eye out for anyone matching this guy's description?'

'Besides height, what description? You can bet that once he was out of our sight, he ditched his baseball cap and just became another guy walking through the streets of Oxford.'

At that moment, Anita appeared behind them, camera bag slung over her arm along with the tripod strapped onto it.

'You didn't catch him, then?' she said.

'Obviously, not,' Joseph said, trying but failing to keep the note of sarcasm out of his voice. 'I don't suppose you have any idea who that might have been?'

Anita gave them a non-committal shrug. 'No idea.'

'And you can't think of anyone who might be stalking you?' Megan added.

'Me?' She pulled a face. 'I don't think so. Anyway, got to go. I have a lecture to get to.' Anita quickly turned and headed away.

'Why do I get the feeling she just lied to us?' Megan asked.

'I agree. Maybe she's trying to protect someone. One thing's for sure, we need to look into the freerunning community here.'

'We seem to have an abundance of leads suddenly. Not only our new mystery stalker, but also this Geoff Goldsmith, even if his motive is a bit unlikely.'

'Then let's make a start with him and see where that goes. That aside, at the very least, he should be able to supply us with a full list of the Assassins' Syndicate guild members.'

'Okay,' Megan said, 'but first can we swing by the Covered Market to grab a hot drink to go, so I can thaw out?'

'God yes, but we need to be quick. We're on the clock here with the deadline to release Ryan being later today.'

As the two detectives headed away together, the stag Anita had photographed watched them go from the cover of one of the nearby trees. Then it turned and silently ambled away into the fog.

CHAPTER TWELVE

THE COFFEE SHOP in the Covered Market was a welcome chance for the two detectives to defrost after their early morning meeting.

Megan took a sip of her coffee, as Joseph's was prepared. 'Wow, you weren't kidding. That's seriously good.'

'Oh, don't I know it?' the DI said, as the barista handed him a cardboard cup. 'Like I told you, they grow their own beans over in Colombia and roast them.'

'It's so good it almost helps to take my mind off the fact that I managed to let that guy get away from me when he vaulted that fence.'

'Don't beat yourself up. I've never seen anyone pull off a stunt like that. I much prefer to chase a criminal who's out of shape and overweight, with a bit of asthma thrown in for good measure.'

Megan smiled. 'Ideally, so unfit they don't even bother to run.'

Joseph chuckled. 'Aye, that's the one.' The DI nursed his own cup of coffee. 'So any thoughts on the why and the wherefore about this guy who got away from us?'

'I guess the question is, and assuming we really weren't the ones being watched, why was Anita being trailed by someone?'

'Maybe it was a rival nature photographer who was determined to stop her from winning that competition by grabbing her camera?' He winked at her.

'Yeah, yeah, but humour aside, whoever it was obviously was very keen not to get caught. That makes me immediately suspicious.'

'Maybe it was as simple as we were in the right place at the right time to prevent that man from grabbing her and...' He shrugged. 'You catch my drift.'

'Possibly, but if we're talking about a would-be rapist, isn't early morning an unusual time to try and grab a woman?'

'Most people like that are opportunists. They see a chance and grab it.'

'Even when two detectives are clearly talking to their potential target?'

'Granted, that doesn't fit the normal MO,' Joseph replied. 'So now we circle back to whether this guy was somehow connected to Gabby's murder, especially as there seems to be some sort of freerunning connection?'

'Hang on, maybe we're overthinking this. What if there's a much more innocent explanation? Maybe it was just part of another Assassins' Syndicate game, and Anita was the guy's target.'

'But surely she would have told us if that was the case?'

'You would think so. Certainly, people playing games seem to be at the heart of this case. But I also can't help but think we're still missing a key piece of information.'

'Then hopefully, we'll learn some more from this Geoff Goldsmith character, especially as he's the one who runs the club.'

'Okay, then time to head straight over to Mansfield College

and talk to the man himself.' The DI gestured to the bag clutched in his colleague's hand. 'But before we head out, and whilst it's still hot, try that Ben's cookie I bought you. I promise you it will be a life-changing experience.'

Megan gave him a sceptical look as she took a bite from the nut and chocolate chip cookie.

Her eyes widened as she brought the biscuit up for a closer inspection. 'My God, where have you been all my life?' Then her eyes flitted to Joseph. 'Would it be wrong to declare my undying love for a biscuit?'

Joseph chuckled. 'You wouldn't be the first. The trick is to get them when they're first freshly baked, so the chocolate is still a little bit runny from the oven.'

'I know you told me about them before, but you could have introduced me to them long before now.'

Joseph shrugged. 'Blame work getting in the way.'

'Same old story,' Megan replied with a grin, before going in for a second bite as they walked out of the Covered Market.

Thankfully, the last of the fog had now evaporated and the autumn sun had taken hold as the two detectives headed across Oxford. It was positively warm by the time they walked towards the main entrance of Mansfield College.

Joseph pointed out a bronze statue of a woman on the far side. 'See that? It's Eleanor Roosevelt, wife of President Franklin Roosevelt.'

'She attended Mansfield?' Megan asked with an impressed look.

'Not quite. Dylan took me on a tour of this college, as he's done with most of the colleges in Oxford, and gave me the rundown. Apparently, Eleanor Roosevelt played a key role in drafting the Universal Declaration of Human Rights. That statue was dedicated to her in honour of her achievement and was unveiled by none other than Hillary Clinton.'

Megan looked suitably impressed. 'Oxford never ceases to amaze me with all the history that's tucked into every nook and cranny.'

'You better believe it,' Joseph said as they headed up the steps and into the entrance.

The detectives entered a lobby area and had a quick conversation with a woman sitting at a desk. A short while later, they were walking along a corridor on their way to the library. At the foot of a large ancient wooden staircase, they passed a large monitor. It was scrolling through a series of slides about Mansfield College, covering its facilities and students.

Megan gestured with her chin towards it. 'That certainly paints a very impressive picture of this place.'

'Would you expect any less in Oxford? Competition between the colleges is fierce, so they always have to be seen putting their best foot forward, if only so the students think their college is the best in the city.'

'And the others don't think that as well?'

Joseph shot her an amused look. 'Of course they do.'

Following the signs, they headed up the staircase and into an impressive library.

A long room stretched away under an arched roof supported by beams and decorated with illuminated painted panels. Sunlight shone in rays through the large stone window at the far end, casting a warm glow over the polished wooden bookshelves lining the walls and alcoves where tables had been placed. Old oil canvas portraits lined an upper gantry, the figures depicted keeping a beady eye on the patrons below. Many of the students were tapping away quietly at keyboards, whilst others had their heads buried in books.

'Bloody hell, talk about a pure Harry Potter vibe,' Megan said, taking in all the details of the ancient library.

Joseph thought fondly of watching the movies with Ellie when she was growing up. 'Aye, isn't it just?'

A man, presumably the librarian, looked up from a desk nearest the door they'd just entered through.

'We're looking for Geoff Goldsmith,' Joseph said in a suitably hushed tone.

The librarian nodded. 'Geoff's in his usual favourite spot; third alcove on the left.'

Megan's gaze swept over the library as they walked through it. 'The students here are so lucky to have somewhere like this to study.'

'That's the truth, but I suppose that's partly what the exorbitant fees are for,' Joseph said, as they reached the alcove they'd been directed towards.

But rather than the corduroy jacket-wearing academic Joseph had been expecting to find, instead was a guy wearing tracky bottoms and a faded sweatshirt with a Space Invaders design on it. The man was sitting at the table, books spread all around him on the desk, some of which looked ancient and were filled with strange-looking writing. However, the student's attention wasn't on any of those, but instead was purely focused on a chessboard before him. Based on the distinct lack of pieces remaining, the game was nearly over.

'Geoff Goldsmith?' Megan asked, a note of uncertainty in her voice. She'd obviously been thrown by the guy's appearance as well.

The man held up a finger as his brow furrowed. Then he reached forward and moved a black knight forward, a wide grin appearing on his face. 'Now let's see you get out of that.' He spun the board around so the white queen and her pieces were nearest him, before turning his attention to the detectives.

'Sorry, I just needed to finish my move. Anyway, to answer your question, yes, I'm Geoff Goldsmith. And you are?'

Joseph and Megan flashed their warrant cards towards the man.

A frown filled Geoff's face. 'What's this about?'

'First of all, can I confirm that you run the Assassins' Syndicate here in Oxford?' Joseph asked.

'Yes, for my many sins, but why's that of interest?'

'We need to ask you about two former members of your club, Ryan Slattery and Gabby Dawson.'

'Oh bloody hell, what have they done now?'

So it seemed Gabby's murder hadn't quite reached the hallowed walls of Mansfield yet, either.

'It's in connection to a current case we're investigating. We're actually here to ask you about an accident that happened last year when Ryan Slattery injured another student, Anita Steadman. Apparently, he ambushed her during one of your Assassin games.'

Geoff grimaced. 'Yes, the guy is a prize idiot. Why? Has Anita finally come to her senses and decided to press charges?'

'No, nothing of the sort. She said it was just an accident.'

'Oh, she would. Ryan can do no wrong in her eyes. Between us, I think she has a bit of a thing for him.'

Joseph immediately filed away that mental titbit of information.

'But you're not a fan?' he asked.

'God no. Ryan got totally carried away with what was meant to be a game. Mind you, Gabby's the same. It was just a matter of time before something bad happened with those two. I should never have let them join the Assassins' Syndicate in the first place.'

'What do you mean, *it was just a matter of time?*' Megan asked.

'Those two are both experience junkies, throwing themselves a hundred and ten percent into any hobby, the more hardcore, the better. Just like they did with Parkour last year.'

'Parkour?' Joseph asked.

But Megan was already nodding. 'It's the formal name for freerunning.'

'That's the one, and apparently, Gabby held the unofficial course record for one of the routes in Oxford,' Geoff replied. 'It may not be exactly legal, but at least, apart from putting their own necks on the line, they didn't hurt anyone else doing it. But for those two, whatever the sport was, the more extreme the better. Thanks to that, they had the wrong attitude towards the Assassins' game from the moment they joined. Between us, I think they both took it a bit too seriously.'

'Seriously enough for Ryan to want to take it further with his girlfriend?' Joseph asked.

'Sorry, what do you mean?'

Joseph weighed up whether to tell Geoff what had happened. But if it was already common knowledge at Blavatnik, it would only be a matter of time before all the colleges in Oxford knew.

'I'm afraid I have to tell you that Gabby Dawson was found murdered in Wytham Woods on Sunday night.'

Geoff put his hands on top of his head. 'Oh fucking hell!' he said loud enough for several other students to turn and stare at him. 'Please tell me you've already arrested someone?'

'Let's just say, we have several persons of interest.'

Geoff's eyes widened. 'Ryan?'

Megan quickly leapt in. 'Why would you assume that?'

'Look, I don't want to get him in any sort of trouble. But Ryan is something of a jealous guy when it comes to other men's interest in his girlfriend.'

So there was confirmation of one of the motives they'd come up with so far.

'Have you got any specific examples?' Joseph asked.

'Oh god, yes. There was one guy in particular, Eddie Foster. He seriously had the hots for Gabby. He hung round those two all of the time, just so he could be closer to her. Eddie even joined the Assassins' Syndicate when they did, like some sort of spare wheel. But eventually, his feelings for Gabby came out when they got drunk together at a gig. Needless to say, Ryan didn't take it well. I think he may have believed Gabby encouraged Eddie. After that, he wanted nothing to do with Eddie and that threesome broke up.'

'And did Eddie keep his distance after that?' Megan asked.

'No idea, but he stayed in the Assassins' Syndicate even after they quit. For any more info, you'll need to ask Eddie himself.'

'Don't worry, we'll follow this up,' Joseph said. 'So, is there anything else you can tell us about Gabby or Ryan?'

'Just that Ryan was always short of money. He'd never buy a round when we were out, claiming he was always flat broke.'

'And Gabby?'

'The rumour was that she had cash and Ryan sponged off her whenever he could, even living with her to save rent.'

Joseph glanced at Megan, who nodded. Geoff was unknowingly confirming the monetary motive. Maybe Derrick had been right about this case after all, and it really was the open and shut case it had seemed at first glance.

'So that must have made things tricky between them?' Megan asked.

'I guess,' Geoff replied. 'Apart from that, I can't think of anyone else who might have an axe to grind.'

Joseph reached into his pocket and took out his phone,

pulling up the image of Gabby's pendant with the hand logo on it. 'I don't suppose you've seen this before?'

Geoff glanced at it, his eyes widening before shaking his head. 'Sorry, no idea.'

Geoff wasn't telling the truth. The man hadn't exactly tugged an earlobe as a tell, but his sudden guarded expression wasn't far off either.

'Are you absolutely sure you can't place it?' he asked. 'Nothing to do with the Assassins' Syndicate?'

'Nope, we don't even have membership cards, if that's what you mean? Why? Is this somehow connected to Gabby's murder?'

'That's what we're trying to work out.' Joseph exchanged a look with Megan. 'One last question. Can you tell us where you were Sunday night?'

Geoff's eyes widened, and he gulped before answering. 'I— I was doing a live stream for my YouTube channel. I was interviewing the designers of a new fantasy board game. You can check online to see that it went out live, and that I was running it.'

'Thank you, and if you could give us the details, we'll have a look. Oh, one thing I needed to ask you. Even though Gabby and Ryan were no longer members of the Assassins' Syndicate, they still seemed to be playing it. You didn't readmit them recently, did you?'

'Absolutely not. They did love the game though, so maybe they were playing their own version.'

Now there's an interesting idea, Joseph thought.

'Okay. We'll also need to see a full membership list for the Assassins' Syndicate.'

'Right...' Geoff replied, drawing out every letter. 'Don't you need some sort of warrant for that?'

'We can get one if you really need us to.' Joseph held the student's eye.

Geoff shook his head. 'No need. It's obviously important. I'll email it to you. Are you sure you can't tell me what's going on?'

'Sorry, it's an active investigation. Anyway, one final question. Any idea where we might find Eddie Foster?'

'I can give you his number, if that would help?'

'It would, thank you,' Megan said.

Geoff nodded and opened his phone, pulling up the contacts and then showing the DC the mobile number.

'He's at Somerville and studies engineering, but I'd try ringing first to see if he's there. He seems to spend half his time out, pursuing his latest sport craze.'

'Thanks, we will,' Joseph said, handing the student his card that included his email details. 'And thank you for your time. It's been most helpful.'

Geoff sat back in his chair and nodded. But before the detectives had even moved, he'd returned his attention to his chess game, hand poised over the white bishop.

'You're playing against yourself?' Megan asked.

'I'm the only person who can give me a big enough challenge. Besides, no one else will play with me as I kept beating them.' Then he gave her an expectant look. 'Why, you don't play, do you?'

'Yes, but obviously not at your level.'

'What about you, Detective Stone?' Geoff asked.

'Sorry, never had time to learn it.'

'You should. It's one of the best games on the planet.'

'I'll have to take your word for it. Games really aren't my thing. Anyway, thank you for all your help.'

'Anytime.'

As the detectives headed out of the library, Megan turned to the DI.

'Did you notice his reaction when he saw the photo of Gabby's pendant? I definitely got the impression he knew something about it.'

'I thought the same. So why not come out and tell us? It certainly has me thinking that whatever that bit of plastic jewellery is about, it might be more significant than we first realised.'

Megan nodded. 'And I can't help but wonder if this whole adrenaline junky angle might have had a part to play in what happened. Maybe Ryan just took what should have been a game too far with Gabby.'

'Or someone wants us to think that he did. Just think of the paintbrush arrow. It will certainly be interesting to see what Eddie Foster has to say for himself, and find out just how deep this infatuation of his ran.'

'You mean he could be our new chief suspect?'

'Let's just put it this way, if Geoff's alibi checks out, I'll be very interested in finding out where this Eddie character was at the time of Gabby's murder. As the clock is ticking, the sooner we talk to him, the better. The only thing for certain is that Derrick isn't going to be happy if we end up releasing Ryan without a charge and no other suspects.'

'You can say that again,' Megan said, her face grim, as they headed down the stairs.

CHAPTER THIRTEEN

MEGAN DROPPED her speed as she drove the unmarked police Peugeot up the ever-narrowing tree-lined lane, towards the top of Shotover Country Park.

'I don't know why we agreed to meet Eddie all the way up here,' Megan said. 'He was more than happy to swing by the station to chat to us.'

'But that wouldn't have been for another hour, and defrosting with cups of coffee aside, every second counts.'

The DC was about to reply when an ancient blue Volvo estate rounded the bend ahead of them and raced at high speed straight towards the Peugeot.

'Watch out!' Joseph bellowed.

Megan just had time to throw the Peugeot into the already deeply rutted verge, spraying mud up the side of the vehicle. Without even braking, the Volvo screamed past.

Joseph had just enough time to see someone as far removed from a crazed, hardened criminal as possible. An old woman wearing a headscarf was at the wheel, her hands gripping the top of the steering wheel she was only just able to see over. Then he spotted a black Labrador in the back as the vehicle sped past. The poor creature gave the DI a slightly helpless look as if to say, *I know, I know,* as his owner's car sped away down the hill.

For once, even Megan looked rattled. 'Bloody hell, what an absolute maniac. I've a good mind to turn on the siren and head after her.'

'Honestly, it's not worth the paperwork. Apart from giving an old lady a stiff lecture about keeping her speed down, she almost certainly wouldn't get charged anyway.'

'Once again, that sounds like the voice of experience,' Megan said, pressing the accelerator and spinning the Peugeot's nearside front wheel in the mud embankment for her efforts.

'Sadly, it is,' Joseph replied. 'And to get us out of the mud, try lowering the revs and rocking the car on the clutch.'

Megan did as instructed. Joseph was just resigning himself to having to push, when the car suddenly gained traction and lurched forward back onto the safety of the tarmac.

He gave Megan an approving nod. 'Nicely done. Do you know where exactly we're meant to be meeting Eddie?'

'He just sent me a map marker that is in the middle of the woods in Shotover. He did say he'd stay in the same spot until we got there.'

'I see...'

Megan caught the bemused expression on Joseph's face.

'What's that look on your face about?'

'Just that, apart from the dog walkers, this particular country park is well away from prying eyes, as well as being close to a city. Let's just say it also attracts a certain crowd at night.'

'Hang on, you're not talking about people meeting up for dogging, are you?'

Joseph grimaced. 'That's the one. I'm still traumatised from when I was called out here with Derrick, back in the day when we were both still PCs. A member of the public made a complaint, and the sergeant stationed the two of us up here in the car park to keep an eye on what was going on. I tell you, some of the things I witnessed that night will traumatise me for the rest of my life.' The DI shuddered.

Megan snorted. 'Let's just hope that Eddie doesn't belong to that crowd then.'

'Feck, I hope not. That aside, the walking paths up here are great. As long as you manage to avoid stepping in all the landmines some of the less than savoury dog owners leave behind to waylay the unsuspecting.'

'You're really selling this place to me,' Megan said, as they reached the end of the tarmac road.

As the car bounced over what had suddenly become a rutted track, the line of trees to the side of the road thinned out to reveal a magnificent view. The city and the surrounding countryside stretched away into the distance, under what had finally decided to become a glorious blue-sky day.

'Wow, what a stunning view from up here,' Megan said.

'Aye, it's pretty grand, and almost makes up for the disturbing association I have for this place in my mind.'

Megan cast him an amused look as they reached the car park and pulled up next to an Audi SUV. A woman was just wiping the mud off the legs of a Cocker Spaniel, before letting it back into her car's pristine boot.

A short while later, with Megan holding her phone like a modern-day compass bearer, the two detectives were heading through the woods towards the marker on the map Eddie had sent them.

Joseph had expected to see the student waiting for them on a bench. What they actually saw was much more surprising.

A man with dark hair, wearing shorts and sporting a blue Somerville College branded hoodie, was balancing on a length of orange strap like a tightrope walker. The nylon line had been stretched out between the boughs of two large trees, a couple of metres above the ground. Arms outstretched, the man was carefully walking along it, the strap bending beneath each foot as he shifted his weight from one to the other.

Megan glanced down at the screen and then at the man before them. 'Eddie Foster?'

The man turned, and the strap immediately bounced sideways beneath him. His arms whipped out as he lost his balance. But all that succeeded in doing was violently shifting him in the opposite direction. The strap oscillated like a guitar string, pitching the guy off. But he somehow managed to land neatly beside it, shaking his head. A grin was already filling his face as he turned his attention to the detectives.

'You'll have to excuse that. Not the most elegant dismount. Anyway, I'm guessing you must be the detectives who wanted to talk to me?' he said, as he headed over.

'Indeed, we are, and you must be Eddie?' Joseph said.

'I am.'

'So what were you doing just now, practising for your audition at the circus?' Megan asked.

A smile filled Eddie's face. 'It's called slacklining. It's a great sport for strengthening your core and obviously improving your sense of balance. It's also a way to spend time outdoors in beautiful places like this. Mind you, I've been partly forced to come up here as I'm being semi-banned from the parks across Oxford. The keepers are convinced my strap will damage the trunks, even though I always make sure I pad it out.'

Joseph glanced at the sacking wrapped around the trees that the strap had been tied over. 'Looks safe enough for the trees to me.'

'Exactly, but try telling an irate warden that. Anyway, why exactly did you need to talk to me? I don't think one of the

University Park staff would be zealous enough to actually report me to the police.'

'You're right. This is linked to an ongoing investigation. First of all, can you confirm that you knew Gabby Dawson?' Megan asked.

Joseph grimaced. The DC had slipped up by referring to Gabby in the past tense.

Eddie was already peering at her. '*Knew?*'

Megan closed her eyes for a moment, before giving Joseph an apologetic look.

He gave her a reassuring smile, before returning his attention to Eddie. There was no point now in holding back. Besides, he was more interested in how the man reacted to the news.

'Yes, I'm afraid Gabby was found murdered in Wytham Woods,' he said.

Eddie's expression widened. 'No way.' Tears were already filling his eyes. 'Who did it?'

'That's what we need your help with,' Megan said.

He stared at them. 'Hang on, that's not why you're here, is it? You don't think I had anything to do with it?'

Joseph narrowed his eyes. 'And why would you say that?'

The student tucked his chin in. 'You tell me?'

Joseph nodded to Megan, partly because he knew she would be desperate to redeem herself after the slip-up.

She gave him a grateful look, before turning to Eddie again. 'We've been informed you had something of an infatuation with Gabby. Is that right?'

Eddie's eyes darted between the two detectives. 'Why, who have you been speaking to?'

'That doesn't matter,' Joseph replied. 'Just please answer my colleague's question.'

'Well, there's obviously no point in denying it, but yes. I did have a bit of a thing for Gabby, but it didn't go anywhere.'

'You mean she rejected you, and based on what we've been told, she did it very publicly?' Megan asked.

'Okay, okay, it definitely wasn't the greatest moment of my life. But I absolutely swear to you I had nothing to do with her murder. Look, I adored Gabby, even if she didn't want to be with me like that. I certainly wouldn't have harmed a hair on her head. Anyway, that whole rejection thing was behind us, and we were finally mates again.'

'I see, so if we were to ask you your whereabouts on Sunday evening?' Joseph asked.

'So I am a suspect.' Eddie shook his head. 'Well, for your information, I was at the cinema with a bunch of mates. They'll all testify I was there. I can give you a list and you can check it if you like?'

'That would be very helpful,' Megan replied.

Eddie spread his hands wide. 'Look, I swear on my mother's life, I had absolutely nothing to do with Gabby's murder. Yes, she might have embarrassed me once, but that's in no way a motive for me to kill her. Even her boyfriend, Ryan, will tell you that things were all cool between us.'

'Then we'll be sure to ask him when we see him next.'

'Please do. Ryan must be devastated.'

'Well, he has just lost his girlfriend,' Joseph replied. 'But talking of Ryan, what can you tell us about him?'

Eddie stared at the DI. 'Fuck, you're not telling me he's a suspect as well?'

'I'm afraid we can't reveal those sorts of details about a current investigation.'

'Which means he bloody is. But Ryan wouldn't kill Gabby. The guy's got a huge heart, and he even forgave me when I made that drunken pass at his girlfriend. And as much as it pains me to say it, he and Gabby really were meant to be together.'

'And you don't know of any problems in their relationship we should be made aware of?'

'Not a thing, and I should know because if there had been, Gabby would have ended up with me. But their relationship was absolutely rock solid.'

'In that case, do you know of anyone who may have wished Gabby harm, including anyone in the Assassins' Syndicate?' Megan asked.

Eddie let out a hollow laugh. 'Absolutely not. Why, you think someone in the club went all psycho and suddenly took what's meant to be a game, for real?'

'That's what we're trying to work out.' Joseph took out his phone, pulled up the image of the plastic pendant, and showed it to the student. 'Have you ever seen this before?' he asked, already alert for any micro-expression that might give the truth away.

The student blinked rapidly, but remained mute.

'Eddie?' Megan asked.

He shook his head. 'Sorry, no. Why? Is it important?'

'We're not sure yet,' Megan said.

'Look, if I knew anything about it, honestly I'd tell you,' Eddie said.

Joseph studied the young man, his instinct already telling him that, like Ryan and Geoff, he was lying about it as well. Once again, that begged the question of why. What was so important about that bit of plastic?

When nothing else was forthcoming, Joseph tried one final question. As Eddie was obviously a bit of a sports fan, there was a reasonable chance he might know something about Gabby's other hobby.

'Do you happen to know anything about the freerunning Gabby was involved with?' he asked.

This time Eddied nodded. 'Not just freerunning but, just

like Ryan, free climbing as well. Those two were like human flies and could scale anything without ropes.'

'So, is this something Ryan and Gabby did as a couple, then?' Megan asked,

'Yeah, they loved their adrenaline highs. But then they got bored with it and moved on to the next big thing, namely the Assassins' Syndicate.'

'But surely, that's a bit tame compared to risking their necks climbing buildings and the rest?' Megan asked.

Eddie shook his head. 'It becomes surprisingly real when you're hunting your target, even if you are only armed with a Nerf gun. Thrill of the chase and all that.'

That expression immediately struck a chord in Joseph's mind. Was that what Gabby's murder had been about? Someone's idea of sport?

Megan had already written that particular insight down in her notebook as well.

'Okay, I think that's all the questions we have for now,' Joseph said. 'If you could just give us the details of your friends who can vouch for your whereabouts, that would be very helpful in clearing you from our investigation.'

'Of course...'

Once Megan had taken down the details, the detectives started back towards the car.

'So what do you think?' she asked.

'Despite what Eddie said about Gabby forgiving him, I think we need to take a closer look at him, especially as Geoff gave us a very different impression about how things were between them.'

Megan nodded. 'It's almost like they're all in on some big secret. And I don't know why, but it has everything to do with that plastic token Gabby was wearing.'

Joseph turned the thought over in his head. 'Yes, some sort

of conspiracy of silence...' But his thoughts were interrupted by his phone warbling. When he saw it was Chris, he took the call.

'How have you got on?' the SIO asked.

'We've managed to gather a few threads together, but nothing conclusive yet about Ryan, or anyone else for that matter.'

'Okay. Unfortunately, we're almost out of time on Ryan. Get back to the station so you can update us in person before we kick off another interview with the lad.'

'A last throw of the dice, in other words?' Joseph said,

'For now, based on the little evidence we have. But I was thinking that as you and Megan have done the most leg work on the case, you might like to lead it.'

'Really?'

'Yes, although I have another reason as well. Derrick is insisting on being in the observation room whilst the interview is being conducted. I thought it would be better if I was in there too so I can manage him if needed.'

Joseph mentally groaned. 'Okay, we're on our way back. See you soon.'

As he ended the call, Megan gave him an expectant look.

'You heard most of that?' Joseph asked.

She nodded. 'I don't much like the sound of the DSU watching us.'

'Me neither. Let's just hope that if Ryan is hiding anything, his time in the cell has loosened his tongue a bit.'

It was then Joseph spotted dog shit on the path and checked his stride before he walked in it.

'For feck's sake,' he muttered, as he veered around it and they continued on their way back towards the car park.

CHAPTER FOURTEEN

JOSEPH AND MEGAN sat across the interview table from Ryan and his solicitor. The DI glanced towards the two-way mirror and, no doubt, the watchful gazes of Derrick and Chris in the room beyond. The problem was, Joseph was under no illusion about who the DSU would blame if this all went tits up.

Unfortunately, beforehand he and Megan had learned that Ian and Sue had come up blank with their search of door cam and security camera footage. Also, the archery club and any shop in the county that sold crossbows had been a bust.

That meant the only tenuous evidence they had was that Ryan had developed a taste for murder when he'd accidentally cut Anita's throat. And, as regards a motive for murdering his girlfriend, the art student had acted out of jealousy, believing she was having some imagined affair. Alternatively, there was the financial angle.

The problem was, they were grasping at straws here. Even if Derrick, in particular, seemed reluctant to accept the fact, they were a long way from a murder charge that would stick.

There was an awful lot riding on the outcome of this interview, and Joseph could feel it like a lead weight on his shoulders.

'Okay, let's get this interview started,' he said, pressing the button on the voice recorder. 'Commencing interview at St Aldates Police Station. Present are officers DC Megan Anderson and DI Joseph Stone, interviewing Ryan Slattery. Also present is the duty solicitor, Ray Edwards.'

As Joseph continued with a repeat of the caution, because of the new information that had come to light, Megan was taking a photocopy of Gabby's bank account out of a folder. As the DI finished, she slid it over the table to Ryan.

'Why are you showing me a bank statement from Gabby's account?' Ryan asked.

'We're hoping you could tell us why that might be relevant?' Joseph said.

Ryan gave the detectives a blank look, then shrugged and began scanning down the statement. 'So she's in debt, aren't we all?'

'Yes, but she shouldn't be because she had an inheritance of thirty thousand pounds, which was meant to fund her through college,' Joseph replied.

'You obviously don't know what it's like being a student these days. Even that sort of money doesn't go far. The fees alone would swallow that up if you don't want to be saddled with student debt by the end of your degree.'

Megan looked up from the notes she'd been taking. 'So what about all the payments she made directly to your bank account over the last year? If you go back through her statements, you'll see all the relevant ones have been highlighted. Altogether, they amount to nearly forty thousand.'

Ryan frowned. 'It was really that much?'

'That's what the bank statements say.'

The student pinched the bridge of his nose before meeting the detectives' expectant gazes again. 'Whenever Gabby lent me some money, she told me not to worry about paying her back.

But I had no idea she was stretched so thin financially. If I had, I wouldn't have accepted it.'

'I see,' Joseph replied. 'So can you tell me what that money was used for?'

'Cover the rent and food, things like that. Gabby had such a big heart and—' His voice caught and he swallowed hard. 'Jesus, I still can't believe she's gone.'

Joseph could tell Ryan's grief was genuine, but that still didn't mean the lad hadn't killed her. He nodded to Megan to jump in.

'Was there anything else the money she gave you was used for?' she asked, even though they already knew the answer.

'Sorry, I don't know what you mean?' Ryan replied.

Megan raised her eyebrows the barest fraction at Joseph.

'Then can you tell me about this?' Joseph took out a betting slip from his folder that Ian and Sue had recovered from Ryan's flat. He slid it across the table. 'Can you tell me what that is?'

'A betting slip?'

'One that belongs to you?' Megan asked.

Ryan glanced down at it again. 'Oh yes, that horse was meant to be a dead cert, too. The last time I listen to a tip on the internet.'

Joseph tapped a finger on the piece of paper. 'And this isn't the first time you've lost a significant amount of money gambling, including investing a large amount in a cyber currency that I believe also didn't go very well for you. So wouldn't it be fair to say you have a serious addiction?'

Ryan tucked his chin in. 'No, because eventually I'll come out on top.'

'And have you so far?'

The student crossed his arms and glowered at them. 'It's just a matter of time.'

'Are you sure about that? Your bank account doesn't make for very pretty reading, either,' Megan said.

For the first time, real anger flashed in Ryan's eyes. 'Fucking hell, I know where you're going with this. You can't seriously be suggesting this was my motive to kill Gabby? Look, we're talking about the woman I loved. That aside, do you really think I would be sick enough to kill anyone for a few quid, anyway?'

The strength of the lad's reaction wasn't lost on Joseph. He knew it was how he'd behave if that sort of insinuation had been levelled at him.

Joseph glanced towards the two-way mirror, easily imagining how Derrick would be leaning forward in his chair, probably pleased to see the suspect rattled by the question. He had to pursue this thread, if only so Derrick wouldn't break his balls about it after the interview.

Playing his bad cop role to a T, the DI crossed his arms and looked at the art student. 'Why don't you tell us? A gambling addict with a serious problem, suddenly becomes aware that his partner has a bit of cash stashed away. Didn't you just tell us you were hard up for money? So let me paint you a little picture. You leeched off Gabby until there was nothing left. Maybe that's why you argued, which is something you've already admitted that you did outside the log cabin. Perhaps it was about all these loans she'd given you or about her having an affair with one of her many admirers. Whatever it was, perhaps it was the catalyst.'

As Ryan balled his hands into fists, his solicitor quickly leaned towards him and whispered something in his ear. The lad took a breath, and lowered his shoulders from where they'd been up around his ears.

'No comment.'

Joseph nodded to Megan again as he sat back in his chair.

She gave Ryan a long look, her eyebrows hitched up, before

launching into a second line of questioning. 'Okay, what can you tell us about the incident with Anita Steadman during an Assassins' Syndicate game? That would be the one where you injured her throat with a plastic knife.'

'Oh bloody hell, I should have known you'd dredge that up.' Ryan shook his head. 'Well, if you've spoken to Anita, you already know it was just an accident.'

Even though the detectives both knew she'd said exactly that, they'd agreed they still wanted to test her version of events with the art student, just in case she was covering for him.

Joseph narrowed his eyes at Ryan. 'Then please explain that to me, because isn't it right that you sneaked up behind Anita and drew your blade hard enough across her neck to draw blood? Doesn't sound like much of an accident to me.'

'Well, it bloody was, and if you're trying to suggest I did it on purpose, why didn't I use a proper knife if I'm the psycho you're trying to make me out to be?'

'But it must have taken a lot of effort to break the skin?' Megan said, the very model of reasonableness.

Ryan's nostrils flared. 'Look, I simply saw an opportunity to assassinate her during a game when she was in town. But I moved a bit too quickly, slipped, and the knife made accidental contact.'

'You *slipped*?' Joseph echoed.

'That's what I bloody said, didn't I?' Then Ryan's eyes flicked between the two officers. 'Hang on, Anita must have told you the same thing because it's the truth.'

The DI didn't respond, and instead steepled his fingers together. 'Okay, moving on.'

'Un-bloody-believable,' Ryan said, throwing his hands up in the air.

Joseph glanced again at the two-way mirror. As cage rattling went, no one could argue they weren't giving it their best shot.

Megan slid over the desk a number of still photos of the man who been stalking Anita, showing him vaulting over the fence to escape. 'Have you any idea who this might be?'

'Well, as I can't see his face, no.'

'Really, even though that's exactly the sort of stunt a freerunner could pull off, something I believe you know all about?'

Ryan's expression became wary. 'I suppose so... Where are you going with this?'

'Isn't it true you used to do freerunning and climbing with Gabby?'

He shrugged. 'So you know about that, and?'

'We're very interested in hearing about what you both used to get up to during these runs,' Joseph said, leaning in.

Ryan cast a glance towards his solicitor, obviously rattled. 'I'm not going to get into trouble over this, am I?'

'No, we have other bigger things to focus our energies on right now.'

'Right...' Ryan glanced towards his solicitor again, who nodded. 'Well, Gabby and I had a number of routes we used to take across the college roofs. Of course, we'd be careful not to get caught by any of the porters.'

'That sounds really dangerous,' Megan said.

Ryan shrugged. 'That was sort of the point of it. The adrenaline hit couldn't be beaten. But we gave up on it about a year ago when Gabby nearly fell. So we weren't totally irresponsible, either.'

'I see, and were there other people who did this activity with you, like the chap in this photo?' Joseph asked.

A wary look filled Ryan's face. 'Nope, just me and Gabby, getting our dopamine hits.'

Joseph fixed the student with his best gimlet stare. 'Are you sure, Ryan? Look, you yourself agreed that leap over the fence looked like the sort of thing a freerunner could pull off. Surely it has to be a small world for people interested in doing that sort of thing. So if you have any idea who this is, we just need to talk to them. I promise, they're not in any sort of trouble, for freerunning at least.'

A bewildered look filled Ryan's face. 'So you think this guy might be linked to Gabby's murder somehow?'

'That's what we're trying to find out,' Megan said.

'I see.' Then Ryan shook his head. 'Look, if I had any idea about who it was, I'd tell you.'

Joseph resisted glancing yet again at the two-way mirror. He'd only one card left to play.

'In that case, I'd like to go through something with you. Didn't you tell us that you and Gabby were playing an Assassins' Syndicate game in the Wytham Woods when she shot you with the foam dart?'

'Yeah, what about it?'

'Well, that's the strange thing. When we spoke to Geoff Goldsmith, who runs the club, he confirmed you'd been thrown out because of what you did to Anita. Then Gabby resigned. Please explain that inconsistency in your story.'

Ryan glanced at his solicitor, who shook his head.

Joseph felt a pulse of frustration. There was an obvious reason for the lie they'd caught him in, but for whatever reason, the solicitor didn't think it was in his client's interest to play ball.

Ryan surprised no one when he said, 'No comment.'

Joseph traded a quick frown with Megan. That was it. The interview had yielded no fresh results, and now they had nothing left to question him about. The DI was pretty sure Derrick would be seething by now. They certainly didn't have enough for the CPS to proceed with, yet, at least.

The DI gave the art student the look a parent might give a child they knew was fibbing. 'In that case, this interview is terminated.' Without ceremony, Joseph leaned over and flicked off the recorder.

'That's it?' Ryan said, looking between his solicitor and the detectives, slightly bewildered.

Joseph nodded. 'Thank you for your cooperation during our investigation. You are free to go, Ryan. However, you'll need to remain in Oxford whilst we continue our enquiries into Gabby's murder.'

Ryan slumped into his chair. 'Oh, thank God for that.'

'An officer will be along in a moment to sort out your official discharge,' Megan added.

The student nodded, before turning to his solicitor, who was patting him on the shoulder.

Joseph took a mental breath as he and Megan headed towards the door and opened it, steeling himself for what was about to happen. Sure enough, Derrick was already standing there waiting for them, with Chris in tow.

'Follow me,' the superintendent said, on the verge of growling.

Chris raised his eyebrows at Joseph and Megan as Derrick marched off ahead of them towards his glass office. The moment his door was closed behind them, the DSU turned to face them with a furious expression.

'That was an absolute shit show, Joseph!'

The DI didn't even bat an eyelid. 'There wasn't a lot more we could do based on the evidence we've unearthed so far. Especially, as we had so few people assigned to the case.'

The way Derrick's face went scarlet, Joseph was pretty sure for a moment that the man's head was going to explode. But thankfully, Chris was already on the case.

'Derrick, we all know CPS wasn't happy with what we had. It wasn't anything like enough to prosecute Ryan. Besides, there is still every chance he really isn't our man.'

The superintendent rounded on him. 'Fucking hell, have you gone soft too? Of course he is. He may be bleating on about how much he loved her, but that doesn't mean he didn't do it. Don't forget, we have his prints all over the crossbow bolt that killed her.'

'Which could have been planted by someone wanting to frame Ryan,' Chris said.

'Who exactly? This mystery man who had a thing for Gabby?'

'We're currently exploring that angle,' Chris replied.

Derrick glowered at the three of them. 'So, in other words, no definite leads yet and, thanks to your collective incompetence, our only major suspect is about to waltz out of this station.'

Joseph had to take a mental breath. He'd never been a fan of the superintendent's behaviour when the heat was on. It was definitely the man's talent to always find someone else to blame. Heaven forbid, one day the great Derrick Walker actually looked in the mirror and questioned his own judgement.

The temptation to confront the superintendent about his own shortcomings was almost too great to resist. But right now, Joseph also knew he needed to keep his powder dry until he had enough solid evidence to take the man down.

Megan jumped in. 'Maybe we need to look at this another way. What if this case really is what it's looked like all along and Ryan really is being framed by someone? Surely our priority now is to find out who it is and as quickly as possible?'

Chris quickly followed that up. 'Megan's right. But I'll need a bigger team.'

Derrick looked between them as the heat in his face ebbed away. 'Let me think about it.'

A knock came from the door, and Graham, the custody sergeant, stuck his head around the corner. 'I'm just preparing the release papers for Ryan Slattery if one of you wants to run your eye over them?'

'I'll do it,' Joseph replied, before the superintendent had a chance to open up on him with round two.

Ryan stood in the reception area of Saint Aldates signing the release form that Graham had just put in front of him. As he put the pen down, Joseph nodded towards the lad.

'That's it, you're good to go.'

Of all the reactions he might have expected, it wasn't for Ryan to head over to him, hand outstretched. 'I just wanted to thank you, Detective Stone.'

Joseph, with a slightly confused expression, took the proffered hand and shook it. 'You're welcome.'

'No, I mean it. You were all just doing your jobs here, and I know how it looked for me. But at least now you can bring the actual murderer to justice.'

'We'll do whatever it takes. Anyway, you look after yourself.'

'I'll do my best,' Ryan said, a waver creeping into his voice.

It was then that Joseph realised that because of everything that had happened since Gabby's murder, the lad hadn't even had a chance to grieve. 'I can put you in touch with a counsellor, if you like?'

'No, I'll be fine,' Ryan said, before turning and slipping some white earbuds in as he headed towards the exit.

Joseph was just heading back to the incident room when John materialised before him. 'Has Ryan already left?'

Joseph cast a glance his way. 'Yes, why?'

'I was just passing your incident room when I noticed a photo on the board of a blue plastic pendant.'

The DI gave him an intrigued look. 'What about it?'

'I saw the same thing just a moment ago when I was getting Ryan's personal effects out of the locker room. He has a red pendant just like it.'

Joseph stared at the man. 'He does?'

'Yes, identical and on a chain. He slipped it over his neck when I gave it to him.'

'But Ryan said he didn't recognise it when we showed him that photo back in the first interview,' Joseph replied, already realising the significance.

'Then he was obviously lying, sir.'

Joseph looked at the closed door to the street. 'Shite, now you tell me!'

The DI rushed outside and looked left and right for any sign of the art student. Then he spotted the lad further along the street, crossing the road.

'Hey, Ryan, hang on there,' he shouted across. But Ryan continued walking along the pavement. Then the DI remembered the white earbuds in the student's ears.

As Joseph broke into a jog, he caught a glint of light briefly flashed from a rooftop opposite. He glanced up and his heart clenched. A hooded figure crouched on the roof, and was aiming a crossbow with a telescopic sight straight down towards Ryan.

Adrenaline roared through the DI as he broke into a sprint. He ignored the car horns and the squeal of brakes as he raced across the road. He was less than a couple of metres away when the hooded figure fired. An arrow blurred through the air and struck Ryan in the shoulder, spinning him sideways into a lamppost. The student's expression twisted into one of shock and confusion.

Joseph saw the shooter was reloading, getting ready for a second shot to finish Ryan off. Heart pounding in his ears, he sprinted towards the art student, closing the remaining distance and leapt towards Ryan, knocking him off his feet. A split second later, a second arrow sped past, slamming into a travel agent's window and shattering the glass.

The few passers-by, who'd witnessed what had happened, froze, their mouths hanging open.

'Get help now!' Joseph bellowed at the group of zombies around him as he continued to shield Ryan's body with his own. He scanned for the shooter again, but the figure had already disappeared from the rooftop. A groan came from Ryan. Joseph looked down to see blood bubbling up around the arrow shaft. The DI pressed his hands on the wound to try and staunch the flow.

'I've got you, lad. Just hang in there. The ambulance won't be long.'

Ryan nodded as John materialised before them, a medical box clutched in his hand.

'What can I do to help?'

Joseph jutted his chin towards the roofline. 'The shooter was just up there. Get after them.'

The PC nodded as he handed the medical box to one of the onlookers, and broke into a run as he dived across the road towards the building opposite.

The DI's heart was hammering as adrenaline thrummed through his system. He already knew one thing for certain— whoever had been up there was used to heights. It had to be a freerunner, and one who'd developed a taste for assassination.

CHAPTER FIFTEEN

THE OVERRIDING EMOTION Joseph was feeling as he walked through the corridors of the hospital was one of fury. Not at anyone else, but at himself.

Megan gave him a sideways look. 'Are you okay?'

'Oh, trust me, I've had better days.'

'Haven't we all, so why do I get the distinct impression that you're taking what happened to Ryan personally?'

'Because I am. If I'd listened to my instinct right from the start, that someone was trying to frame the lad for murder, he might not have ended up being shot in broad daylight less than a hundred metres away from our fecking police station.'

'You're not psychic, and we have procedures to follow. Even though he may have been innocent, like always, we had to follow the evidence. That was always going to mean that Ryan was a suspect. Besides, if he hadn't been in the cell, the real murderer would have probably got to him long before now. And you wouldn't have been there to save him.'

Joseph blew out his cheeks. 'Aye, you're probably right. But why did they come after Ryan at all? Surely, whoever it was had plenty of opportunity to kill him back in Wytham Woods after they killed Gabby?'

'Who knows? Maybe our investigation got close enough to rattle whoever was responsible, and they were worried about Ryan saying something.'

'You think it's somebody we've already spoken to?' the DI asked.

'That would be my guess. We need to take a closer look at everyone. But hopefully, if Ryan has been holding something back from us, he'll finally come out and tell us.'

'And then there's this business about the plastic pendant Ryan was wearing.'

'I would have said it was some sort of club membership badge for the Assassins' Syndicate, apart from the fact that Geoff Goldsmith was adamant their club didn't have one,' Megan replied.

'So maybe it's another club, and this plastic pendant is how members identify themselves to each other. Maybe even one Ryan and Gabby came up with themselves.'

'Yes, and they used them like player tokens,' Megan said, almost to herself.

'What's that?'

'You know, like tokens you get in a board game.'

'Actually, now you mention it, that's exactly what they look like. Whatever they are, let's just hope Ryan's in a talkative mood now that he was nearly killed.'

'Keeping everything crossed here,' Megan replied, as they reached the doors of the ward and buzzed.

After checking in at the nurses' station, the two detectives headed towards the armed tactical unit officer standing in front of a closed door.

'Wow, Derrick really wasn't messing about when he said he

was going to do whatever it took to make sure Ryan was kept safe,' Megan said.

'Well, it's never a good look when somebody who was being held as a potential suspect is shot just outside your own station. But at least he's given Chris the manpower we should have had in the first place.'

Megan sighed. 'Same old story.' The two detectives showed the armed officer their warrant cards hanging from the lanyards around their necks.

'Anything to report?' Joseph asked him.

'Nothing at all, sir. But bearing in mind how the lad was shot, we've taken the precaution of keeping the blinds shut.'

'Good thinking. We certainly don't want a repeat performance.'

The man nodded and stepped aside to let them pass.

The last time Joseph had seen him, Ryan had been hooked up to all kinds of monitoring equipment. Now there was just one solitary drip line hooked up to a pump. A large bandage covered the wound in his right shoulder. However, his eyes were shut and he looked as grey as a British summer's day.

'Ryan?' Joseph asked quietly.

The lad's eyes fluttered open. 'Ah, the man who saved my life,' he said, slurring his words. 'Sorry, I'm a bit out of it. Pain meds.'

'Can we get you anything?' Megan asked.

'Maybe a time machine to avoid getting shot,' Ryan said.

That raised a small smile from both officers.

'Apart from that, anything else?' Joseph asked.

'Some water would be great. I'm so bloody thirsty.'

'That will be the general anaesthetic. Makes you as dry as a cracker in the Sahara.'

Ryan almost managed a grin as Joseph poured him a glass of

water and handed it to him. The lad took a sip, his hand shaking and spilling some of it down his chin.

'Here, let me help,' Megan said, steadying the glass. The student took several greedy gulps before settling his head back into his pillow. He shot the DC a grateful look. 'Thank you, not quite back to the top of my game yet.'

'We're not surprised after everything you've been through,' Joseph replied, as he and Megan sat in seats on either side of the bed.

'According to the doctors I'm lucky to be alive,' Ryan said. 'That crossbow bolt managed to pass through my chest just beneath the clavicle. If you hadn't rugby tackled me to the ground, that second shot would have almost certainly killed me, Detective Stone.'

'I'm just glad I was in the right place at the right time. But I'm sure you realise we need to ask you some questions after what happened.'

Ryan's expression tightened. 'You want to know who shot me?'

'That would be an excellent place to start.'

'I wish I knew. Why some maniac would want to take me out in the middle of Oxford, especially right outside a police station, I've honestly no idea. But you have to be thinking what I'm thinking. It has to be the same psychopath who killed Gabby. And using a crossbow, too. That has to fit, what do you guys call it, his MO?'

Joseph smiled. 'Modus operandi, and I agree. It certainly seems unlikely that the two events aren't linked somehow. So, the natural conclusion is that it's the same person who targeted you both. If so, have you any idea of why that might be?'

Megan's notebook was already out, looking at the lad expectantly.

'If you mean can I think of anyone who would hate us enough to do that, then absolutely not,' Ryan said.

'You seem very certain about that,' Megan said.

'That's because I am,' Ryan replied, his expression tightening.

'Then what about your money situation?' Joseph asked. 'Looking at your bank account, it's clear you've been short of cash for a long time. You or Gabby didn't take out any loans from anyone you shouldn't, to cover your gambling habit?'

'If you mean a dodgy loan shark, then no. Why do you think I turned to gambling in the first place? It was all about making enough money to be able to afford to stay in Oxford with Gabby.'

'Well, gambling is a fool's game, as I'm sure you've already learnt,' Joseph replied.

Ryan sucked the air through his teeth. 'Getting there, but maybe not fast enough.'

'I just hope you do eventually, for your sake. Anyway, getting back to your assailant. There's one interesting aspect we're wondering if you have an opinion on, and that's where your assailant took the shot from, namely the top of a roof.'

'I already see where you're going with this. You think he's a freerunner, then?'

'Well, it's not exactly the average place to try and shoot someone from, is it?'

'I suppose not. If he is, he would have dozens of ways he could have escaped. Plus, as I know from experience, all those security cameras in Oxford are pointing down towards the street, rather than covering anything that happens at roof level. Thanks to that, unless someone spots you up on a roof, there's never going to be much chance of getting caught.'

'Oh, we already know all about the lack of camera footage. We've already checked that,' Megan replied.

Joseph nodded. 'It seems a bit of a coincidence that you and Gabby were freerunners yourselves, and just happened to both have been attacked by someone who would seem to be into the same pastime.'

'I grant you, that really is weird.'

'And you're sure you can't think of anyone? The freerunners in Oxford have to be a small group, aren't they?'

Ryan's expression clouded. 'Sorry, no idea. It was just something Gabby and I did.'

Joseph knew the student was lying. But why, even now, if he had an idea of who it might be, would he protect them?

The DI tried a different tack and gestured towards the student's chest. 'So, are you still wearing it?'

Ryan gave him a blank look. 'What?'

'That red plastic pendant.'

The student grimaced. 'So, you know about that?'

'Yes, and now we're intrigued about why you said you didn't recognise the blue version of the same pendant.'

Ryan broke eye contact as his expression became more guarded. 'I was embarrassed.'

'Sorry, what do you mean?' Megan asked.

'Gabby borrowed them from a board game called Eliminator at the Games café and made pendants from them. It's a game a lot of members of the Assassins' Syndicate club are into playing.'

'So, when you say she borrowed, you actually mean she stole them?'

Ryan shrugged. 'There are lots of player counters in the box, so she didn't think they'd really mind. Besides, we're not the only guild members who've helped themselves.'

'Okay, so why be embarrassed about that?' Megan asked.

He met their gazes again. 'Would you want to tell two police officers that your girlfriend had basically lifted something from a board game café as a keepsake?'

Joseph couldn't help the smile that formed. 'Aye, I don't suppose I would.'

'I know this sounds stupid, but if it's okay, I'd like to have Gabby's pendant back.'

'I'm sure at some point that will be possible, but it's still evidence.'

'Thank you so much...' Ryan blinked. 'Sorry, I really am desperately tired and need to sleep.'

'Okay. We'll let you get some rest. But if you think of anyone or anything that might be relevant, you contact me day or night.' Joseph placed one of his cards on the bedside cabinet.

'Will do...' Ryan said, as the two detectives stood. Even before they'd reached the door, Joseph glanced back to see that the lad's eyes had fluttered shut again.

'So, what are your thoughts?' he asked Megan, as they left the ward.

'His explanation for the plastic pendants seemed plausible. The only thing is, if this game is so popular with other members of the Assassins' Syndicate, why didn't one of them mention it to us when we spoke to them?'

'Maybe they were covering for the other members who also stole the tokens from the café?'

'Possibly. That theory aside, I definitely got the impression he was covering for someone,' Megan said.

'I agree, but once again, why? If I'd been shot by someone and knew who they were, especially as they'd already killed my girlfriend, I'd be pretty damned keen to see them locked up before they could try it again.'

'I would have said we should take a closer look at Eddie Foster, especially as we know he had a thing for Gabby,' Megan replied, 'but both his and Geoff's alibis checked out.'

'I know, and I thought we might be onto something there with Eddie. So who else might Ryan be covering for?' Joseph sighed. 'We also can't rule out the possibility that the murderer chose someone, or in this case, a couple, randomly. After all, there have been plenty of serial killers who've done just that over the years. So, I suppose in this instance we can't ignore the possibility Gabby and Ryan were just unlucky.'

'Maybe that's exactly what they were,' Megan replied as they reached the lift.

But Joseph still didn't feel it in his bones. There was still something they were not seeing in this case, but what exactly?

CHAPTER SIXTEEN

Tux was sitting on top of *Tús Nua's* roof when Joseph finally rolled up home much later that day. If the cat had picked up his paw and tapped an invisible watch, the DI wouldn't have been surprised. Instead, his feline companion gave him the *look*.

'What can I say, little guy, but it's been a long day,' Joseph said, reaching out his hand to try to rub the side of his cat's neck, who ducked away from his touch. Yes, the cat was definitely peeved at him. Tux gave the paper carry bag the DI was carrying an inquisitive sniff.

'That would be the takeaway fish casserole for my dinner, but I doubt you'd like it,' Joseph said.

Before Tux could give him a cat response equivalent to *I won't know until I try it*, there were two barks. Max and White Fang, Dylan's dogs, appeared on the towpath, their eyes firmly locked onto the DI's takeaway.

'You two, on the other hand, would scoff the lot in a heartbeat,' the DI said. He dug into the tin he kept for just such emergencies and tossed a couple of dog biscuits to them, followed by a cat treat to Tux. 'Good, are we all happy now?' Joseph asked his animal audience. They continued looking at him expectantly, and with a sigh, he handed out three more treats.

'And what have you got there?' Dylan asked, gesturing towards the takeaway bag, as he appeared behind his dogs, their leads in his hands.

'A fish casserole from that new place in St Clements. If you've not eaten, feel free to join me. I've got it on good authority that it's very good.'

'I've actually already eaten, but could probably manage a small portion. That's if I won't be intruding? No Amy tonight?'

Joseph shook his head. 'She's had a bit of a long day as well. Ryan, the boyfriend of the woman who was murdered in Wytham Woods, got shot with another crossbow bolt while leaving the police station.'

'Flipping heck, is he okay?'

'Yes, but now our investigation has reached something of a dead end. Meanwhile, we have some psychopath running around, taking potshots at people. And this time from an Oxford rooftop. It's just a matter of time before the press gets hold of this. There were plenty of eyewitnesses this time round.'

'Then you need to tell me all about it, and I can bring the gin.'

Joseph gave Dylan a perplexed look. 'I'm sorry, but even you can't conjure up a gin that goes with fish.'

'Oh, ye of little faith. Of course, I can. It's Dà Mhìle from Llandysul in Wales and is made from seaweed.'

'Seriously?'

'Yes indeed. It's infused with seaweed for three weeks, giving it a fresh, salty taste. It even has a hint of green colour to it. Apparently, it's just the thing to be had with seafood.'

'Then we better put that theory to the test.'

'I'll go and get it, and I'll be with you in three shakes of a lamb's tail.' The professor gave Tux a scratch behind the ear, who, in stark contrast to Joseph, was rewarded for his efforts with a very loud purr. Yes, his cat knew how to make him suffer.

The dogs had made themselves at home in front of a radiator, along with Tux, who was treating them as two warm, doggy pillows. The cat had certainly never been fazed by White Fang and Max. The three of them seemed to get along famously, although Tux wasn't averse to bopping them on the nose to remind them who was boss if they got a bit too enthusiastic around him. Meanwhile, the humans were finishing off the last of the fish casserole.

'That smoky paprika really elevates this dish,' Dylan said.

Joseph nodded as he scraped the last of the sauce with some freshly baked wholemeal soda bread the professor had turned up with. 'You'll get no argument from me. That was grand. In fact, almost as good as that Welsh gin you brought with you.'

'Yes, they were right, that slightly salty flavour of the Dà Mhìle really hits it off with the fish.'

'I can't disagree. So tell me, have you got a gin pairing for every sort of food then?'

'Well, I like a challenge, although even I would have a problem with coming up with something for pickled eggs.'

'Thank God for small mercies. I loathe the things.'

'I give you, they're certainly something of an acquired taste. Anyway, back to your latest case.' Dylan poured himself another measure of gin. 'You do seem to have reached rather a dead end with your investigation.'

'Don't I know it. But at least we've got enough manpower now, thanks to Chris's efforts, to put the hours in to try and track whoever's responsible down.'

'Have you thought about asking for the public's help?'

'In a word, yes. The story is about to break anyway. Chris has already organised a press conference for first thing tomorrow. Gabby's mum and dad are also going to put in an appearance to ask anyone who might have any information to step forward.'

'Needless to say, I'll ask around with my college contacts as well to see if anyone has any useful information,' Dylan said.

'I'd certainly appreciate any help you can give us.'

'As always, I'm delighted to be of assistance. Has Kate been able to dig up anything? Someone might have previously seen this mysterious freerunner in Oxford and reported something to the press?'

'I haven't seen Kate in ages.'

Dylan's look zeroed in on him. 'And why would that be, Joseph?'

'Our paths just haven't crossed in a while.'

'I see...' The professor's eyes narrowed even further, like a headteacher dealing with an obstructive child.

'Honestly, nothing more to it than that,' the DI replied, avoiding his friend's hardening stare.

'Hmm.' Then the professor tapped his fingertips together, not saying anything else, but letting the silence in the cabin linger.

Joseph wasn't sure if it was his subconscious determined to trip him up, but he inadvertently glanced at his evidence board, which was turned around to the other side. He tore his gaze away the moment he realised what he'd done, but it was already too late.

The professor gave him a knowing look. 'You've got some sort of personal investigation going, haven't you? But it can't be anything to do with the Midwinter Butcher case, as that's been long since solved. So...' He clicked his tongue against his teeth. 'This is something to do with Kate, or at least part of the reason you've been avoiding her...' Then his eyes widened. 'Hang on, you're not investigating the Night Watchman in your own time, are you?'

Joseph already knew there was no point in denying it. When Dylan got his teeth into something, he was as tenacious as one of his dogs with a bone.

'Jesus, I really can't keep anything from you, can I?' he said.

'Absolutely correct, but what's puzzling me is why you would want to. Also, if you're still looking into the Night Watchmen, surely you and Kate would be as thick as thieves?'

'Ah, you're forgetting she agreed to let her own investigation drop when the NCA took over.'

Dylan gave the DI a straight look, raising his eyebrows a fraction.

'Look, Kate personally promised me she wouldn't, after that email threatening her.'

'Have you ever known your ex-wife to give up on anything?'

'Rarely, I grant you that.'

'Okay, putting that aside for a moment. Have you shared with her the fact you're still looking into it?'

Joseph sighed. 'No, I haven't.'

'I see, so this is something you don't want to tell her, because...' The professor's eyes travelled to the hidden incident board again.

'Bloody hell. At this rate, you'll have worked it all out.'

'So just tell me already.'

Joseph slowly nodded. 'To be honest, I could do with someone to talk to about all of this because it's been doing my head in.' He stood and headed to the pinboard and turned it over.

Dylan's gaze swept over it. Then he stood for a closer look at the photo of Derrick in the pub car park and then the line connecting him directly to the Night Watchmen heading.

He turned to stare at Joseph. 'You're not trying to tell me that Derrick is working for this crime syndicate, are you?'

'I couldn't be sure until recently, but that photo you're interested in was taken from a video I shot last weekend. If nothing else, it basically confirms something is definitely off with the man.' He took his mobile out and handed it to Dylan. The professor watched the video of the superintendent throwing the cash back at the woman in the Mercedes.

'I recognise that woman from somewhere,' he said.

'That's because it's none other than our esteemed Chief Supt Kennan.'

'I see, and what's exactly happening here?'

'I'm as sure as I can be that Derrick was refusing a bribe from her. I may be jumping to conclusions here, but to me that suggests she's involved with the Night Watchmen, too. But maybe Derrick's conscience finally caught up with him, because I'm certain he's been under the syndicate's thumb for a while now.'

'Based on what evidence exactly?'

'Well, I haven't got any, as such. But remember when our suspect in the Burning Man case, Daryl Manning, was killed during transport?'

'Of course, you were ambushed by those two Night Watchman thugs and John and another police officer were badly injured. I'm not about to forget that awful ordeal in a hurry. Why, you can't be saying that Derrick was involved in that?'

'I'm afraid that's exactly what I'm saying. Remember, there was plenty of speculation at the time that we had a leak at St Aldates. Eventually, the assumption was that Daryl's solicitor, who was almost certainly paid for by the Night Watchmen, had tipped them off and maybe our convoy was followed from the station. But what if...' Joseph deliberately let his words trail away.

'You're suggesting Derrick would have also known all about it and could have been the source of the leak?'

'Exactly, and what makes it even worse was that Chris actually asked for armed officers to protect the convoy, but Derrick refused him point blank, saying it wasn't necessary.'

'Flipping Nora, Joseph. That's a bit of a mental leap, isn't it?'

'Maybe it is, maybe it isn't. But that photo of Derrick in the pub car park definitely tends to make me think the latter.'

'However, just as you've already alluded, it's not conclusive evidence of that either, not by a long shot.'

'Oh, don't I know it. But enough to make me very suspicious about Derrick. There's been something off with the guy for a long time. Even Kate said so, and that he was drinking a lot, even at work sometimes. Tell me that's not the sign of a guilty conscience?'

'I suppose it could be. Okay then, tell me what your next step's going to be?'

Joseph took a long sip of the gin. 'I don't actually know yet.'

'In that case, I have a suggestion for you.'

'Go on?'

'You need to talk to Kate, and do it sooner rather than later. If you have these sorts of suspicions about her husband, you need to discuss it with her.'

'But I can't. At least not yet.'

'Then just imagine what will happen if you do dig up enough evidence to get Derrick prosecuted. How do you think Kate will feel when she eventually finds out you've been withholding something so important from her? She has a right to know, Joseph.'

Joseph dragged his hand through his hair. 'But it won't be pretty, will it?'

'Absolutely right. It won't be, and it could destroy your relationship with her beyond repair. I suppose the real question is, even knowing that, are you prepared to take the risk?'

The DI sighed. 'I suppose I have to. I don't think I could cope with the endless lectures you'll give me if I don't.'

The corners of the professor's mouth twitched. 'So you'll talk to Kate, then?'

'Aye. I'll even have the perfect opportunity. She'll be at the press conference tomorrow.'

'In that case, good man,' Dylan said, raising his glass to the DI.

Joseph retrieved his own drink and clinked it against the professor's. 'I can't tell you what a relief it is to finally share this with you. It's been weighing me down for months now.'

'Then let that be a lesson, right there. You should know by now I'm here for you, my friend, and always will be. This is exactly the sort of thing you should be confiding in me.'

'Maybe you should set up a confessional on your boat that I could use.'

'If you're going to be a frequent flyer, then maybe I should,' Dylan said, winking at him and making Joseph roar with laughter.

CHAPTER SEVENTEEN

JOSEPH FELT a real pull in his gut as Gabby's mum, Mary Dawson, had tears streaming down her face. She was sitting next to the DI at the press conference, looking out at the reporters gathered there. Her husband, Joe, glassy-eyed and mute, was on the other side of her, flanked by Chris.

No one had asked Gabby's parents to be there, but as soon as they'd heard about the press conference, they'd insisted on attending. Mary had told them that they wanted to help in any way they could. Despite the detectives wanting to shield them from the press, they also knew a request for information coming from the grieving mother's lips would help to get the message out there like nothing else could.

The DI noticed Megan giving him a thumbs up from the back, before spotting Kate sitting among the other journalists. His ex-wife caught his eye and gave him a grim look. Of all people, she knew just as well as he did this was the worst sort of grief for a parent. Joseph certainly doubted that in Mary's place, he could hold it together long enough to get any words out. He was always all snot and tears when it came to anything happening to Ellie. But Mary Dawson, it seemed, was made of sterner stuff.

Despite her hands visibly trembling as she looked down at her notes, Mary raised her head to look out at the audience and the video cameras and the photographers taking photos of her.

The woman took a shuddering breath and began. 'Our beautiful daughter, Gabby, was murdered with a crossbow last weekend in the woods just outside Oxford. Our loss has destroyed our family, but now we need the help of the public to try and bring her killer to justice. Only yesterday, her wonderful boyfriend, Ryan, was nearly killed by someone who fired a crossbow at him. If it hadn't been for the swift action of DI Stone sitting next to me, he almost certainly would have been killed, too.'

Dozens of cameras turned towards the DI and shutters whirred. But he studiously ignored them, not feeling in any way a hero.

'You are probably wondering why Joe and I are here today, but we both felt we needed to do something to help the investigation,' Mary continued. 'You see, right now, no one knows who the murderer is, but someone out there must. The police have reason to believe the suspect is someone called'—she looked at her notes—'a freerunner. These are people who love to vault, jump, and climb through cities and over rooftops. They view it as a form of sport and call it Parkour. Much to our surprise, it turns out that Gabby and Ryan took part in this as well, despite the danger. But of course, our daughter loved to live life to the fullest, doing things like bungee jumps with Ryan, so maybe we shouldn't be so surprised.'

Joseph noticed how Mary's voice was growing stronger the longer she'd been speaking. Yes, she really had needed to do this, not for herself, but for the sake of Gabby's memory.

She smeared away some of her tears with the tissue clutched

in her hand. 'The police believe the murderer might actually be another freerunner, based on the fact the person who shot Ryan was on a rooftop at the time. The problem is Ryan, who is now recovering in hospital, has no idea who this might be. This is where you, the public, can help.' She looked straight at the BBC's video camera. 'If you know anyone who is a freerunner in Oxford or the surrounding area, you need to come forward and let the police know so they can be interviewed and eliminated as a suspect.'

Mary's shoulders rose. 'I appeal to you as parents who have lost their daughter, please, if you know anything, anything at all, get in contact with the investigation hotline. We need to catch this person before they do this to anyone else and break another parent's heart. Thank you for your help.'

As she sat back, Joe cradled her hand in his and she took another long breath. It was clear that this stoic performance had taken every ounce of mental reserves the woman had left.

A barrage of questions exploded from the pack of journalists, aimed towards her, but Chris was already leaning forward.

'Mr and Mrs Dawson won't be taking any questions. However, I will take a few before wrapping things up.'

It was Kate who the DCI picked first. 'Can you tell us if you have uncovered any clear motive about why Gabby and Ryan might have been targeted?' she asked.

That's so my Kate, straight to the core issue, Joseph thought to himself.

'At this time, we have no clear motive,' Chris replied.

'So you're saying it could have just been a random killing?' Kate said.

'That's certainly still a possibility, although maybe less so now that Ryan was targeted as well.'

Joseph's ex-wife nodded as another hand shot into the air. Then the DI's heart sank when he saw who it was. Ricky Holt, the lowest of the low tabloid pond scum, who even gave the gutter press a bad name.

Kate was already glowering across at Ricky before he'd even opened his mouth. Joseph knew that had to do with the run-in they'd had with the festering toerag of a man. It had been at a similar press conference about the Midwinter Butcher, where he'd tried to imply that Ellie had something to do with the murders. Joseph wasn't at all surprised when the slimeball from the shallow end of the gene pool swivelled his attention towards him.

'How is it that Ryan Slattery was shot almost right outside the police station when you were by his side, Detective Stone?'

'There wasn't a lot I could do about it, as the crossbow shot came out of nowhere,' the DI replied.

'I see, and why didn't you give chase to the shooter?' the weasel-faced man asked.

It took some considerable act of will for Joseph not to eye-roll the gobshite. 'Unfortunately, they were too far away to apprehend as they were on a rooftop at the time.'

'Besides, DI Stone was doing his best to save Ryan Slattery's life,' Chris quickly added. 'PC John Thorpe did give chase, but the assailant was long gone by the time he was able to gain access to the roof where the suspect had been spotted.'

'Right, but there must have been other people around who could have helped Ryan, DI Stone?' Holt asked. 'Surely, this is a dereliction of duty and, thanks to that, we now have a murderer on the loose in Oxford.'

Joseph felt a ball of fiery anger growing in his stomach.

'In fact, wouldn't you say that this investigation has been run incompetently from the start and that you even managed to briefly arrest the wrong man over Gabby's murder, her own boyfriend, Ryan?' Holt continued. 'If he hadn't been arrested and then released, then he wouldn't have been shot.'

Chris glowered at the reporter and was opening his mouth to say something when a voice spoke up from the back.

'That is pure conjecture, and this investigation has been absolutely thorough from the very start,' Derrick said.

All eyes turned towards the big man standing at the back of the room, his hands clasped behind his back.

'I certainly have every confidence in my officers, and I can assure everyone that no stone will be left unturned in the pursuit of this murderer.'

Although a certain Stone will be thrown under the bus if the heat gets anywhere near me, Joseph couldn't help adding to the end of Derrick's comment.

'Anyway, I think we'll wrap things up there,' Derrick continued. 'I'd like to thank all of you for coming.' He nodded to Chris, who turned to Gabby's parents and quickly ushered them out of a door as dozens more questions were fired at their departing backs.

As the meeting broke up, Joseph valiantly resisted the urge to march over and grab the steaming turd of a reporter by the scruff of his neck. Instead, he headed towards Kate. Compared to the press conference, the DI felt far more nervous about what he was about to broach with her.

He certainly wasn't surprised to see Kate giving Ricky dagger eyes as he headed past her, smirking.

'That man never gets any better,' she said, as Joseph reached her.

'Aye, tell me about it. Anyway, long time no see.'

'Yes, it's almost like you've been avoiding me.'

Joseph took one of the largest mental breaths of his lifetime. 'About that. We really need to talk, Kate.'

She shot him a surprised look.

'Okay, I'm all ears.'

Joseph scanned the room, but there was no sign of Derrick.

Of course, he wouldn't hang around longer than strictly necessary in case a reporter started asking him one too many difficult questions.

'No, not here. Somewhere a bit more private,' he said.

'Can it wait? I need to head over to the AI Research Unit in the Department of Computer Science in Parks Road, to cover a breakthrough they've made.'

'No, not really, but I can walk with you, presuming you're heading over there on foot?'

'I am. Let's go,' Kate replied, giving him a questioning look as she gathered up her things.

'Look, I don't really know quite how to tell you this. It's about Derrick,' Joseph said, as he headed away from St Aldates Police Station with Kate.

'Oh hell, you've got your, *I'm about to tell you bad news,* face on,' Kate replied. 'What is it?'

'Look, before I say anything more, I need to preempt it by saying I don't have any hard and fast proof, just circumstantial. Well, that, along with a gut feeling.'

'Okay. I learned a long time ago to take your instincts seriously, so please, just tell me what this is about.' Then her hands flew to her mouth. 'Oh God, please don't tell me you've discovered Derrick's having an affair?'

'No, nothing like that.'

Kate's shoulders visibly dropped. 'At least that's something I can relax about. Although, that would explain why he's been so sharp with me recently, biting my head off about the smallest thing. So, what is it, then, Joseph?'

He gave her a sideways glance as they turned onto the High Street crammed full of buses and cyclists.

'You know when that prisoner transfer of Daryl Manning during the Burning Man case all went spectacularly south, when we were attacked by those masked gunmen?'

'I'm not about to forget something like that, especially when John was badly hurt, let alone the fact that you and Megan nearly got shot as well.'

'You probably also recall we thought Manning's solicitor probably tipped the Night Watchman off?'

'Yes...' She caught Joseph's tense expression, and her eyes widened as her well-honed journalist's instinct kicked in. 'Hang on, you're not saying my husband had anything to do with that? That would mean he's working with the Night Watchmen, and that's... that's just ridiculous.'

Joseph held up his hands to stop her. 'Look, as I said, I don't have any hard proof, but there are some things that haven't added up over this last year.'

She searched his face. 'So, this is just pure conjecture, then?'

'Not entirely. For months now I've been trying to find evidence either way. I was almost ready to throw in the towel when this happened last weekend.' He took out his phone and handed it to Kate.

She started watching the video of her husband getting out of the white Mercedes. 'What exactly am I looking at here, Joseph?'

'Derrick met someone in the Printing Press car park while you were still at work on Sunday night. At first, I thought the same as you did, that he was having an affair. But keep watching.'

Kate watched intently as Derrick threw the envelope of money back into the car and she listened to her husband's response, '*I don't want your bloody money!*'

'What does that look like to you?' Joseph asked, not wanting to put ideas into his ex-wife's head.

'That he was refusing some sort of bribe? And, correct me if I'm wrong, isn't that Chief Superintendent Kennan?'

'Indeed, it is.'

'Hang on, surely that's good news. If anything, it paints Kennan in a bad light. This is certainly a long way from proving that my husband has any connection to the Night Watchman.'

'Maybe, maybe not. If we were talking about this in isolation, then I'd say you might have a point. But when you yourself have told me many times that something's been off with Derrick for a while now, maybe that points to him being involved with them somehow and it's been taking its toll. Don't forget, your husband was one of the few people who knew anything about that prisoner transfer and the route we planned to take.'

'But I'm sure that, as his superior, Kennan would have known that as well. Maybe she's the one who we should be looking more closely at here,' Kate said, crossing the road and dodging the traffic, as they headed into Catte Street.

Joseph couldn't help feeling a little surge in his heart at the phrase *we*. 'Yes, that's certainly possible, but nothing is clear at this point.'

Kate shot him a penetrating look. 'And just how long have you been sitting on these suspicions, Joseph?'

'Three months or so; since the end of the Burning Man case.'

'Bloody hell, and you're only telling me now? I thought, even after everything that had happened between us, we were still friends.'

'Of course we are. I just didn't want to tell you anything in case I was totally off the mark here.'

They had reached the edge of Radcliffe Square and Kate turned to stare at him. 'So, let me get this right. You were trying to protect my feelings?'

It sounded incredibly lame hearing her say it, but that was exactly what he'd been trying to do.

Joseph sighed. 'Right or wrong, I'm afraid that's about the measure of it.'

'Oh, trust me, that was very much the wrong call when we're talking about the man I'm married to.'

The DI put up his hands. 'Okay, I hear you. But what do we do next?'

'Absolutely nothing before I've had a chance to talk this over with Derrick.'

'Sorry, but you can't do that. What if it turns out he really is involved with them? That would tip him off before I've had a chance to build a solid case.'

What, seriously? You expect me to keep this from him? You have to know that's not an option. If anything is going to poison our marriage, it's that.'

'Look, as hard as this is, you need to sit on this until we know more,' Joseph said.

'No, you're completely and utterly wrong there. I'm going to have this out with Derrick tonight, but I will do you one favour and keep your name out of it.'

'But what about the video of him and the chief superintendent?'

Kate pulled up the share option on Joseph's phone and tagged the video, then emailed it to herself. 'I'm going to say I was suspicious he was having an affair, so I had a private investigator follow him. Then I'll listen to him as he explains what this meeting with the chief superintendent was really all about.'

'But if he is working for the Night Watchmen, this could be dangerous for you. Don't forget that email you received warning you off.'

'I don't bloody care, Joseph. This is my marriage, and maybe my one and only chance of saving it.'

'But Kate—'

'Don't you dare bloody *Kate* me. This is the end of the discussion. Do you understand me? I'm doing this and you had better get used to the idea.'

She turned on her heel and stalked across the square.

'Please, don't do anything rash,' Joseph called out as she headed away.

Without turning around, she lifted a hand in the universal sign of no more.

Joseph watched her go, a feeling of dread filling his chest.

What the hell have I just done?

He watched until he lost sight of her down the side of the Bodleian Library, then, with a heavy heart, he turned and headed back to the police station.

CHAPTER EIGHTEEN

IT HAD BEEN A VERY long day at work, and Joseph spent much of it forcing himself to focus on his job. Despite all the people now assigned to the case, thanks to the press conference, the investigation had shifted to filtering through the flood of information that had poured in from the public via the hotline.

Despite interviewing every single member of the Assassins' Syndicate, each had come up with an alibi for where they were during Gabby's murder. They'd even dug deeper into Eddie's cover, but his friends had stuck to their stories that he'd been with them on Sunday night. Even Geoff Goldsmith's alibi had stood up to scrutiny. Ian had checked the video of the student talking to the board game designers live on YouTube. According to him, the date and time stamp proved it had been streamed at the time of her murder. So right now there were no other leads.

But it wasn't the creeping air of despondency in the incident room that had got to Joseph. All the DI could really think about was what would happen when Kate talked to Derrick later that night.

It was with that lead weight of guilt and worry dragging his soul down that he'd arrived back at *Tús Nua*.

Dylan appeared the moment he'd dismounted his bike, giving him a cheery wave. But as soon as his friend saw the expression on Joseph's face, the professor shot him a concerned look.

'What on Earth is wrong with you?' he asked. 'You've got a face like you just discovered you're out of coffee.'

When Joseph didn't so much as smile, the professor looked even more worried. 'You followed my advice and told Kate about Derrick, didn't you?'

'To a T. And guess what her reaction was?'

'She didn't take it well?'

'The understatement of the century, and now she's going to have it out with Derrick tonight.'

'Ouch, so if it turns out he is involved with the Night Watchman, what then?'

'Exactly. The fallout could be enormous.'

'Oh, Joseph, I'm so sorry. I can only begin to imagine what you're feeling right now.'

'Basically, bloody powerless and unable to do anything about it.'

'Alright, but this was always going to happen at some point. Look, Kate has got a good head on her shoulders and will find a way to navigate this.'

'You think?'

'I do. Besides, there's still a chance that Derrick is innocent. Don't forget you actually witnessed him refusing what, on the surface at least, looked like a bribe.'

'You're not wrong but, dealing with the fallout firsthand with Kate when I told her, has left me wishing I'd never stuck my nose into the whole fecking mess. I've a good mind to go into my boat and rip down my incident board.'

Dylan gave him a straight look. 'Don't be ridiculous. You're just a good cop who wants to do the right thing. Because of that, you could never leave it alone. And if you tried, you wouldn't be able to sleep at night. I'm afraid it's just the way you're wired.'

Joseph sighed. 'Maybe you're right, but look at the cost of all this.'

The professor's forehead ridged. 'What do you mean?'

'I mean that I could have destroyed my relationship with Kate. She won't want to have anything to do with me after this.'

'Don't be so melodramatic. Of course she will.'

'You weren't there when I told her. The look she gave me...' Joseph's eyes closed briefly as he relived that awful moment for the hundredth time that day.

The professor shook his head, reached out, and patted his shoulder. 'Trust me, Kate will. All you did was tell her the truth. Look at it this way, if you'd sat on the information and it finally came out some other way, she wouldn't have thanked you, either. Much better she heard it from the mouth of someone who really cares about her.'

'I suppose you may have a point there.'

Dylan gave his friend a long, thoughtful look.

'What is it now?' Joseph asked.

'Well, if ever a man needed cheering up, or at least distracting from his own thoughts, it's you. Otherwise, all you'll end up doing is pacing up and down your boat tonight.'

'Very true. So what did you have in mind? Finishing up the rest of that seaweed gin?'

'No. I don't think that would be much good for you right now.'

'Aye, you're probably right, so what then?'

'Playing a board game.'

Joseph stared at his friend as though he'd just totally lost the plot. 'Come again?'

Dylan chuckled. 'Okay, I can see by the look on your face that you think I've got a screw loose. But there's a method to my madness. You see, I've finally struck gold with that pendant design Gabby was wearing when she was killed.'

'Oh, you little beauty. But save your breath because I know what it is now. It's just a token from a board game.'

'That may well be true, but I found something else out about it as well. One of the college lecturers at Keble College told me he had to discipline some students recently when one of them shot another in their library. When it emerged that this was a hit as part of the Assassins' Syndicate game, he showed the pendant design to the students who'd been involved. They were reluctant to tell him what they knew, but when pressed, one of them thought it was to do with a club called the Hidden Hand.'

'And who are they when they're at home?'

'This is where it gets really interesting. Apparently, years ago, a group of students decided the Assassins' Syndicate was far too tame for them, and decided to take things to the next level. However, it was invite-only to play the game.'

'In what way?'

'That's as much as the student knew, other than it was seen as the ultimate game, and with some sort of cash prize up for grabs.'

Joseph felt some of the fog lifting from the case. 'Okay, that may be the breakthrough we've been looking for.'

'How so?'

'It turns out, Ryan and Gabby were both wearing those pendants, suggesting they were both players in this Hidden Hand club. We also know they were both adrenaline junkies, who happen to have money problems, so I can see why that kind of game might have appealed to them.'

'And you think one of the players might have taken it literally about taking it to the next level?' Dylan asked.

'That's my guess based on what you just told me. Is there anything else you know about this mysterious club?'

'No, but as we're talking about games, there's one group I know who are experts in all forms of gaming. And they just happen to hang around in the very place I want to take you tonight, the Games Emporium Café in Gloucester Green. If anyone knows anything more about the Hidden Hand club, it will be someone there.'

'That's the second time the name of that café has come up regarding this investigation.'

'How so, exactly?'

'Ryan told us that's where those plastic tokens came from. The story he spun was that Gabby stole them from a board game called Eliminator as keepsakes for the two of them to wear.'

'Did he, now? Then I would hazard that was a lie, and they're actually players in this Hidden Hand club. So what do you say about joining me in a game at the Games Emporium? I really do think it's the best place to dig up more information.'

'Then you've persuaded me to come,' Joseph replied.

'Wonderful, but one last thing. We'll need to rustle up three other players. It's a special six-player variant of the Catan board game tournament tonight that uses expansion packs.'

'Hang on, your maths are out. Three plus us two is five.' Joseph was very taken aback to see his friend actually blush.

'That's because I play with an old friend there, Professor Iris Evans.'

'Oh, right,' Joseph replied, intrigued by his friend's obvious embarrassment at even mentioning the woman's name. 'Hopefully, I can rope Amy, Ellie, and John into this as my plus three.'

'Excellent, then we're all set.' Dylan peered at him. 'So, did this help?'

'Help what... Oh. You mean, take my mind off Kate for a few minutes? Yes, it did. Cunning, very cunning indeed.'

'You know me. Anyway, you'll need your wits about you, as

neither Iris nor I take any prisoners when it comes to our board games.'

'Challenge accepted,' Joseph said, smiling at his friend.

Joseph and Dylan's breaths clouded in the frosty autumnal air as they approached Amy, Ellie, and John, waiting just outside the Games Emporium Café in the corner of Gloucester Green.

'Why on Earth aren't you already inside when it's this cold?' Joseph asked.

Amy gestured towards the glowing windows where they could see lots of people packing out the tables and hunched over board games in progress. 'And enter the lion's den filled with all those geeks without any backup? I don't think so.'

Dylan laughed. 'So let me get this straight. You're not intimidated by dealing with the most grizzly of murder scenes, but the most delightful group of human beings you could hope to meet puts you all on edge?'

'Don't look at me,' Ellie replied. 'I was all for heading straight in, but...' She shot John an amused look.

He shrugged. 'Let's just say it's not exactly my usual crowd.'

'Then let me educate you about what you've been missing out on, rather than standing out here freezing our nether regions off,' Dylan said. 'Besides, Iris is already holding a table for us, and if we're late, we'll lose our slot.'

'Seriously, you have to book to get into this place?' Joseph asked.

Dylan nodded. 'It really is that popular, and by the end of this evening, I promise you all, you'll see why.'

Like a shepherd herding a reluctant flock of sheep, Dylan took up the position at the rear of the group, flapping his hands at them and towards the door.

'So about this mystery woman, Dylan,' Ellie said, as she opened the door.

'Oh, Iris and I are just old friends who go a long way back,' the professor said, avoiding her eye as he ushered everyone in.

Joseph had been expecting, much like Amy it seemed, to see a bunch of die-hard geeks in the gaming cafe, some of whom might even be wearing costumes. What he wasn't expecting was that everyone looked relatively normal, and of every age. They ranged from groups in their twenties and parents playing with their children to a more senior clientele. It was one of these, a woman who was maybe in her late sixties, who was waving enthusiastically at them. She had a sweep of grey hair and the sharpest, almost iridescent blue eyes. But most arresting of all was the beautiful smile lighting up her face as Dylan walked over.

She reached up and squeezed his hands in hers. 'Thank goodness you've finally turned up. I've had to fight this rabble tooth and nail to hang onto this table.'

'Good work, Iris,' Dylan said, leaning over and kissing her on the proffered cheek.

Joseph cast a second look around him at the people in the café, but they were as far removed from a *rabble* as he could possibly imagine.

Iris's attention switched to the DI. 'So, you must be the famous Joseph. Goodness, you're a bit of a dish, aren't you?' She grinned at Dylan. 'You somehow managed to leave that little detail out all these years.'

Dylan sighed. 'You'll have to excuse Iris. She's one of those people who says whatever is in their head without any sort of filter.'

'Nothing wrong with being a straight talker,' Joseph replied, already warming to the woman. 'But I'm afraid you have me at a disadvantage. Dylan here has made sure your good self has been a well-kept secret all these years.'

'Has he now?' Iris said, casting an amused look at the professor, who was looking distinctly uncomfortable. Then her laser-like gaze swept over the rest of the party. 'And who are the rest of you?'

'I'm Ellie, Joseph's daughter.'

'Oh my goodness, you're as beautiful as your dad is handsome. I almost feel like I know you. Dylan has told me how well you're doing at college and how proud of you he is.'

Ellie beamed at Dylan as she mock-punched him on the arm. 'Oh, shucks.'

'Well, I am,' he replied, returning her smile.

Iris looked at John. 'And you must be Ellie's brave boyfriend?'

'Brave?' John said, looking confused.

'From what I've been told, you have to be *brave* to dare to date Joseph's daughter.'

'Hey, I'm standing here, you know,' Joseph said, chuckling.

'Tell me it isn't true,' Iris replied.

Joseph winked at John. 'Guilty as charged.'

Then Iris zeroed in finally on the last member of their party. 'And you must be Amy. I've been so looking forward to meeting you. With your razor-sharp mind, you sound like a woman after my own heart. I hope Joseph isn't giving you too much trouble.'

'No more than usual,' the SOCO replied.

'Yet again, still standing here,' Joseph replied, shaking his head at her.

Iris, smirking, sat back down in her chair. 'Now, with all the introductions out of the way, are you all prepared for a night of gaming and high jinks? Because I warn you now, I'm a bit of a demon at Catan and intend to crush you all, showing absolutely no mercy as I kick your collective behinds.'

Amy raised her chin at the woman. 'We'll see about that. I used to play it with my parents all the time back in Germany, and if I say so myself, I'm rather good at it.'

Iris rubbed her hands together. 'Challenge accepted.'

Even though Joseph was losing spectacularly badly, he was surprised just how much he enjoyed playing—it was really stretching his grey matter. As the rest of the players had fallen behind, including, much to his own surprise, Dylan, Amy and Iris were still slugging it out in the lead. A small crowd of onlookers had even gathered around their table as people watched the epic battle unfold. It was Amy's move, and she gave Iris what could only be described as a smug look as she turned over a card she'd kept hidden for most of the game.

'Oh goodness, a victory card. That takes you up ten points for the win,' Iris said, shaking her head. Then she reached over the board to shake her opponent's hand.

There was a smattering of applause as the small crowd dispersed and headed back to their tables.

'Very well played indeed, Amy. Although I will obviously need a rematch at some point to regain my honour.'

'I'd be delighted to,' Amy replied.

'Well, that's certainly as good a game of Catan as I've ever seen played in here,' Dylan said. 'The question is, did you all enjoy yourselves?'

'That was huge fun,' Ellie said, as John nodded. 'We should make this a regular thing.'

'I'd certainly be up for that,' Amy said.

All eyes turned to Joseph.

He held up his hands. 'Maybe when I can, work allowing.

'Anyway, that aside, Dylan, we should start picking some brains about that club.'

'Who?' Ellie asked.

'That's exactly what we're trying to find out.'

'And you're asking the players in here, because?' Iris asked.

'We thought the regulars of the Games Emporium would count as Oxford's greatest experts in all things games, and might know something about a mysterious club called Hidden Hand,' Dylan said. 'Apparently, it's meant to be a step up from the Assassins' Syndicate played by Oxford students.'

'Oh, all that nonsense where the members try to shoot each other with foam darts?' Iris asked.

'That's the one. Apparently, members use tokens from the Eliminator board game and use them like some sort of membership badge.'

'I see,' Iris said, looking intrigued. 'Then I know the first person we should ask, and that's Neil Tanner. He's studying computer science at Balliol College. He's also a white hat hacker in his spare time and the go-to person when anyone needs anything technical sorting out.'

'What's a white hat hacker, then?' John asked.

'They're the good guys who try to detect the vulnerabilities in computer systems and let people in charge know about them,' Ellie said.

Iris nodded. 'That's right. You'll find him over there in the corner playing Mysterium with his friends. He certainly has his finger on a lot of pulses when it comes to anything to do with games in all their varieties.'

'Including the Assassins' Syndicate?' Dylan asked.

'Well, as it's a game, of course he does,' Iris replied.

'Then he sounds like the perfect man to ask.'

Iris nodded and waved a hand. 'Neil, dearest, can we pick your brain about something?'

The man with curly blond hair and a neatly clipped beard looked up from the board game he was playing, said something to the other players, then headed over.

He glanced at the game board. 'So I see you're beating everyone at Catan as usual, Iris,' he said.

Iris shook her head and gestured towards Amy. 'Not this time, I didn't. This good lady here gave me rather a good thrashing.'

Neil shot the SOCO an impressed look. 'Anyone who can beat Iris, immediately has my respect. Anyway, what can I do for you, Iris?'

She gestured for him to get closer and looked around conspiratorially as Neil lowered his head towards her.

'What do you know about the Hidden Hand club?' she whispered.

His eyes widened. 'How do you know about them, and perhaps more importantly, why are you asking?'

'It's something to do with an ongoing investigation,' Joseph explained.

'You're a policeman?' Neil asked, surprised.

'I'm actually one of several officers sitting at this table.'

Ellie quickly held up her hands. 'Don't look at me.'

'So now you're going to tell me you're working undercover in a board game café?'

Joseph gave Neil an amused look. 'No, unless you're about to tell us this is all a front for some sort of criminal activity.'

'The only whiff of that is the price they charge for their coffee.' The smile faded from his face as he drew up a chair and sat down at the table. 'So what do you want to know?'

'Anything at all,' Joseph said.

'Well, to start, the Hidden Hand club story has been swirling round for years,' Neil replied. 'It's one of those folk tales that's been handed down through the years and told to new members of the Assassins' Syndicate. It's said that it's a game where nothing is banned as long as no one gets seriously hurt. So rather than pretend to stab someone, you actually did, well, at least enough to draw a drop of blood. Or rather than use pretend poison, you slipped them something to make them have epic diarrhoea, that sort of thing.'

'You said it was just a story, though?' John said.

'Exactly. Until recently. Suddenly a rumour started doing the rounds this year. Apparently, a group of people who'd been in the Assassins' Syndicate, joined, or perhaps created, the Hidden Hand club for real. There was even a cash prize on offer.'

'So why hasn't anyone told us any of this before?' Joseph asked.

'Because it was invite only. People who were approached to take part were also threatened with consequences if anything about it ever got out.'

John leaned forward. 'What sort of *consequences*?'

Neil shrugged. 'I doubt anyone wanted to find out.'

'And do you know who runs this club?' Ellie asked.

'No idea. Whoever it is, they've done their best to keep it well under the radar, which only adds to the mystery.'

'So what about the game tokens the players wear?'

'They're apparently used like a dog tag. When a player is assassinated, the person has to retrieve the pendant from the target. That, along with the action camera footage they have to take of the kill, helps them prove it was a successful hit.'

Joseph exchanged a knowing look with Amy. Suddenly, the pendant being torn from Gabby's neck made sense.

'So how does someone playing this Hidden Hand game win, then?' he asked.

'It's simple. The last person left metaphorically standing, takes the prize pot.'

'Or not so metaphorically,' Amy said, casting Joseph a knowing look.

'Sorry?' Neil said, looking confused.

'Do you know any members of this club?' Joseph asked.

'No idea. It's all very hush-hush. But if anyone knows about it, it would be Eddie Foster. The rumour is he might be a member. He has some major debts he was trying to clear.'

'Oh, has he now?' the DI said, as another missing piece of the puzzle fell into place. 'And any other students you know who might also be members?'

Neil shook his head. 'Not that I know of. But like I said, it's meant to all be very hush-hush.' He tapped the side of his nose.

Joseph nodded towards Amy. 'We should go.'

'Sorry, is something wrong?' Iris said, looking between them as they stood up.

'No, far from it. You've been incredibly helpful, Neil.'

'Anytime,' he said, looking nonplussed.

'Can someone please explain to me what's going on?' Ellie asked.

'Later,' Joseph said, leaning down and kissing her on the top of the head.

John also stood. 'Ellie, if you don't mind, I'm going to go with them.'

'You go do what you have to,' she replied, in a way that made Joseph think her boyfriend had discussed the case with her. Exactly what he would have done with Kate back in the day.

With a wave to Dylan, Iris, and Neil, he headed towards the door with the others. Joseph almost collided with Geoff Goldsmith, who was entering the café.

The student gave Joseph a surprised look. 'I didn't have you down as a board game fan, Inspector Stone.'

'I'm a freshly minted one, but no surprise seeing you here,' he said as the others headed past him.

'Absolutely, this is the chapel at which I come and worship,' Geoff replied with a smile. 'Anyway, always good to see a new face in here. If this is going to become a regular thing for you, perhaps we could play sometime?'

'Maybe another day. But right now there is somewhere I need to be in a hurry. Anyway, enjoy yourself.'

'I always do,' Geoff replied.

The DI nodded and headed out of the door to join the others who were waiting.

'So, what's the plan?' Megan asked the moment the DI emerged.

'If you're thinking what I'm thinking, then we need to investigate Eddie further.'

'But what about his alibi?' Megan asked. 'His mates confirmed it.'

Joseph shrugged. 'Maybe they were lying to protect him. Either way, we need to check any CCTV footage from the cinema to be sure. The one thing I know for certain is the sooner we have Eddie in custody, the happier I'm going to be. We need to organise a search warrant, pronto.'

'But we only have hearsay from Neil to go on at this point.'

'Right, so we need to establish probable cause for a search warrant. So far, we already have proof from Eddie's own mouth he was rejected by Gabby. So, despite what he said, and I know this is pure conjecture at this point, but that could have been his motive for killing her. Then there's the prize money for taking part in the Hidden Hand game. That might be enough to convince a judge to at least issue us a warrant to check out his bank account. If that proves Eddie was seriously in debt, the judge might then be more amenable to giving us a search warrant for his home, especially if any of the CCTV footage casts doubt on or disproves his alibi.'

'In that case, it sounds like we're going to have a busy night of it, especially Chris,' Megan said.

'That's why he gets paid the big bucks.' Joseph winked at her. 'Anyway, Amy, you'll need to have your team ready to go the moment we get that search warrant.'

'Don't worry, I've already called them and primed them, based on the assumption you'll get that search warrant somehow.'

'Then let's do this,' Joseph said with a fresh pep in his step. As they headed back to St Aldates, he called Chris.

CHAPTER NINETEEN

It had taken several hours of painstaking work to jump through the necessary hoops to obtain a search warrant. The clincher had been when the cinema's CCTV footage hadn't shown Eddie with his mates. The only problem was the cameras didn't have an exhaustive view of the lobby area, so there was still a chance that the student simply hadn't been picked up by them.

Luckily, the judge had agreed it was enough to raise suspicion about Eddie's alibi. That, combined with the fact that his bank account had been heavily overdrawn, and with much persuading from Chris, had finally convinced the judge to issue the search warrant.

After that, and without a moment to waste, things had moved quickly and everything had been put in place to raid Eddie Foster's flat.

Chris, Joseph, and Megan were standing outside the student-shared house where Eddie lived. Because he might be armed with a crossbow, PS Erol Kentli and his armed tactical unit were getting ready to lead the way in.

Megan looked uncertain as she eyed the MP5s the officers

were holding clutched to their chests. 'Isn't this a bit overkill? Surely we could have just tried knocking first?'

Chris shook his head. 'Not when we're dealing with someone who might be armed.'

'Yes, far better to play things on the safe side, rather than end up with an officer being shot,' Joseph added.

Megan grimaced, no doubt thinking of her last armed encounter with the prisoner transfer convoy. 'Of course.'

Erol, his earpiece in, turned to the SIO. 'My team is in position, including two men round the back if Foster tries to make a run for it.'

'Then let's get this operation started,' Chris replied.

Erol nodded and spoke into the walkie-talkie strapped to his chest.

An officer armed with a battering ram aligned it with the lock and, with a hefty swing, shattered it with one blow, sending the door crashing inwards.

'Armed police, stay where you are!' Erol bellowed, as he charged into the house with his men.

There were several cries of surprise, followed by shouted orders as the team swept through the property.

In less than two minutes, Erol was back on the doorstep. 'The house is secure, sir. But I'm afraid there's no sign of Foster. Only his housemates are inside.'

'Shit,' Chris muttered.

'Well, we can still interview them to see what they know,' Joseph said. 'We can also check out Eddie's room for any evidence, whilst we're waiting for Amy to get here.'

'Okay, I'll handle the interviews of his housemates, whilst you and Megan check out Foster's room,' Chris replied.

As Joseph entered the house, he caught sight of several people in the dining room with their hands on their heads. One of the armed officers was standing over them.

'You can all relax, I just need to ask you a few questions about Eddie,' Chris said to the group as he walked in.

Joseph turned to Erol. 'Any idea which room belongs to our suspect?'

'First door on the right at the top of the stairs,' Erol replied.

'Thanks.' With a nod to Erol, the DI and DC headed up the stairs, already slipping on their blue latex gloves.

Joseph's first impression as he entered the bedroom was that everything inside it was incredibly neat and ordered. Books were carefully stacked in a series of square bookshelves running along one wall. A large well-cared-for palm took up most of one corner. A collection of trainers filled a shoe rack, next to piles of neatly stacked clothes in an open white wardrobe, along with a stack of dumbbells on a rack.

'Bloody hell, this looks like it's straight out of the pages of an IKEA catalogue,' Megan said.

'Well, if Eddie did take that shot at Ryan, based on this room, he'll certainly keep his prison cell tidy,' Joseph replied. His gaze alighted on a laptop. 'Aha, the digital gold chest.'

Megan began searching through the desk, even looking under it. She shook her head. 'No sign of any password.'

Joseph spotted the Apple logo on the laptop. 'Aye, no doubt that thing has Touch ID or some such. Nothing Amy and her team won't be able to crack.'

Megan nodded as her eyes swept the room. She walked past the DI, turned her phone's torch on, and aimed it beneath the perfectly made bed. The sheets were so crisp Joseph had a sneaking suspicion the man had actually ironed them.

The DC's eyes widened. She reached underneath the bed and dragged out a large T-shaped fabric bag.

'Shite, that can only be designed to carry one thing,' Joseph observed.

Megan nodded and neither of them was surprised when she

unzipped the bag to reveal a hunting crossbow inside. It had been equipped with a scope and had a dozen barbed hunting bolts strapped into the lid. There was also an action camera in one of the inside pockets.

Joseph felt a surge of relief. 'Thank God for that. Seems we have our man. But don't touch anything else. We'll leave that to Amy and her team in case there's any DNA evidence lurking in here as well.'

Megan nodded as they heard footsteps on the stairs.

Chris opened the door, his eyes widening the moment they fell on the crossbow bag on the floor.

'Wow, you've hit the jackpot.'

'It's looking that way, Boss. Now all we need is to arrest the man himself and find out for sure.'

'We may have just had a break in that regard. One of his housemates just told us two very interesting facts. The first is that one of Eddie's hobbies is freerunning and free climbing.'

Joseph pressed his hand to his forehead. 'So someone who would have been very much at home on any rooftop. Why didn't I realise this before?'

'Why would you?' Megan asked.

Joseph sucked air through his teeth. 'Think of what he was doing when we found him—balancing on a strap. That now strikes me as exactly the sort of thing a freerunner would do.'

'Bloody hell, you're right. But surely Ryan must have known he was a fellow freerunner, as well as another member of the club, so why cover for him?'

Chris scratched his neck. 'Whatever the answer is to that particular riddle, we have an arrest to make to find out. Thankfully, thanks to Foster's housemates, we have a good idea where he is tonight. Apparently, someone bet him he wouldn't have the balls to climb the spire of St Mary the Virgin in Radcliffe

Square. But to prove he actually did it, he was challenged to tie a blown-up sex doll to the top of the spire.'

'Feck, what an eejit,' Joseph replied. 'Foster sounds like as big of an adrenaline junkie as Ryan and Gabby.'

'There's definitely a pattern of behaviour that links the three of them,' Chris replied.

'And by process of elimination, right now everything points towards Foster,' Megan said.

Chris nodded. 'Okay, well the good news is the bet is meant to happen before eleven. If we head to St Mary's right now, there's every chance we'll be in time to have Foster tucked up in a nice cell before the night's out. So let's get going and arrange a reception committee, people.'

Joseph was doing his very best not to look down from the outside balcony of St Mary's. Instead, he was trying to concentrate on the beautiful nighttime view of Radcliffe Camera and the Oxford colleges stretching away beyond it. Then, the DI made the mistake of glancing down to see if there was any sign of Foster approaching the church, and his stomach swirled.

'For feck's sake, this is too high for me,' he muttered.

'Yes, but imagine what it would be like trying to climb the steeple above us,' Megan replied, gesturing up with her chin to the spire towering over them.

'Well, if this is Foster's idea of great craic, he's definitely certifiable in my book.' At that moment, the walkie-talkie in Joseph's hand squawked.

'All the teams are now in place round Saint Marys, Boss,' Ian's voice said.

'Roger, everyone stay hidden until you can lay hands on

Foster,' Chris's voice said over the open channel. The walkie-talkie crackled, then fell silent again.

Megan looked through the binoculars she was holding, scanning the surrounding rooftops.

The DI glanced at his watch to see there were only ten minutes left until eleven, which was when Foster would forfeit the bet. As the DI waited on this longest of days, another important question filled his mind. How had Kate got on with Derrick?

Perhaps even now the big man was packing his bags. Of course, there was still a faint chance the superintendent was innocent. Either way, Joseph just wished he was there in person to support Kate. Whatever happened, he would be there to help her pick up the pieces, if she let him.

'Hey, what's that?' Megan asked, breaking his train of thought. She had her binoculars trained on the tip of the spire directly above them.

Joseph was about to ask what, when he saw for himself. A pale, naked caricature of a woman was flapping in the breeze as it was being tied to the summit by a shadowy figure.

'Feck!' Joseph stabbed the button on his walkie-talkie. 'We have eyes on Eddie. He's already on the spire!'

'How the hell did he slip past us all?' Chris said. 'St Mary's is well away, and we already did a sweep for any ropes tied to the side of the church?'

'That's the skill of a free climber for you. They don't need any,' Megan said into her own radio.

'Okay, make your presence known but try not to surprise him. We don't want this operation going tits up and him falling to his death,' the SIO responded.

'Roger that,' Joseph replied, before cupping his hands around his mouth. 'Eddie, stop what you're doing—we have the church surrounded.'

The figure froze.

'We need you to make your way down here right now, nice and carefully.'

The figure looked down and Joseph found himself eyeballing Foster.

'And you can bloody well bring down that doll whilst you're at it,' Megan said.

'Yes, that would have been a bizarre call out for the fire brigade,' Joseph said, feeling the tension he'd been carrying easing. At last, they were going to crack this case wide open.

Foster nodded, and set to work untying the doll, but seemed to be having problems with the knot, his movements slow.

'Will you get a move on? We haven't got all day.'

'Trying,' Foster said, his voice slightly slurring.

Then he shook his head as though he was trying to clear it.

'Are you okay?' Megan asked.

But then the student's head seemed to slump, his right foot sliding down the spire before he managed to gain purchase again.

'Whoa, careful there, lad,' Joseph called out.

Foster tried to clamp his hand onto the edge of one of the tiles to steady himself, but his fingers didn't seem to have any strength.

The next moment, everything kicked into horrifying slow motion.

The student above them slipped again, sliding straight down the spire, gathering speed as he came, and dragging the inflatable doll behind.

With no thought for his own safety, Joseph desperately leaned right out from the balcony to try and grab him as he shot past. His fingertips briefly caught the edge of Eddie's flapping hood. The DI's arm was almost yanked out of its socket as he took the weight of the student and somehow managed to stop his fall.

Meanwhile, Megan only just had time to lock her hands around the DI's waist and steady him before he was pulled over the edge.

Joseph found himself looking down at Eddie, the tip of his hood dangling from his right hand, the lad slowly turning beneath him like a human mobile, and from the student's hand, the inflatable doll doing the same.

Gritting his teeth, DI felt burning through his fingers as he willed them not to lose their grip. He could already feel the fabric starting to slip. He groaned, his whole arm vibrating with the effort. He knew he was fighting a losing battle. Then the last millimetres of the hood finally slipped free and the impossible weight was released.

Helplessly, he watched in horror as the student plummeted towards the ground, the lad's eyes closed. Eddie looked at peace, as if he'd given in to the inevitable. A split second later, there was a sickening thud as he slammed into the cobbles far below them.

'Fuck!' Megan said, and pulled Joseph back onto the balcony.

Joseph, nausea filling him, turned, and together they ran back down the twisting spiral staircase.

By the time the two detectives reached the outside of the church, Chris, Ian, Sue, and a handful of officers were already standing around the crumpled figure of Eddie. He was sprawled onto the ground face-first, blood pooling around his shattered body. Next to the student was the incongruous sight of the inflatable woman lying next to him, her hand still grasped in his.

It was then Joseph spotted the black cord hanging around his neck. He squatted next to the body and took out his pen and used it to hook the cord, pulling it gently to one side. Just as he suspected, the plastic Eliminator game token appeared. This one was green.

'This bloody Hidden Hand game,' Ian said, shaking his head.

With a tight expression, Chris pressed the button on his walkie-talkie. 'We need an ambulance, but no need for them to rush.' He turned to the team. 'It doesn't look like there's going to be any trial after all.'

The DI returned his gaze to the dead man before them. 'But what a stupid waste of a life, and for a bet of all things,' he said, shaking his head.

CHAPTER TWENTY

THERE WERE a lot of drawn faces the following morning at the briefing in the incident room, as they waited for Amy to join them for a forensic update. Of course, Joseph was feeling more wrung out than usual, and not just because of Foster's death. The icing on the cake of this already shite twenty-four period, was that so far he hadn't seen any sign of Derrick. That was making him really worried about what had happened with Kate. But Dylan, who Joseph had already briefed about last night's developments, had warned him off.

'*She'll contact you when she's good and ready,*' had been his advice. But trying to stick to that was easier said than done. Joseph's fingers were literally twitching, desperate to grab his mobile and ring her.

'Are we absolutely certain that Foster was our man, Boss?' Ian asked during the team briefing.

With some mental effort, the DI forced his attention back to the task in hand.

'A crossbow hidden under his bed is pretty conclusive,' one of the detectives at the back of the room said.

'Also, Amy is on her way over right now with what she says

is compelling evidence,' Chris replied. 'So, I think it's safe to assume that's going to be the end of the matter.'

Megan, who'd been looking at the evidence board with the grim photo updates of the student's shattered body lying next to St Mary's, frowned. But if she had any reservations, she wasn't sharing them for now.

'I was literally just talking about you,' Chris said to Amy as she walked into the room. 'So, have you got that conclusive evidence you mentioned?'

'Yes, and it's very interesting indeed,' the SOCO replied, holding up the USB stick in her hand. 'Shall I go ahead and show the team what we've uncovered?'

'Please, be my guest,' Chris replied.

Amy headed over to a computer and slotted the memory stick in it. A few clicks later, the Thames Valley Police logo had been replaced with a paused video on the large screen. The static frame showed an open window looking out over the night-time rooftops of Oxford.

'What are we looking at here, Amy?' Chris asked.

'This is footage retrieved from the action camera found in Eddie's bedroom.'

Joseph peered at the aerial view of the city. 'Hang on, this isn't the start of one of those freeruns across Oxford, is it?'

'Just so,' Amy replied. 'Let me play you this clip. It shows something rather surprising towards the end.' She hit play.

The video burst into life as the view headed out of the open window onto a pitched roof. Just to emphasise how high whoever was filming this was, they glanced down at what looked like Broad Street. The pavement looked a very long way down indeed, and Joseph had an immediate flashback to the previous night. The sound of the wind gently blowing could be heard in the background.

Joseph noticed a lone black cab coming into view, picking

up a group of revellers who had just tumbled out of the White Horse pub, made famous by being *Inspector Morse's* local. The view swung back up and then started to move up towards the apex of the pitched slate roof.

'Eddie obviously had a death wish long before tonight's events,' Megan said.

'Oh, you haven't seen anything yet,' Amy replied.

The end of the roof was coming up. The next building was a good ten feet away and slightly lower.

Rather than slowing down, Eddie accelerated, his breath audible, coming in short regular bursts.

'He's not bloody going to make that leap,' Ian said.

'He *bloody* well is,' Amy replied with a small smile.

Joseph's stomach rose as a surge of sympathetic adrenaline swept through his body, as Eddie sprinted even harder towards the edge of the roof.

The student leapt.

A few people in the room whistled and shook their heads as for the longest moment Eddie was suddenly hurtling through empty air, and plummeting down towards the next flat roof. Just when it seemed it was going to be impossible for him to reach it and he'd fall to his death, the tip of his running shoe briefly came into view and made contact with the ledge of the next building.

Suddenly, the camera view of the world briefly gyrated as Eddie absorbed the impact of the leap by going into a roll. Then it settled again as he stood up. Two people emerged from the shadows, grinning at him.

Joseph shook his head when he saw Gabby and Ryan approaching Eddie, their arms reaching out to slap him on the back.

'I thought you would bottle that leap,' Ryan said.

'No way am I going to let you two steal all the glory,' Eddie's voice could be heard replying, removing any doubt that the person shooting the footage was actually him.

'Wow, you really have turned into an adrenaline junkie just like us,' Gabby said. 'Anyway, that was just the warm-up. Ready for some serious Parkouring?'

'Always,' Eddie replied.

'Then try to keep up,' Ryan said.

Gabby turned and set off at a run, with Ryan right behind her. She bounded like a gazelle over the rooftops, with her boyfriend close on her heels, and Eddie bringing up the rear. The video stopped abruptly when Amy hit the pause button. 'Okay, we don't need to see any more. Feel free to watch the whole thing in your own time. But I warn you, some of their stunts will have your toes curling with the risks those three took.'

'If nothing else, it proves just how reckless they were,' Sue said.

Ian nodded. 'Isn't that the truth? And this footage more than proves that Ryan definitely knew Eddie was a freerunner.'

Chris looked at Joseph and Megan. 'Yes, I think you might need to pay Mr Slattery another visit.'

'Don't worry, after seeing this I was already planning to,' Joseph replied. 'The lad must have had a reason for lying to us, just as he did about that pendant they all wore.'

'Then I will leave you to ferret out the *why* of all this,' Chris said. He turned to Amy. 'Anyway, great work, as always, and very insightful.'

She held up her hand. 'Actually, I'm not done yet. I have a second freerunning video from Eddie's action camera that you're definitely going to want to see.'

She selected a file from the menu and double-clicked it. This time a daytime video of the rooftops appeared, centred on a college tower off to one side.

'Hang on, that's Christ Church College, right next door to us,' Megan asked.

'It is,' Amy said.

Joseph already had an inkling about what they were about to see. That only grew as the view swung around and settled on the street near the entrance to St Aldates Police Station. 'I'm going to skip forward from this point because Foster was in this position for at least thirty minutes.' She pressed fast forward, and sped-up footage of cars and pedestrians passing the station played, officers coming and going from the doors.

'This is about the right point,' Amy said, hitting play again.

A few seconds later, a distant figure could be seen emerging from the police station.

'Got you,' they heard Foster whisper, confirming it really was him recording the footage.

Megan turned to Joseph. 'Hang on, isn't that...?'

Joseph finished her sentence for her. 'Ryan, when we released him.'

Then, as the DI already knew Foster would, they watched the student's gloved hands reach for something that had been out of sight on the roof next to him. The hunting crossbow, the same one they currently had in the evidence locker, was lifted into view. No one in the incident room said a thing as the crossbow was aimed down at the distant figure of Ryan and began tracking the student as he crossed the road.

Foster's breath settled into long, regular breaths as he got ready to take the shot. Then they all saw Joseph emerge from the police station, looking up and down the street. A few officers in the room glanced at the DI as the distant figure on the video cupped his hands around his mouth, before running after Ryan.

A long exhale could be heard on the video as Foster's gloved finger squeezed the trigger. With a loud *thwack*, the weapon's arms recoiled, hurling the bolt forward. Ryan, far below, bucked as the projectile hit him in the shoulder.

Eddie was already loading a second bolt. Thankfully, on the video Joseph had closed the distance and hurled himself at Ryan, throwing him to the ground. At exactly the same moment, Foster fired again, and the travel agent's window behind the two prone figures shattered.

One thing of note from the video footage was that Ryan looked very dead.

'Sorry, mate, you know I had no choice,' they heard Eddie say, as he ducked down and slid backwards from the edge of the roof, dragging the crossbow with him.

Amy stopped the video and nodded towards Joseph. 'So, as we all just witnessed, if it hadn't been for your swift actions, Joseph, Ryan would have been killed.'

The DI nodded, but his thoughts were a whirlwind, and it was Chris who was the first person in the room to voice what he was thinking.

'This proves that Foster attempted to murder Ryan. But that still leaves us with a question. Are we safe to assume he was also responsible for Gabby's murder?'

'Actually, we have new evidence to suggest exactly that,' Amy said. 'We handed the crossbow over to ballistics, and much like they can match a bullet to a gun, they were able to match it with the paintbrush crossbow bolts that killed Gabby, along with the bolts that were fired at Ryan. Scratch marks along their shafts indicated they were all fired from the crossbow we recovered from Eddie's bedroom.

'Okay, compelling as that is, something still doesn't quite stack up here,' Megan said. 'Why did Foster risk filming himself shooting Ryan? Even if that's what they were meant to do for the Hidden Hand game, surely he must have known that it was evidence that would help convict him?'

'Maybe he was the sort of guy who got his kicks from watching that sort of thing?' Ian suggested.

'I suppose that's always possible,' Chris replied. He glanced at Amy. 'Did you find anything on the laptop in Foster's room to support that idea?'

'Well, one interesting thing we discovered was evidence that he'd accessed a site on the dark web,' the SOCO replied. 'The real problem is the website has a high level of security on it, so we can't access it. That in itself is suspicious.'

'Surely the DFU team can crack that?' Chris asked.

'No. It seems to require a physical encryption key to unlock the site. Unfortunately, there isn't a sign of that anywhere. There is evidence to suggest that the footage from the action camera was uploaded somewhere on the dark web, but we don't know where exactly.'

'This has to be connected to the Hidden Hand game,' Joseph said.

Amy nodded. 'Yes, no doubt. The question is if that's what Eddie uploaded, surely whoever was organising the game would have seen he was playing the game for real, so why not report it?'

'Unless that's the point of the game,' Megan suggested.

'Also,' Amy went on, 'the use of the dark web suggests whoever's behind the Hidden Hand didn't want anything traced back to them.'

'Which is suspicious behaviour in itself,' Joseph said. 'We need to track down whoever is behind this fecking game and ask them a few pointed questions.'

Amy nodded. 'Unfortunately, the use of a Tor browser is going to make life difficult. However, there's an avenue I'm now exploring to possibly help us get past that particular problem.'

'Which is?' Chris asked.

'I'm considering using a freelance computer expert I met

recently to analyse the laptop to see if he can unearth anything. He also just happens to be a white hat hacker.'

'Neil Tanner, that guy we met in the Games Emporium?' Joseph asked.

Ian shot him a look of surprise. 'Why were you in there?'

'Long story, for another time,' Joseph replied. 'Anyway, Amy?'

'Yes, him. We're just running some background checks on Neil, but if he passes and is agreeable, his skills could be useful for this and future cases.'

'That sounds promising,' Chris said. Then he turned to face the room. 'Okay, is there anything else anyone can think of that's relevant before we finish?'

Everyone shook their heads.

'In that case, Megan and I better go and have another chat with Ryan, pronto,' Joseph said. 'Maybe because of some sense of misguided loyalty, he was trying to protect Eddie. But one way or another, we'll get the truth out of him this time round.'

'Do it with my blessing,' Chris replied.

Joseph nodded as he and Megan grabbed their coats and headed to the door. As they walked out, the DI couldn't help but glance at Derrick's fishbowl office as he passed it. The lights were off, and there was no sign of the big man anywhere. On a hunch, he paused as he spotted Jake, the desk sergeant, walking towards him along the corridor.

'Isn't Derrick in yet?' he asked.

'He's rung in sick,' Jake replied.

I bet he fecking has, Joseph thought as he headed away with Megan. No doubt the superintendent was desperately wondering about how he was going to stop his career and marriage from imploding, probably in that order. But as soon as things were wrapped up with their current case, the DSU would get Joseph's undivided attention.

CHAPTER TWENTY-ONE

Joseph paused by the armed officer before they headed into Ryan's room at the John Radcliffe Hospital.

'How's it been going here?' the DI asked him.

'Apart from Ryan's parents who came to visit, nothing else to report, sir.'

Joseph nodded as he and Megan stepped into Ryan's room. They found the student looking at his phone, which had been recently returned to him after Amy's team had found nothing of interest on it.

'How are you doing there?' Joseph asked as they sat down on either side of his bed.

'Actually, okay. The doctors are very pleased with my progress. As long as I promise to look after my shoulder, they said I should be able to go home by the weekend.'

'That's good to hear, but I'm afraid we have some bad news for you.'

Ryan's face paled. 'It's about Eddie, isn't it?'

'You've already heard about what happened to him?' Megan asked.

The art student nodded. 'One of his housemates messaged

me first thing this morning. You guys trying to arrest him last night is already all over a WhatsApp group. I suppose you've got him in custody and he's confessed to Gabby's murder, right?'

Joseph traded a look with Megan. 'I'm afraid it's worse than that. I'm sorry to say that Eddie fell from the spire of St Mary's last night. Apparently, someone had bet he couldn't get to the top and tie a blow-up doll to it.'

Ryan inhaled sharply. 'He's dead?'

'I'm afraid so,' Joseph said. 'But you don't seem surprised he was climbing the spire.' The DI fixed his gaze on Ryan. 'Why exactly is that, Ryan?'

The lad looked warily between the two detectives. 'What do you mean?'

'Look, there's no point in denying it any longer. We've seen video footage of you and Gabby freerunning with Eddie,' Megan said.

Ryan opened his mouth to say something, but then closed it again and his shoulders sank.

'Yes, he used to Parkour with us. He was turning into a real athlete, too. Even though he hadn't been doing it for long, he would always push himself to do better.'

'In that case, why deny knowing anything about Eddie being a freerunner before now?'

'Because he's a mate and I know how it would look if I dropped him in it.'

'Even though we suspected he might be the man who killed your girlfriend?' Megan asked.

'I just knew he wouldn't do something so sick. Eddie wasn't like that.'

Just like Eddie said about you, Joseph thought to himself. And there it was rearing its head again—the misguided sense of loyalty this group seemed to have towards each other.

The DI stared at the lad before him. 'I'm afraid that's not what the evidence is pointing towards.'

'Sorry, you're really saying Eddie killed Gabby?'

'We do have compelling evidence to suggest he might have.'

Ryan gave him a sceptical look. 'What evidence?'

Joseph gave Megan the barest nod and she took a tablet out of her bag and pulled up a video on it. She pressed play and handed the device to Ryan.

He watched Eddie's action camera footage, his eyes widening at seeing the rooftop view looking down at the entrance of the police station.

'No, he wouldn't do that,' Ryan whispered, as he watched the crossbow being brought up and aimed down at him. Ryan gasped as his friend fired. He blinked several times after the video finally ended, and then focused his attention back on the detectives. 'Where did you get this?'

'From an action camera recovered from Eddie's bedroom, along with the same crossbow used to murder Gabby,' Megan said.

'I'm afraid we strongly suspect he tried to frame you for her murder with the converted paintbrush bolts. Eddie also knew we were holding you and that's when he must have staked out the police station. So when we released you, he was already in place, ready to assassinate you when you eventually emerged.'

The student balled his hands into fists. 'But why?'

'That's what we're hoping you can help us out with,' Joseph said. 'Is there any reason he would have a personal vendetta against either you or Gabby?'

'None at all. The only thing...' He shook his head.

'What is it?' Megan asked gently.

'I didn't want to say anything, but Eddie did have a bit of a thing for Gabby.'

'Yes, we know all about that and the incident at the gig where she very publicly rejected him.'

'Shit, you really have been doing your homework.'

'It would have helped our investigation a lot had you just told us about it in the first place. Maybe if you had, Eddie would still be alive now,' Joseph said.

Ryan gave him a pale look. 'That's not down to me, is it?'

'Well, you didn't exactly help him. Your friend obviously wasn't thinking straight.' Now was the moment the DI knew he had to push Ryan to get him to open up about the other key thread to the investigation. 'Isn't it about time you fully opened up about the Hidden Hand club? Isn't it a fact that just like you and Gabby, Eddie was also a member? And before you attempt to deny it, we know the three of you were wearing tokens from the Eliminator board game, identifying each of you as a player.'

Ryan moved his hand to his neck, where they could see the telltale bulge of his own pendant beneath his T-shirt.

'I suppose there's no point in denying it. Yes, you're right.' Then his eyes widened. 'Hang on, you're not seriously suggesting any of this has anything to do with that game?'

'You tell us. Isn't it true that just like you and Gabby, Eddie had significant money problems? Maybe he felt his were big enough to warrant crossing the line into murder to make sure he won the cash prize on offer. Then, after Gabby's murder, there was no going back, and he thought he had to keep going.'

'Anywhere, anyhow,' Ryan whispered.

'Sorry?' Megan said.

'That's the motto of the game, but surely Eddie wouldn't be stupid enough to take that literally?'

'I know this must be hard to hear, but it's exactly what the evidence is pointing towards,' Joseph said.

Ryan squeezed his eyes shut and pinched the bridge of his nose. 'I still can't believe he would do this. I mean, he was always going on about being short of cash, but this? Only a psychopath would take things that far.' He opened his eyes to wipe away a tear beading his eye.

'Even people we think we know can have a dark side to them. But apart from Eddie, we also need to talk about whoever was responsible for organising the game and putting together the prize fund.'

Ryan gave them a blank look. 'I honestly don't know.'

'Are you sure, or are you still trying to protect someone else from the fallout?' Megan asked.

'No, I mean, I literally don't know. We were all sent anonymous texts. It said that each of us had been identified as the best of the best in the Assassins' Syndicate, and if we were interested, there was another much more exclusive game with ten thousand pounds going to the last person standing. All we had to do was respond to the email and say yes. Then we would be told who the other players were before the game kicked off.'

'And the other players being?'

'Gabby, Eddie, and myself.'

'That's not exactly a lot of players, is it?'

Ryan met the DI's stare without so much as blinking. 'As I said, it was meant to be an exclusive game.'

'I see. And you really have no idea who set this club up?'

Ryan shook his head. 'That was all part of the cloak-and-dagger nature of the game, and only added to its mystery.'

'But surely whoever was behind this would reveal themselves when they handed over the cash to the eventual winner?' Megan said.

'No, the prize was going to be left buried in a box in University Park. All part of the cool role-playing vibe.'

'Interesting,' Joseph said. Yes, it could all be just part of the game, but this, along with Eddie's use of a Tor browser, makes something seriously feel off here.

Tears were freely rolling down Ryan's face as the reality of what had happened hit home.

Joseph's heart went out to the lad. 'I realise how painful all of this must be for you.'

Ryan nodded, but just stared at his hands, lost somewhere inside himself.

'Okay, I think we've asked you enough questions for now,' the DI said, nodding to Megan.

A short while later, the detectives were heading out of the ward towards the lifts.

'So, what do you think?' Joseph asked.

'That Ryan seemed genuinely shocked about Eddie's involvement with Gabby's murder. But the thing I can't get out of my head is whether there really was any cash prize. After all, being told there's money to be won is very different from actually seeing it with your own eyes.'

'You think the organiser behind the game might have been lying to them about it?' Joseph asked.

Megan frowned. 'All I know is a ten thousand pound prize sounds a bit improbable, doesn't it?'

'Yes. I suppose people believe what they want to, especially where money is concerned. It sounds to me like the only way we're going to get the answers to that is by tracking this individual down. Like they say, follow the money, or maybe even a lack of it.'

The DC pushed the lift call button. 'It's certainly strange that whoever it is, is so keen to remain in the shadows.'

'Then I look forward to asking them why they are so keen to stay out of the limelight when we get our hands on them,' Joseph replied, as the lift pinged and the doors opened.

CHAPTER TWENTY-TWO

Joseph didn't quite know how he managed to keep the shock off his face when he and Megan headed back into the incident room to see Derrick standing there, actually smiling and patting Chris on the back like he didn't have a care in the world.

'Ah, there you both are,' the superintendent said, smiling at Joseph as they dropped their things off on their desks. 'I was just congratulating the rest of the team on a job well done. You better help yourselves before Ian scoffs the lot.' He gestured to the almost empty box of Krispy Kreme Doughnuts.

Ian waved a chocolate-covered one at them, grinning. 'Sorry, none of these left for you two.'

What fecking parallel universe have I just fallen into? Joseph thought. What he'd expected when he next saw Derrick was for the big man to look hollowed out from the inside. Certainly not someone in a good enough mood to actually stick his hand in his pocket to buy fecking doughnuts!

Then things got even weirder, making Joseph briefly question his sanity. Derrick headed over and shook first his hand, and then Megan's.

'From what Chris tells me, you're both to be congratulated

on your part in working out Eddie was the murderer. The press is going to lap this up.'

Joseph was so shocked, it took him a moment to find his voice as he stared mutely back at the DSU.

Thankfully, Megan jumped in. 'Thank you. But there are still some loose ends to tie up. Specifically, who was behind this Hidden Hand group. We really need to ask them some questions.'

'Yes, and I'm sure that you'll get to the bottom of that in good time. But today, we celebrate.' Derrick raised his cup of tea in a toast to the room, and a few of the team responded with raised doughnuts.

The superintendent headed past Joseph, out of the room with the expression of a man for whom Christmas had come early. He even patted Joseph on the shoulder like he actually liked him. That only deepened the DI's sense of bewilderment, which must have shown on his face, because Chris headed over and chuckled.

'Yes, our illustrious leader has obviously got out of bed on the right side this morning,' he said.

'But I thought he was off ill,' Joseph replied.

'Apparently, just a bad headache which wore off. Mind you, I do think it's a bit premature to be celebrating. As Megan just said, there are loose threads to be gathered up. Talking of which, how did you get on with Ryan?'

'Pretty much what we expected,' Megan said, heading over with three doughnuts stacked in her hand, only one of which she handed to Joseph.

'Then you better get me up to speed,' Chris said.

But the DI's thoughts were now on a spin cycle. Why was Derrick so fecking happy? By all rights, even if the man was completely innocent as regards any involvement with the Night Watchmen, he couldn't have just brushed off the money incident in the car park. The only thing certain was Kate would have kept his name out of it. Otherwise, there was absolutely no way that the big man would have been all rainbows and sunshine with him just now. To hell with waiting for Kate to contact him. He needed to talk to her right now.

'Actually, Megan, can you brief Chris. Talking of headaches, I've got a migraine coming on,' Joseph said, before turning to the SIO. 'If it's alright, I need to head home, Boss.'

Chris gave him a concerned look. 'Not like you, but it's definitely been a bit of a rollercoaster this week.'

'Aye, that it has,' Joseph said, handing his doughnut back to Megan. 'I'm not sure I can even manage this right now.'

'Don't mind if I do. I can run you home if you like? You shouldn't be cycling with a migraine threatening.'

'No, I'll be fine. The bike ride might actually help.'

'Okay, but only if you're sure?' Megan asked.

'I am.' Joseph grabbed his things and as he turned to head for the door, caught the questioning look in both their eyes. If only they knew.

Kate still hadn't returned any of the dozen messages Joseph had left on her mobile's answering machine, let alone the countless texts he'd sent. His worry had turned into a tight knot in his gut after heading to the Oxford Chronicle offices, only to discover she hadn't come to work that day. That was why he was heading up the steps to her home. To find out, most importantly, how she was, and secondly, what the hell had happened with Derrick.

The DI buzzed the doorbell and almost waited a whole five seconds before buzzing it again. When at least another three seconds had passed, he went all in, leaning on the button.

Then his heart lifted a fraction when he saw someone

approaching the door through the rippled glass. But when the door opened, it wasn't Kate standing there, but Ellie.

'Blimey, Dad, where's the fire?' she said.

'Sorry, but where's your mum? I need to speak to her,' he asked, looking over her shoulder.

'She's still at work.'

'No, she isn't. I've already been and they haven't heard from her all day.'

'Then she's probably following up on a juicy lead. You know what she's like.'

Joseph's concerns had now grown to the weight of a lead ball inside him, and that worry was now reflected on his daughter's face.

'What's wrong, Dad?' Ellie asked.

'Nothing, I just wanted to pick her brain about something,' he replied, realising he needed to quickly deflect her. 'Anyway, why are you here?'

Ellie pointed to the large blue IKEA bag full of clothes behind her in the doorway. 'Just catching up with my laundry.'

Joseph raised an eyebrow at her. 'In other words, making use of the free electricity and soap powder.'

Ellie grinned at him. 'That's the one. Anyway, do you want to leave a message for Mum for when she gets back?'

'No, I'm golden. I'll just give her a call later.'

'No problem. Oh, how is it going with the investigation into Gabby's murder? John was telling me it's all hands to the pumps. I also heard the shocking news about Eddie's death last night. Is that anything to do with this Hidden Hand group we heard about at the game café?'

'You really should consider becoming a police officer with those instincts of yours.'

She smiled at him. 'In another life, maybe.'

'Well, you'll get a glowing testimonial from your old man should you ever decide to take the leap.'

Before Ellie could respond, Joseph's mobile rang, and he couldn't help but feel disappointed when, rather than Kate's name, he saw Amy's on the display.

'I'd better take this,' he said.

His daughter nodded as he pressed the accept button.

'Joseph, there's been a couple of last-minute developments in the Gabby Dawson investigation,' Amy said. 'I was at St Aldates just now, briefing the team about what we found on Eddie's laptop, thanks to Neil Tanner's efforts. He did something he called a cold boot attack, and was able to recover some data from the RAM storage. That impressed our digital forensic team, no end.'

'Excellent. What did he discover?'

'The destination of that video clip he had of Ryan's attempted murder. We knew before it was uploaded to some site on the dark web, which as you know we were unable to access because it need a hardware key, but...'

'Neil was able to somehow get past it?'

'Yes, and what he found was a single image file from the Dark Web site. It had a heading of the Hidden Hand Club with an instruction beneath it. The webpage seems to have been solely set up with the purpose of uploading the videos to it. But that's not the reason I'm ringing, because while I was there, a call came through from Doctor Jacobs with a very interesting finding from the autopsy. It turns out he went the extra mile and analysed a tissue sample from Eddie's body, which threw up a surprising result.'

'Which is?'

'Apparently, something very suspicious indeed. Chris and Megan are heading over there right now to be fully briefed. The only thing Rob would reveal over the phone is it throws a large question mark over Eddie's death. So I was thinking, headache or not, you might want to drag yourself over there as well.'

'You, Amy, as always, are bang on the money, and thanks for the heads-up. And at some point, we must arrange that date night.'

'We really must,' she replied. 'Now, go off and have some fun at the autopsy.'

'Only you would say that and actually mean it.'

Amy chuckled. 'See you soon, handsome.' The phone line clicked off.

'Oh, interesting,' Ellie said, as Joseph pocketed his phone.

'You heard most of that, then?'

'Yes, *handsome.*' She grinned at him.

'Away with you already,' Joseph said. 'I have things to do and people to bother.'

Ellie leaned in and kissed him on the cheek.

Joseph headed back down the steps. He waited until he heard the front door closing behind him before ducking over the road to retrieve the hidden trail camera from the bush opposite. The problem was, he couldn't shake the feeling that something was badly wrong with Kate. Yes, she might just be making him sweat by not taking his calls, but until he'd seen her with his own two eyes, he wouldn't be able to relax. He also needed to gather his thoughts, because the longer he hadn't heard from her, the more he was certain he would have to tackle Derrick directly. And that could get messy very fast indeed.

As urgent as tracking down Kate was, right then he needed to know what Rob had to tell them. Unfortunately, he had the feeling their superintendent had been premature in celebrating the end of the case.

By the time Joseph headed into the post-mortem lab, Megan and Chris were already with Doctor Jacobs and his assistant, Clare. The DI had been so focused on finding out what they'd discovered, he hadn't mentally prepared himself for the state that Eddie Foster's body would be in after such a fall. The one saving grace was the badly deformed body was thankfully face-down on the examination table. That hid the worst of the damage. But the rest of the lad's torso, which was mottled with bruising, was a different matter.

'Fecking hell,' Joseph said, already reaching for his Silvermints in his pocket.

Megan and Chris looked up from the briefing they'd been in the middle of with the doctors.

'What are you doing here? You're meant to be resting up at home,' Chris said.

'The fresh air on the ride home worked wonders on my migraine,' Joseph said, popping a mint into his mouth under his mask. Then he proffered the pack to Megan, but she waved him away. The student had become the master.

'Well, you've timed your entrance perfectly. Doctor Jacobs is about to do the big reveal,' Clare said.

'Although you have missed my explanation of the victim's wounds from the impact.'

Joseph caught Megan's eye, and she shook her head at him, indicating he really didn't want to know anything about that.

'No, I'm grand, and you can spare me all the gory details,' Joseph said.

'Spoilsport,' Rob said, raising his eyebrows at him. 'Anyway, let's cut to the chase. As I was about to tell your colleagues, we missed this during the initial autopsy. However, the biopsy work came back from the lab with a very interesting result.'

'I'm certain a lot of other doctors would have missed this,

but my mentor is nothing if not thorough,' Clare said, beaming at Rob.

'Oh stop now, you'll make me blush,' Rob replied. 'Anyway, as Doctor Reece alluded to, I do like to kick the tyres on what looks like a straightforward cause of death. That certainly paid dividends in this case.'

'What do you mean?' Chris asked, peering at him.

'I ordered both gas and liquid chromatography-mass spectrometry tests run on the fluid, blood, and tissue samples. Thankfully, we took those soon enough after the victim had ingested the drug because it's rapidly metabolised, normally leaving no trace behind.'

'Drug?' Joseph said. Then he remembered how the student had stumbled and his eyes had been closed as he'd plummeted to his death. At the time, he thought that was purely instinctive for someone not wanting to see what was about to happen.

Megan's forehead ridged. 'From what you've already said about the drug leaving no trace behind, are you describing the date-rape drug, Rohypnol?'

Rob positively beamed at her. 'Your talents are so wasted as a detective. You should seriously consider switching careers and joining us here.'

Megan couldn't help but smile at the man, who Joseph knew definitely had a bit of a thing for her. 'No, I'm good, but thanks for the offer, anyway.'

'Yes, no poaching members of my team, thanks all the same,' Chris said.

Rob chuckled. 'You can't blame a man for trying.'

Joseph looked at the doctors as he turned the thought over in his head. 'So let me get this absolutely clear. You're saying that Eddie was already drugged before he climbed the spire?'

'Yes, and based on the lab report, a good thirty minutes before it fully kicked in,' Clare replied.

'In other words, just long enough for the Rohypnol to affect him during his climb?' Chris asked.

'Exactly,' Rob said. 'So, assuming he didn't take it himself, that could mean someone may have deliberately timed slipping him the drug when they did, so it kicked in at the worst possible moment.'

Joseph's thoughts sharpened. 'That means someone wanted to make Eddie's fall look like an accident. In which case, we need to seriously consider that not only Ryan was framed, but Eddie, as well.'

'You mean someone planted that crossbow in his room?' Chris replied.

'Exactly. Also, don't forget, we didn't actually see who shot that crossbow on the video.'

'But we heard Eddie's voice on it,' Megan said.

'Did we, though?' Joseph replied. 'Isn't that the sort of thing you can fake these days with AI?'

Chris stared at him. 'So, are we really suggesting that the murderer is still out there?'

'Aye, Boss, I'm afraid it seems we are.'

Megan held up her hands. 'Hang on, didn't Ryan literally only just tell us that he, Gabby, and Eddie were the only three players in the game?'

'Yes, but once again, the lad may have lied to us. He certainly seems to have a talent for it. But even so, there's every reason to believe Ryan's life is still in danger, armed guard or not.'

'Then we need to move quickly,' Chris said. 'First of all, we need to check Eddie's whereabouts in those thirty minutes before he fell from St Mary's spire. Do that and maybe we'll discover who drugged him. We'll need to go over all the CCTV footage covering Radcliffe Square and the immediate area to see if we can retrace his steps.'

'We should also interview his housemates again. See if they knew if he was meeting anyone before the steeple challenge,' Joseph said. 'It might even be the same person who bet Eddie couldn't do it.'

'Bloody hell, that all makes perfect sense,' Megan replied.

'Then stuff this for a game of soldiers,' Chris said. 'We'd all better head to John Radcliffe to interview Ryan and see if he knows anything about a fourth player. On the way there, I'll ring in and get Ian to brief the team about this latest development. But Derrick certainly isn't going to be thrilled to hear we need to reopen our murder investigation.'

My heart bleeds for him, Joseph thought.

'You won't stay for a cup of Earl Grey first?' Rob said to Megan, as though she were the only person in the room.

'Work calls,' she said.

Joseph caught the amused look on Clare's face, only for her to hide it after catching him looking at her. So, he wasn't the only one who realised Rob was keen on the DC.

'Then maybe another time,' the pathologist replied.

Joseph leaned in and whispered to Megan as they headed out of the lab, 'Despite what you keep telling me, that you two are just friends, your luck is so in there.'

Megan just gave him an eye-roll as they headed outside.

As they walked over towards the Volvo V90, Joseph's thoughts were elsewhere. He checked his phone, but there still wasn't any update from Kate. So why the radio silence? The one thing that Joseph knew for sure, if he hadn't heard from her before the evening was out, he would be talking to Derrick directly, to hell with the consequences.

CHAPTER TWENTY-THREE

THE FIRST THING Joseph registered as he, Chris, and Megan entered the corridor of the hospital where Ryan's room was located was that there was no sign of the armed officer who should have been standing guard.

'Where the hell is the policeman who should be here?' Chris said, voicing what Joseph had been about to articulate.

Megan had already headed over to the nurses' station. 'Do you know where the officer is?'

The woman looked up from the screen she'd been staring at intently. 'That's strange, he was there literally a minute ago. I know, because I took pity on him and made him a cup of tea. Maybe he's just popped to the loo.'

Under any other circumstances, Joseph would have agreed that was the most likely thing, even though the man wasn't meant to leave his station. But the thing was, his well-honed instinct, perfected over the years, was already yelling at him that something was wrong.

The DI was the first to reach Ryan's room, but when he went to open the door, it didn't budge.

'Feck, give me a hand,' he said.

Chris shot him a frown as he put his shoulder to the door. Together, both officers pushed hard. With a shudder, the door started to open as something on the other side shifted.

'Ryan, are you okay in there?' Megan called out the moment a crack appeared in the door.

There was no response.

Chris and Joseph traded worried looks, and then they really put their backs into it. The door groaned open, and at last they all saw what was propped up against it—the police officer, slumped on his side on the floor, his eyes closed.

'Shite on a fecking bike!' Joseph said, as Megan squeezed through the gap in the door, followed by him and Chris.

Even as Megan crouched to check that the officer was okay, Joseph's gaze swept over the room. No sign of Ryan.

'Okay, he's got a pulse,' Megan said.

Chris nodded and shouted through the door. 'We need help in here!'

They began to carefully move the downed officer away from the door as a nurse rushed into the room. Seeing the officer on the floor, she immediately slammed her palm onto the alert button on the wall. An alarm shrieked out in the corridor, and in what seemed like seconds, the room filled with medical staff.

In the chaos, Joseph headed to the en suite bathroom, but he wasn't surprised to find it empty. When he returned, Megan and Chris were standing back to let the medical team work. Then he noticed the closed blinds on the windows gently rocking inwards.

In three strides, he crossed to them and pulled the blinds back. The outside window had been pushed wide open. The safety arm that should have prevented it from being opened so far, had been sheared off. A dented metal water bottle, presumably used to do that, lay discarded on the windowsill.

'Feck's sake!' he muttered, sticking his head out of the gap, to see a small ledge beneath the window and the four-storey drop to the pavement below.

A groan came from behind the DI, pulling his attention back to what was going on inside the hospital room.

The policeman had his eyes open as one of the nurses checked his blood pressure.

'The bastard hit me.'

'Ryan?' Chris asked.

The officer waved the nurses off as he struggled into a sitting position. He nodded, but immediately regretted it based on the way his mouth twisted into a tight line.

'Yes, Ryan called me into the room. But he was behind the door and clobbered me over the head with a bloody chair. The last thing I saw before I blacked out was him scrambling out of that window like a regular Spiderman.'

Chris already had his phone out. 'Hi, we need a general alert put out across the Oxford area to be on the lookout for Ryan Slattery. He's done a flit from the JR hospital after injuring an officer. Yes, you heard me right...'

As the SIO continued to relay the shocking turn of events, Megan turned to Joseph. 'So does this mean what I think it does?'

'Well, it's hardly the actions of an innocent man, is it?'

'Okay, so we're now asking whether Ryan killed Gabby after all? But if so, what about drugging Eddie, because surely he was stuck in hospital at the time?'

'A good question. But first things first. We need to check with the security team here to see what, if anything, their cameras picked up of Ryan's escape.'

'Good idea,' Chris said, catching the end of their conversation as he ended his call.

The three detectives returned their attention to the officer, who was now kicking up a fuss with the female doctor who'd just entered the room and was shining a light into his eyes.

'I'm okay, I just need a minute,' the PC said.

'I think I'll be the judge of that,' the dark-haired female doctor replied, who, according to her lanyard, was called Kelley Stanbridge.

'You better listen to her, and that's an order,' Chris said.

'Absolutely right,' Doctor Stanbridge said. 'You've had a head injury and you'll need a CT scan and we'll need to keep you in for observation.'

'It's a lot of fuss about nothing if you ask me,' the officer said.

'Which it seems no one is, so do as you're told,' Joseph added, making the doctor grin.

The officer scowled at him before turning to the doctor. 'Well, tell me where I need to go, and I'll walk over there right now.'

'You'll do no such thing—we'll call a porter to fetch you,' the doctor replied.

The officer opened his mouth to argue, but Kelley just raised her eyebrows at him. He sighed and nodded, before looking at Chris.

'I'm sorry. This is all my fault,' he said. 'I'll write it up in a full report. I take full responsibility for what happened.'

'You can do the paperwork when you're good and ready, but as for taking responsibility, this isn't on you,' Chris replied. 'Remember, you weren't guarding a prisoner, but someone we thought was a victim in all of this.'

'But not any longer?' the officer asked.

'Maybe not,' Joseph replied for all of them.

'That video caught by the hospital CCTV was pretty conclusive,' Megan said, as she drove the Volvo back to St Aldates.

'Yes, it seems that despite his shoulder injury, Ryan is just as skilled as Eddie in freeclimbing,' Chris replied. 'But good on you, Joseph, following up on that hunch to check the footage from last night as well.'

Megan nodded. 'Otherwise we wouldn't have known that this wasn't the first time Ryan had done a flit from his room. At the very least, it now puts him in the time frame for Eddie's murder and slipping him the drug. Especially as he made sure he left and was back again before the nurse did her usual rounds to check in on him.'

'And he had the perfect alibi because no one knew he was even gone, including the police officer stationed outside his room,' Chris added.

The DI raked his hand through his hair. 'It seems that Ryan has pulled the wool over all our eyes.'

'But he seemed genuinely upset about Eddie's death, just like he did with Gabby,' Megan said. 'Surely no one is that good an actor?'

'I wouldn't discount it, although maybe part of Ryan genuinely regretted what he'd done,' Chris said.

'Aye, but the thing that I'm puzzled about is why make a run for it now?' Joseph asked. 'If anything was going to focus our attention back on him, it would be this and as things stood, he was in the clear.'

'Perhaps he just wants to pick up his winnings before going on the run?' Megan suggested.

'Ten thousand is hardly enough to start a new life with. So that leaves me thinking there's another reason in play here.'

'Such as?' Megan asked.

'No idea, but the sooner we catch the little fecker, the sooner we can get to the bottom of it.'

'Well, apart from posting patrols in University Park to check Ryan doesn't turn up there to get his prize, there isn't exactly a lot more we can do,' Chris said. 'So for now, we'll head back to St Aldates so I can break the news to the team. After that, I want the two of you to head home, so you are fighting fit and ready for whatever tomorrow brings. We're going to have to intensify our investigations tenfold, especially regarding Eddie's last movements before he died. And for that, I want everyone as sharp as possible. But don't worry, if there are any developments, I'll pull you both in sharpish.'

'Sounds like you intend to pull an all-nighter, Boss,' Megan said.

'That's the breaks of being the SIO on a case.'

'That doesn't mean you can't follow your own advice,' Joseph said, giving his superior a pointed look.

'True, but not on this occasion.'

Joseph actually rather respected that. He would have probably done the same in Chris's position. He also wasn't going to look a gift horse in the mouth, because he'd still not heard anything from Kate all day, and was trying to suppress his growing sense of panic.

The nightmare scenario gradually gaining traction in his imagination was that, trapped by her accusation, Derrick had acted out. Maybe his whole Mr Charming performance at work earlier was just that, an act, intended to throw people off the scent. If Joseph even caught a whiff of that, God help him, he wouldn't be responsible for his actions.

CHAPTER TWENTY-FOUR

As the sun set, the fallen autumn leaves crunched under Joseph's feet as he headed down the towpath towards his boat. His growing unease that something had happened to Kate was on a spin cycle in his gut, making him nauseous. The DI's plan was to freshen up, and head straight over to Kate's house again to see if she was okay.

Then he spotted the figure next to his boat. A split second later, his heart leapt when he realised it was Kate making a fuss over Tux sitting on the cabin roof.

It was all Joseph could do not to break into a sprint and throw his arms around her. Instead, he somehow managed to keep his stride in check. He walked up to her as casually as a man who hadn't been on the verge of having a complete emotional breakdown just a moment ago.

But any sense of relief was swept away when he saw how drawn her face was. Her attention was so focused on the blue tits on Dylan's bird feeder as she stroked Tux, she actually took a moment to register Joseph was standing before her.

'Kate, are you okay?' he asked gently.

She looked around, blinking. 'Oh, I've had better days.'

'Derrick?'

'Yes, Derrick,' Kate echoed in a flat voice.

'You do know I've been going out of my mind with worry about you after you went dark on me all day?'

'I just needed space to gather my thoughts after what happened. I've been walking the streets of Oxford since this morning, trying to do exactly that.'

'Then you better come inside and tell me all about it,' Joseph said, taking his key out to unlock the cabin of *Tús Nua*.

A short while later, with the boiler cranked up to full to take the biting chill out of the air, Kate sat opposite Joseph with Tux curled up on her lap and purring like a steam train.

Joseph sipped his freshly brewed Guatemala Antigua coffee, a solid nine out of ten on any day, and let the silence linger. He knew Kate well enough to know she'd begin the conversation when she was good and ready.

After several minutes had passed, Kate finally met his eye. 'Is this one of your interrogation techniques? Not saying anything, so I'll end up filling in the silence?'

He gave her a small smile. 'Something like that.'

The corners of her mouth briefly rose before falling again. 'I don't know what to think about my husband, Joseph.'

'Go on,' he replied, with an encouraging tone.

'Then cutting to the headline of this breaking story, when I confronted Derrick, he denied being mixed up with the Night Watchman. He even laughed in my face.'

Joseph felt surprised at hearing that. 'That's good then. But how did he explain away his clandestine meeting with Kennan?'

'He didn't. I didn't show him the video you took.'

The DI stared at his ex-wife, feeling nonplussed. 'But why? That was your ace up your sleeve that he couldn't deny.'

'Exactly,' Kate said, concentrating on rubbing Tux's neck. 'If

I did that, there would be no way back because I would have caught him in the lie. Then what?'

Joseph slowly nodded. 'There wasn't any way for it to end well.'

'Exactly. If I had thrown that piece of evidence into the mix, there would have been no saving our marriage.'

'But you're still convinced he's lying about not being involved?'

'More than ever. Derrick has never been the most accomplished liar. I can always see right through him. The trick is not to let him know that, which he never does. Even now, I can guarantee he's absolutely certain he's pulled the wool over my eyes.'

'Aye, based on the ridiculously good mood he was in at work, I think that's probably the case. But surely you're not going to leave things there?'

'Of course not. That video is exactly what you said it was, the ace up my sleeve. But I'm only going to hit Derrick with it when I'm good and ready. That's why I'm going to restart my own investigation into the Night Watchmen.'

Joseph gaped at her. 'But you can't do that, or have you forgotten their email warning you about not sticking your nose in?'

'Of course I haven't. I'm still all too painfully aware of that little detail. However, that's not going to stop me. My marriage is on the line because of it. Ideally, I'll unearth something that will help Derrick extract himself from whatever he's got himself mixed up in. And if I can't...' She raised her shoulders in a small shrug.

'Jesus, Kate. You could end up risking your life.'

'So be it. But please don't worry, I'll be extremely careful. And this isn't exactly my first rodeo, either.'

'Maybe, but I'm still not happy about this.'

'I know. But you know me well enough to understand I have

to do this. Besides, what's good for the goose is also good for the gander. Haven't you been the one looking into Derrick, despite your suspicions he was somehow wrapped up with the Night Watchmen?'

'Yes, but I'm paid to take that sort of risk.'

'Not when it's off the books, you're not. Besides, would you be doing this at all if Derrick wasn't my husband?'

'A bent copper is a bent copper, so yes, I would.'

'But not like this, you wouldn't. Tell me, you wouldn't have handed over what you had to the Counter Corruption Unit, rather than try to investigate it yourself. So my question to you is why?'

Joseph waved his hands around in the air. '*Because* it was Derrick, and the man's your husband. You deserve better than that.'

'So you did it partly out of kindness to me?'

'If you want the honest truth, yes. But part of me still can't believe that Derrick would be so bloody stupid as to get involved with them. That's a big part of why I'm doing this. Believe it or not, part of me is relieved that I saw him rejecting that cash. If it's what it looked like, then that means there's still hope for the man.'

'Exactly, and which is why like you, I will do my own digging before I'm ready to torpedo our marriage. Call it blind loyalty, but none of this is the man I know.'

Joseph took a long sip of his coffee and nodded. 'Aye, that's the thing. Derrick might be a right royal pain in my arse some days, but this...' He spread his hands and met her eye. 'So can I talk you into letting me do this while you—'

Kate held up a hand to silence him. 'Don't waste your breath.'

A smile flickered across his face. 'In that case, what do you intend to do next?'

'Oh, that's easy. Even though I was meant to park my own Night Watchmen investigation, I kept digging.'

Joseph shook his head. 'Dylan was so right about you.'

'Sorry?'

'Don't worry, carry on.'

'Well, one of my sources told me about a slave smuggling gang based over in Cheltenham that runs a haulage business operating right across Europe.'

'Are you sure? Cheltenham doesn't exactly shout it's the place for a people smuggling operation.'

'I think that's the whole point, so they could keep a low profile. Anyway, the rumour is this gang is linked to the Night Watchmen and has paid key members of the police force to turn a blind eye. I'm going to find out if there's any truth to it.'

'How, without making yourself a target again?'

'Trust me, I will do everything to keep off their radar.'

'Kate, I'm not happy about this.'

She reached over and squeezed his hand. 'I know, but I need to do this, Joseph. But don't worry, this is just a quick research trip and I'll be in and out of Cheltenham before anyone even realises I was there.'

'Like a ninja.'

A real smile lit up Kate's face. 'But without a sword.'

Joseph's heart sank a fraction as she withdrew her hand from his, and he couldn't help but think that feeling was a betrayal of Amy. But the woman before him, trying to save her husband from God knew what, would always be the love of his life.

'There's no way I can talk you out of doing this?' he said.

'I'll answer that with a question. Are you going to stop until you unearth the truth?'

'Not whilst there is still breath in my body.'

'There you go then.'

She held his gaze a moment too long, but then Joseph's mobile rang, breaking the spell. Then he almost jumped when he saw Amy's name on the display. He couldn't help but glance out of the window at the towpath, half expecting to see her standing out there, peering in on the two of them with a thunderous expression on her face.

With a considerable sense of relief when he saw she wasn't there, Joseph took the call.

'Hi, Joseph. You're going to want to get yourself into work. There's been another development in the case.'

'What is it this time?'

'Neil Tanner just got back to me after hacking Eddie Foster's mobile. He unearthed some real gold with his last attempt. It turns out that Eddie recorded a conversation with someone talking about the Hidden Hand club, and it's very enlightening. It appears there is a fourth player, after all.'

Before Joseph could reply, his phone buzzed again. 'Sorry, hang on, someone at St Aldates is trying to ring me on the other line.'

'I'm heading in there now and will talk to you about this when you get there.'

'See you soon,' Joseph said, before switching to the incoming call.

'Joseph, I hate to do this to you, but it's all hands to the pump,' Chris said. 'I need you to come in, so I can brief you and the rest of the team.'

'Don't worry, Amy just called. I'll be there as fast as I can.'

He hung up and returned his attention to Kate.

'Sounds like a promising development?' she said.

'Hopefully, but I'm afraid I'm going to have to dash.'

'Nothing new there then.' She shot him an amused look.

'I know, and I'm sorry. But please, from now on keep in

regular contact and let me know what's happening. No more going dark on me and worrying me stupid.'

'I promise.'

'Thank you.' He put down his coffee and picked up his jacket. But when Kate went to do the same, he shook his head. 'No rush, take your time and finish your coffee. Besides, Tux will appreciate the company.'

'Then I don't mind if I do.' She reached out again and squeezed his hand before letting it go again. 'You mean so much to me, Joseph.'

'And you to me,' he said, before turning and heading out of the door with a far lighter sense of being than when he'd first boarded his boat.

CHAPTER TWENTY-FIVE

The incident room was already full of officers by the time Joseph turned up at St Aldates. Amy beamed at him the moment she saw him, only tightening the sense of guilt hanging over the DI. How could he be dating her when he was so clearly still infatuated with his ex-wife?

Megan materialised in front of him, eating of all things, a Pot Noodle.

'Jesus, you're not actually voluntarily putting that bloody stuff in your mouth?' he said, welcoming the distraction.

'Needs must. I haven't eaten. Besides, these curried noodles almost taste edible.'

'You must have been desperate,' Joseph said as he slipped his coat off.

Ian, the last of the team to arrive, appeared in the doorway munching a pasty, and nodded at Joseph as he headed to his desk.

'Is there anyone here not filling their faces?' Joseph asked.

Megan slurped up a whole noodle in one go, like a blackbird eating a juicy worm. 'Well, it's dinnertime, so what do you expect?'

It was at that moment his stomach decided to rumble, making him realise he hadn't had a chance to eat anything, either. He briefly considered asking Megan if she had another Pot Noodle in her desk, but quickly thought better of it. A radioactive sandwich would have been more appetising.

Chris, who'd been deep in conversation with Amy, clapped his hands together. 'Okay, let's get this show on the road. To kick things off, I'm going to show you the footage Sue managed to recover from a security camera on the corner of Broad Street. It was taken thirty minutes before Eddie fell from St Mary's. In the video, I want you to concentrate on who emerges from the King's Arms.'

Ian gave Sue a soft handclap, to which she responded with a royal wave and a grin to the gathered officers.

Chris hit the play button.

Joseph and the rest of the officers in the room watched the camera feed covering the doors of the pub. He sat up straighter when Eddie Foster walked out, followed by a woman. She had a hoodie raised over her head, obscuring her face thanks to the high camera angle.

'So you're saying that Eddie was with that woman in the timeframe he was drugged with Rohypnol?' Megan asked.

'Exactly, and that means, despite what Ryan told us, we now have a new potential fourth player to throw into the mix,' Chris replied. 'The only problem is that, as you can all see, we can't actually see her face. Fortunately...' He nodded to Amy, who was already selecting a file on a computer linked to the large display screen.

'It turns out Neil Tanner is just as skilled hacking phones as he is computers,' Amy said to the room. 'What you're about to hear is a recording he managed to find hidden on Eddie Foster's mobile. It's a five-minute recording taken with a timestamp that matches when he would have been in the King's Arms.'

'In other words, recorded when he was with this mystery woman?' Joseph asked.

Amy nodded, and pressed play.

'I can't believe that someone in the club went as far as killing Gabby,' they all heard a voice that was clearly Eddie's say.

Everyone in the room exchanged glances.

'It's all getting way out of hand, and for what?' a woman's voice replied. 'I know it's a lot of money now that the prize pot has been upped to twenty thousand, but to murder Gabby? What sort of sicko would do something like that?'

Joseph felt a crackle of electricity pass up his spine. He knew that woman's voice from somewhere. He just couldn't quite place it.

'Someone who really needed the money and was prepared to do whatever it took to make sure they won,' Eddie replied. 'The question is, was it you?'

You could have heard the proverbial pin drop as all the detectives in the room waited to hear the answer.

'No, but I could ask you the same,' the woman replied. 'I mean, that kind of money could tempt someone to do something really stupid if they were hard up.'

'Not me,' Eddie replied. 'But I know you're as desperate for cash as I am, which puts you squarely in the frame as well. And the problem is, the only other member of our game who's left is Ryan. It obviously can't be him, because our mystery murderer tried to kill him and he's now in hospital. And I didn't do it, so that only leaves you.'

'I didn't do it either, but I'll do whatever it takes not to be your next victim,' the woman replied.

'Ten out of ten. You almost sound convincing. But I warn you, if you try anything, all bets are off. I will do whatever it takes to survive, the prize money be damned.'

The woman laughed. 'Oh really? So why are you taking on this side bet to climb the steeple?'

'Well, if someone is stupid enough to bet me to do it, they obviously don't know me very well. Besides, it's easy pickings and I need the money, especially if I don't win the jackpot. A bird in the hand and all that. But at least I won't have to hurt anyone to win the bet. Unlike this bloody Hidden Hand game. One of us is a certifiable psychopath and I know it isn't me.'

'Yeah, yeah, yeah. Then we've got nothing more to say to each other. Just keep well clear of me, Eddie, and I'll do the same until Saturday at midnight, when this whole bloody nightmare will be over.'

'Done, not that I believe you.'

'And vice versa.'

'Okay, I've wasted enough time on this face-to-face you were so desperate to have. I need to get going and win myself some easy cash.'

They heard a clink of a glass being set down before the recording ended.

Chris looked expectantly at the detectives gathered together in the room. 'First of all, does anyone know who that woman's voice belongs to?'

Joseph realised he knew exactly who it was, but before he could even open his mouth, Megan beat him to it.

'I would lay good money on it being Anita Steadman. We interviewed her about being injured by Slattery during an Assassins' Syndicate game. What do you think, Joseph?'

The DI was already nodding. 'I was about to say the same thing. Certainly, she would have had ample opportunity to slip Eddie some Rohypnol in the pub, despite what she just said about not going round killing people.'

'And in the right time frame for the drug to have kicked in

when he was climbing the steeple,' Amy agreed. 'She was knowingly sending Foster to his death.'

Chris nodded. 'So it seems we have a new chief suspect.'

'He obviously suspected her based on the conversation we just heard, and the fact that he even took the extra step of recording it,' one of the other detectives in the room added.

'Okay, this is all starting to add up, but why did Ryan run then?'

'Actually, I do have a new theory now about that,' Megan said. 'After Eddie's death, Ryan would have known Anita was the last player in the game. By a process of elimination, he would know she had to be the murderer. Perhaps he was worried she was deranged enough to try to get to him in hospital, despite our police protection.'

'But why not just tell us?' Sue asked. 'Then we could have arrested her and none of this would have happened.'

Joseph looked at his fellow officers. 'What if he's still playing? Perhaps, realising that Anita must have murdered Gabby, Ryan wants to take matters into his own hands.'

'You mean he's now prepared to kill her?' Sue asked.

'Grief can push the most rational people over the edge. Or maybe he just doesn't trust us to keep him safe. That's not surprising after what happened right outside. Perhaps until that moment, like Eddie tried with Anita, Ryan wanted to confront her. But here's the thing, we now know that whoever organised this whole shite show, apparently increased the prize pot.'

'Like they're egging the players on by upping the cash on offer?' Ian said.

'Exactly, and like watching the action cam footage of the assassinations, this is how they get their kicks. Pitting the players against each other, upping the stakes. There's also the deadline Anita mentioned. My guess is that's when this'—Joseph made air quotes with his fingers—'"*game*" ends.'

'Ends how?' Chris asked.

'Maybe it's killed or be killed now,' Sue suggested. 'After all, this was meant to be an assassination game taken to the next level. Quite literally, the last person standing wins everything.'

'You're really trying to say that an everyday student in Oxford, like Anita, could be motivated enough to commit actual murder?' Ian said.

'I know it doesn't make much sense, but that's what this new evidence is suggesting.'

'And for all we know there's something in her history that set her on this path, and she took the criteria literally,' Chris said. 'So that's exactly what we're going to look into, in addition to obviously pulling Anita in for questioning immediately.'

'And what about Ryan?' Megan asked.

'We'll just have to hope we get to him before he does something really stupid.'

Sue blew out a puff of air. 'Just how sick do these people have to be to take part in something like this in the first place?'

'Put enough money on the table and people who are desperate enough will often surprise you,' Amy said.

No one argued with the SOCO.

'Okay, who would like to go with me to bring Anita in?' Chris asked. 'We'll take an armed unit as well, just in case she's got another crossbow.'

Megan's hand was already in the air. 'Joseph and I have already spoken to her, so I'd like to do that. I can't help but feel we let her slip through our fingers.'

'We had no reason to suspect her at the time,' Joseph replied.

Chris nodded. 'This certainly isn't on either of you.'

'Leading from the front, that's what I like to see,' Derrick said from the doorway.

The man looked practically jovial, smiling in at them.

Joseph had to fight hard not to glare back at the little fecker. Of course, Derrick had every reason to look relaxed now that he believed Kate was off his case.

The big man nodded to Chris and ducked back out of the door.

'Okay, everyone, I'm going to set the wheels in motion with tactical unit support,' Chris said. 'In the meantime, everyone get kitted up.'

But Joseph barely heard what the boss said, because his mind was still focused on Derrick. The DSU was a career man, first, second, and third. So why risk all of that by getting involved with the Night Watchmen? It couldn't be for money. He'd watched the man throw an envelope full of the stuff back at Chief Superintendent Kennan, a woman presumably also involved somehow with the crime syndicate...

'Joseph?' Amy's voice said.

'Sorry?' Joseph looked up from the notepad he'd been doodling on.

'You looked a million miles away.'

Joseph grabbed onto the first excuse he could think of. 'Just wondering who the people or person is behind this game. Who can afford to lose twenty thousand pounds if someone wins?'

'That's a very good question. But at least you have a promising suspect now. Anyway, you better get yourself to the storage room to pick up a stab vest like the others.'

Joseph looked around to see Megan, Chris, Ian, and Sue had already disappeared.

'The boss isn't taking any chances then,' he said, as he stood.

'Just as it should be,' Amy replied. 'For all we know, you'll be greeted by a crazed woman ready to shoot you dead when you raid her home.'

'Aye, good point.'

Amy's gaze lingered on him.

Joseph peered at her. 'What?'

'Just if we weren't at work right now, I'd be leaning in to kiss you and wishing you luck.'

'Yes, that would get the tongues of the office gossips wagging.'

'And...' She smiled at him, just touching his arm lightly, but still enough to send a tingle through his body.

'Maybe afterwards,' he said, matching her smile with his own.

'I'm going to hold you to that,' Amy replied, her smile sharpening into a grin.

A surge of lust wasn't exactly what Joseph needed right then, and he turned away before she started to really push his buttons. But as the DI headed after the others, he couldn't help but wonder at himself. On one hand, there was Kate, who would always mean the world to him. But now Amy was very much part of his life. But if so, why was he continually pulled back to Kate, like a moth to a flame? That was the question he was still trying to work out in his head.

CHAPTER TWENTY-SIX

'Another day, another fruitless raid, and what could be seen as a waste of police resources,' Chris said, shaking his head as Erol Kentli led his tactical unit out of the flat in Cowley.

'Only because Anita wasn't at home,' Joseph said. 'But if she had been armed as well, going in with armed officers was always going to be the right approach.'

'Yes, much better to head in with an abundance of caution, rather than risk an officer getting shot,' Megan said. 'Besides, who knows what evidence we'll find when we head in there ourselves.'

'Thanks for the pep talk,' Chris said, raising his eyebrows at her. 'At least I manage to keep the locksmiths of Oxford busy with the repair work I send their way,' he said, looking at the shattered door frame.

Joseph chuckled as he slipped on a pair of blue latex gloves. 'I'm sure they all thank you for it on a daily basis. They probably have a shrine set up in your honour by now.'

Chris gave him a wry look as they entered the flat.

The first thing the DI registered were the framed animal photographs filling all the walls. There were countless bird shots, some hares, along with ones of small rodents like shrews and mice. There was even one incredible photo of an otter in a small stream that Joseph recognised. But the pride of place went to a series of large black and white shots of deer.

'Bloody hell, Anita really is good,' Megan said, casting an appreciative look over the pictures. 'You could easily imagine these adorning the cover of one of those nature magazines.'

Chris's eyebrows arched as he leaned in for a closer look. 'Anita took all of these?'

Joseph nodded. 'I'd lay good money on it. She is seriously into wildlife photography. The last time we saw her she had one of those cameras with a huge, *take a closeup of a flea's arse at three hundred paces*, lens.'

'Then if she really is our woman, it's a shame she didn't stick to just shooting animals with a camera,' Chris said, as he handed both of them evidence bags.

The three detectives set to work, systematically checking everywhere in the one-bedroom flat. A laptop and iPad were soon secured, along with a journal that had been hidden under her mattress.

Megan gestured towards a camera bag. 'Is it worth bringing that in to check for evidence?'

Joseph nodded. 'Best to leave no stone unturned, especially as there doesn't seem to be any action camera anywhere around here. For all we know, she may have an incriminating photo on her camera. At least we know by it being here she's not off shooting deer again, or some such.'

'Whatever else Anita is, she isn't exactly a master criminal,' Chris said, coming out of the bathroom holding a small white bottle. 'Look what I just found in her medicine cabinet, a bottle of Rohypnol.'

'So that's pretty conclusive,' Joseph said.

Megan nodded distractedly, as she looked past the two other detectives. Excusing herself, she went by them to a photo on the wall. She pointed at the selfie of Ryan and Anita. The art student's arm was wrapped around her waist and he was kissing her neck. She was beaming at the camera like the happiest woman on the planet.

The DI frowned. 'Those two look rather cosy together.'

'Oh, I'd say it's way more than that,' Megan replied.

'What, you're saying Anita and Ryan were having an affair?' Chris asked, joining them.

'Look how lit up she is. They certainly seem like a couple to me.'

Joseph stared harder at the photo. 'Jesus H. Christ. And just like that, we have a possible motive for one or both of them murdering Gabby. Maybe they wanted her out of the picture. We thought this might all be about money for the murderer, but what if it was this?'

'If that's true, why kill Eddie?' Megan asked.

Joseph rubbed his neck. 'Maybe he found out about their affair and they realised they needed to silence him, so there was no way to connect her to Gabby's murder.'

'Hang on, what about the action camera footage of Eddie shooting Ryan, or are we going with the idea that Eddie's voice was edited into it?' Megan said.

'It's as good a theory as any. Also, don't forget, we just saw the arms and hands of the person who fired that crossbow and with the baggy top they were wearing, that could have just as easily been a woman.'

Megan nodded. 'Anita could have planted that action camera in his room to make sure we discovered it, confirming our suspicions about Eddie. Remember, she's only in the frame now thanks to Eddie being paranoid and taking the extra step of recording their private conversation in the pub.'

'Then there's one thing that's for certain, we need to get our hands on her and fast,' Chris said.

'We may still have an opportunity to grab her tonight,' Megan said. 'Unless Anita saw us entering her flat, or a neighbour tipped her off about a group of armed officers storming the place, she still doesn't know we're onto her.'

Chris nodded. 'We should clear out of here as fast as possible and put someone on stakeout duty in case she turns up.'

'You've got a locksmith on speed dial, right?' Joseph said.

Chris just gave him the *look*.

The three of them sat in the unmarked Volvo V90, watching the steps that led up to Anita's maisonette flat.

'I can't believe we're on a stakeout without food,' Megan grumbled from the backseat.

'I'm sure even you can survive a few hours without needing to fill your face,' Joseph said.

'What about a Silvermint to stave off my imminent starvation?'

'Those are only for emergencies.'

Megan made with the puppy dog eyes. 'Pretty please.'

'Bloody hell, what are you like?' Joseph offered her the pack and didn't raise his eyebrows too high when she helped herself to two. Then he offered one to Chris, who also took one.

'Is she always like this?' the DCI asked.

'Let's just say, if you come between Megan and her grub, she's likely to trample you to death.'

Megan scowled at him from the back seat. 'Hey! That might be true, but even so.'

Chris chuckled.

The DC pulled a face at them, before returning her attention to what she'd been doing just a moment before. Latex gloves on, she'd slowly been working her way through Anita's journal.

'Have you found anything useful in there yet?' Joseph asked.

Megan nodded. 'Well, we were right about Ryan and Anita being an item. She is absolutely infatuated with him. There's also plenty in here to confirm she and Ryan were having an affair behind Gabby's back. She even visited him in that artist's studio in Wytham after he invited her there to have sex with him.'

'So it seems whatever Ryan Slattery is, he's something of a dark horse when it comes to women,' Chris said.

'Or, if you pardon my language, just a two-timing shithead thinking he could have a bit on the side and get away with it,' Megan replied with considerable vehemence.

That suggested to Joseph that maybe Megan had suffered through something similar with an old boyfriend, but he couldn't help squirming at hearing her harsh words. Was that what he was doing to Amy with Kate? Wasn't that a form of being unfaithful?

'Men like that give the rest of us a bad name,' Chris said. 'Isn't that right, Joseph?'

'Aye, isn't that the truth,' the DI replied, looking anywhere but at his colleagues.

'Hey, I'm not condemning all men, just the few who think it's a good idea to be players,' Megan said.

That only helped add to the DI's growing discomfort. Fortunately for him, the subject was about to change.

'Oh, what have we got here?' Megan said, as she shone her phone's torch down at the journal open on her lap.

'More about Anita's affair with Ryan?' Chris asked.

'No, actually, this is about the Hidden Hand club. There's an entry here where she talks about finding a message on her phone, saying if she wanted to find a way to make a lot of money from playing assassination games, she should log onto a secret website to find out more.'

'Hang on, is that the dark website that Neil Tanner found on Eddie's machine?' Chris asked.

'I assume so. Listen to what she wrote next, *'I don't know whether this is some big wind-up from one of the other members of the Assassins' Syndicate, but the website looked legit, even though I had to use a dodgy browser and encryption key shoved through my letter box with instructions on how to log in. But when I saw how much the prize pot on offer was, I thought it had to be a hoax, especially as I thought the Hidden Hand club was just an urban legend. After all, who would pay out that much money for letting a bunch of people run round Oxford, playing a game? It all seems too good to be true.*

The snag is the message on the website that said if I want to know more, I would have to sign up first. They also said if I told anyone about being approached, I'd be automatically banned from taking part. The question is, do I? And why approach me? They said some bullshit, obviously intended to flatter, saying I was one of the best players in the Assassins' Syndicate. But the more I think about it, the more I think it's a scam. Oh, just enter your credit card to learn more. Yeah, right. Do I really look that naive?'

'Onto her next entry,' Megan said, turning the page.

'Okay, curiosity caught the cat and here I am up to my neck in whatever this is. Much to my surprise, I haven't had to hand over any money. But now for the catch—for a hit in this game to be viewed as successful, all contestants (there are only four) have to wear an action camera to record the hit.

'Any footage we take has to be uploaded to the Hidden Hand's secret website. The only thing I don't know yet is who the other players are. I'm desperate to talk to Ryan about this, but once again the rule states that if I do, the organisers say they will

know and I'll be thrown out. The sensible part of my head is telling me to walk away. But the woman who wants to pursue a career in nature photography and needs that money isn't so sure. I really feel pulled both ways by this.'

Megan looked up. 'That certainly clears a few things up.'

'Yes, but it's still a long way to actually murdering someone. So what changed?' Joseph asked. 'You better keep reading to see if we can gain any insight into the *why* of this whole situation.'

The DC nodded and started to read again.

'Well, if I had reservations before, they've been swept away. I now know who my fellow players are. None other than Ryan and Eddie. But here's the real kicker. Gabby's the fourth player. I'm not sure how I feel about that, seeing as I'm having an affair with her boyfriend.'

Megan looked up again. 'So what are we thinking?'

'That this isn't looking good for Anita, especially since we just found Rohypnol in her home,' Chris said.

Megan's eyes widened as she had turned the next page. 'Bloody hell, we've had this all wrong. Here, let me read it to you...'

'After what happened to Gabby and now Eddie, I tried to ring Ryan, but he didn't pick up. Who is the psycho behind all of this?'

Megan was already turning the next page. 'This is the last entry.'

'Let's just hope it fills in the missing pieces,' Chris said.

The DC nodded as she began reading again. 'I still can't believe Gabby was murdered, and then someone tried to kill Ryan. And now Eddie's dead. To think, I thought Eddie was going to murder me, even though I told everyone I wanted nothing more to do with their stupid game. None of this makes any sense. It's just me, and Ryan is still stuck in hospital. I know I should go to the police, but for all I know, whoever took a potshot at Ryan outside the police station, will do the same thing *to me. No, to be safe, I need to drop off the grid until the game's deadline finishes at midnight on Saturday. Then I'll tell the police everything that's happened and this nightmare can finally be over.'*

Megan closed the journal. 'I'm afraid that's it.'

'So Anita's gone into hiding, and of course what she doesn't know is that Ryan has left the hospital,' Joseph said.

'But I thought they were meant to be in love?' Chris added. 'And what about the Rohypnol we discovered?'

'Exactly. A bit careless don't you think, keeping evidence in your home that could link you to a potential murder?' Joseph said.

'You're saying she's been set up like Eddie was?' Chris said.

'Think about it. Who else would have a key to her flat and could let themselves in to plant evidence, apart from her lover?'

'But we thought Ryan had been set up as well,' Megan said.

Joseph turned the thought over. 'What if it were a double bluff, and he deliberately went out of his way to make it look like he'd been framed?'

'Bloody hell, that's really devious,' Megan replied. 'Especially since he probably knew it would make it near impossible to secure a conviction based on that alone.'

'So you're saying Ryan could be trying to track down Anita right now?' Chris said.

The DI shrugged. 'For all we know, he could have already killed her. A twenty thousand-pound jackpot is certainly enough to do a flit with.'

'Maybe, but I have another theory to throw into the mix here,' Megan said.

Chris dipped his chin towards her. 'Go on.'

'What if Anita is the one playing us? She could have deliberately left her journal hidden in her home, knowing we'd find it.'

'You're saying she's left us a false trail?' Chris said.

Joseph slowly nodded. 'For feck's sake, this case is making me dizzy. For every step forward, we seem to take another one back. This investigation is trickier than a game of Snakes and Ladders. It's as clear as the Irish Cliffs of Moher in a sea mist.'

'I'll have to take your word for that,' Chris said. 'The only thing I'm certain of right now is this stakeout is a bust. A much better use of our time is to head back to the station and regroup. The Saturday deadline is looming and is now only two days away. That may be all the time we have left to save a life, whether it's Ryan's or Anita's, is still open to debate.'

Joseph pulled a face. 'That is, if it isn't already too late.'

'We can't afford to think like that,' Chris said, casting a scowl in the DI's direction as he started the Volvo.

CHAPTER TWENTY-SEVEN

Nearly two fruitless days later, Chris was standing in front of the whiteboard, pen in hand, looking out at the room full of detectives, most of whom looked exhausted thanks to it being nearly two o'clock on Friday morning.

'Okay, our number one priority is to try to go over all the evidence we've uncovered. I think, as we all now realise, it's anything but straightforward.'

'Tell us about it. It's become as tricky as a game of Twister with my wife,' Ian said.

A very unfortunate mental image filled Joseph's imagination.

Chris just frowned at Ian before continuing. 'Right now, we have two potential suspects on the run. Ryan Slattery and Anita Steadman, either of whom could be our murderer, or equally, a potential victim. The question is which way round is it? What's complicated this investigation further is that it appears deliberate false evidence trails have been planted. That started with the original attempt to frame Ryan with the crossbow bolts made from one of his brushes. Once again, that may or may not have been Ryan.'

'Whoever our murderer is, they've been enjoying themselves at our expense,' Sue said.

Joseph squinted, staring into the middle distance. 'The more I think about it, the more I feel that whoever the murderer is, not only have they been playing against the other contestants but against us as well, going out of their way to confuse the investigation,' he said.

Chris nodded. 'I completely agree. All we can do in the small window of time left to us today is concentrate our efforts on Ryan and Anita. So what have we found from looking into their backgrounds?'

'Well, there's nothing in Ryan's history to suggest he could fall into this sort of pattern of extreme behaviour,' one of the detectives standing in the back of the room said. 'He came from a happy family and excelled at school. According to his parents, he's someone who could have chosen any career and succeeded in it, but decided to pursue art.'

'Which is never going to be an easy path for anyone to follow,' Megan said. 'I have a friend who's an artist and struggles to make a living, but for all that, wouldn't have it any other way.'

'So it sounds like Ryan is very driven, despite the obstacles in his path,' Chris said, as he wrote *'Driven,'* next to the art student's name on the whiteboard.

'You can certainly imagine his temptation to win that prize money when he was in such dire financial straits,' Sue said.

'Yes, but being a struggling artist isn't the same as being prepared to act out and murder someone,' Megan said.

'I would normally agree, but we really do have to look at every possible motive here that might tip even a normal, everyday guy over the edge,' Chris said. 'And that also applies to Anita. Is there anything there to suggest she could become a murderer, given the right situation?'

'Once again, there's nothing obvious,' another detective said.

'Other than being a bit of a loner, and being fanatical about wildlife, which all Anita's social media feeds are filled with, she seems like an everyday woman. Like Ryan, she was never in trouble with the police. She got good grades in school, and both her parents were teachers. The only red flag is, there's next to no money in her bank account. She seems to spend every penny she had on expensive camera gear.'

Chris wrote, 'Loner with money troubles,' on the board next to her name.

'But that's still a huge leap to becoming a murderer,' Megan said.

'I actually agree, but we have to look at everything, however tenuous,' Chris said. 'Murderers sometimes have problems fitting into society and often resent others to the point they want to kill them.'

'And just as often, they're not,' Joseph interjected. 'Don't forget, they can just as often be high-functioning individuals, the life and soul of the party, even. Face it, Boss, we're still clutching at straws here.'

'I know, but do you have any other suggestions?'

The *Cliffs of Moher* sea fog had started to lift a fraction from the DI's mind. 'Actually, I can't help but feel we've been looking at this back to front,' he said. 'What if the mystery person who started the Hidden Hand club took the urban myth and made it real because they have a grudge against the four players and they're the actual murderer?' At the blank looks the others were giving him, he added, 'Like I said before, it feels as though whoever is responsible is also playing the police. Shouldn't we at least consider the idea that the contestants are also being played? If so, that leads us back to the mystery game organiser. We know they've gone out of their way to remain anonymous, even getting the players to use Tor browsers. Maybe that's the real reason.'

All eyes were on the DI, and several people nodded.

'Think about it,' Joseph continued as the idea started to gain traction in his mind. 'They lure students in who were desperate for money with an offer of a large prize fund. Okay, not a fortune I grant you, but enough to grab the interest of people who think they're just playing another version of the Assassins' Syndicate game, and with the potential to win the money they so desperately need. *Fine*, Ryan, Anita, and the others think, *sign me up now*. But this is the really clever part. The money on offer wasn't a large enough amount to raise alarm bells at that point, even though none of the players knew who was behind it.'

'Which has to be significant,' Megan said.

'Exactly, someone who was desperate to stay in the shadows. So my guess is that when the game started, none of our players knew what they were really getting themselves into.'

'So you're saying the money was just a honey trap to lure them in?' Chris asked.

'It makes sense if you're setting out to turn a bunch of regular students into murderers. Then doubling the prize as the danger ramped up was to make sure they all danced to the organiser's tune.'

'Actually, everything you're saying makes sense,' Chris said. 'Think about how the contestants have to upload the footage to a dark website.'

Sue nodded. 'And they could have been the one getting their kicks out of watching these four being slowly corrupted and turned into murderers.'

'Oh great, now I have a mental image of a guy in his underpants watching the footage and getting turned on,' Ian said.

'Sometimes I worry about where your mind goes,' Sue said.

'You're not the only one,' Joseph said, shaking his head at his colleague. 'But maybe that's the real motivation behind all of this shite show.'

'Sorry, I'm still having a problem understanding how normal people could be suckered into trying to kill each other,' an officer at the back of the room said.

'If they were made paranoid enough, convinced their own lives were on the line, then maybe they'd cross that line,' Megan replied. 'The law of the jungle, and the winning criteria of the game, kill or be killed.'

'If true, it could be argued that the real murderer, even though they may not have directly murdered anyone, is the puppet master, organising all of this,' Joseph replied.

'The only solid connection we have so far in any of this is that members or former members of the Assassins' Syndicate were approached,' Chris said. 'That, to me, suggests this mysterious founder comes from their ranks. Based on the assumption that it's someone who knows all the players and their financial situations, I think we need to look at the Assassins' Syndicate again and re-interview all their members. In particular, we need to look for anyone who has any reason to have some sort of vendetta against the four players, and who might want to see them turn against each other. Maybe, like Joseph suggested, that was the real motivation in forming this Hidden Hand club all along.'

'But we have twenty-two hours left until the midnight deadline,' Ian said. 'That doesn't exactly give us a lot of time to pin someone down for this.'

'Well, that's what we're going to try to do anyway, because it's definitely a line of enquiry we need to pursue with real urgency,' Chris said. 'That's why I want you to get the club members out of their beds if necessary, and also find out how healthy their bank balances are and if they have money to burn. Joseph is right; we may have been looking at this back to front all along. Unless we get lucky and either Ryan or Anita drop into our laps, there isn't a lot more we can do from that angle. That is, apart from issuing a general press release in the morning, asking the public to let us know if they spot either of them. What we can do is put some real effort into kicking the tyres on Joseph's theory.'

'And what if Ryan or Anita have already been corrupted by the game and one of them is our murderer?' Sue asked.

'Then, they will have to face the consequences for their actions when we eventually catch up with them.'

If we catch up with them, Joseph couldn't help thinking.

'Is there anything else we should be considering?' Chris asked. When no one said anything, he nodded. 'Then let's put our backs into this new angle and let's see if we can't unearth the truth before it's too late for the remaining players.'

As the meeting broke up, Joseph turned to Megan. 'I'll get the coffee in, because this is going to be another long day.'

Joseph's shoulder was being gently shaken. He felt briefly disoriented when he lifted his head from his desk only to realise he was still in the incident room, surrounded by his exhausted-looking colleagues. It was still daylight outside, and when he managed to focus on the wall clock, he saw it was six p.m.

'Jesus, how long have I been out?' he asked.

'About two hours, which is hardly surprising after working nearly thirty-six hours straight,' Megan said, placing a cup of coffee bearing the Steaming Cup logo on the side.

'You should have woken me,' Joseph said, sitting up.

'And deprive the team of your epic snoring? I don't think so.'

'Oh feck, really?'

She grinned. 'Just winding you up. Anyway, you needed a nap. You were practically dropping when your body finally gave into the inevitable.'

'What about you? Have you managed to catch any shuteye?'

'Not yet, but I'm good for a bit longer. I'm younger. Better staying power.'

'Okay, no need to rub it in.' Joseph took a sip of the coffee. 'Ah, that hits the spot.'

'I thought you probably needed the good stuff to get you firing on all cylinders again.'

'You're not wrong,' Joseph said, as he took a second grateful sip of the rich dark roast. 'So what have I missed?'

'Not a lot. We're still as stuck as we were a couple of hours ago.'

'So no fresh leads for any of the members of the Assassins' Syndicate?'

'No. I'm afraid that as strong as your theory was, we haven't got anything tangible to go on so far. It's also an awful lot of bank accounts for the digital forensic teams to go through.'

'Shite, so there goes our last chance of making a breakthrough before the deadline.'

'We still might, and Chris has bent Derrick's ear and brought in lots of Uniforms to be on the lookout for Ryan and Anita. But as for our detective team, Chris is telling the vast majority to head home and get some rest.'

'But we've only got six hours left until midnight!'

'And there's nothing more we can do now,' Chris said, overhearing their conversation and joining them. 'So far, there's been no leads or sightings of Ryan or Anita from the plea to the public. We've also tried interviewing all their friends, but everyone swears they haven't seen them for days.'

'So that's it then, we're just giving up?' Joseph said.

'Not giving up, just taking a breather before the last push,' Chris said. 'What else would you have me do?'

The DI felt a twist in his gut. 'Sorry, that wasn't a criticism aimed at you or anyone else on the team. It's just so fecking frustrating.'

'Tell me about it. But you and Megan are top of the list to go and grab some proper sleep. For now, we've already got as many warm bodies as we need prowling the streets of Oxford.'

'You think the final murder will happen somewhere in the city, then?'

Chris shrugged. 'If at all. Don't forget there is every chance that the killer won't find the remaining player. But if they do, there's no reason it couldn't still happen here on our patch.'

'You do realise that's very long odds?' Megan said.

'Tell me about it, but if you have any better ideas, I'm all ears.'

Both Joseph and Megan shook their heads.

'In that case, get yourselves some kip somewhere other than at your desks, and I'll see you back here around nine, ready for that final push to midnight,' Chris said.

Joseph, clutching his coffee, stood. 'You heard the man, Megan.'

The DC nodded and, as she went to fetch her things, Joseph checked his phone. There was still no update from Kate about how she was getting on. Maybe she was still in Cheltenham, or better still, maybe she was waiting to update him in person back at his boat. He quickly slipped his jacket on and headed for the door.

CHAPTER TWENTY-EIGHT

FOR THE SECOND time in as many hours, Joseph awoke suddenly from an impossibly deep, dreamless sleep.

He dislodged Tux, who gave him an indignant miaow as he leapt down from where he'd been snoozing on his chest.

'Give a man a break,' Joseph said.

In response, Tux just raised his tail, pink arse aimed back at Joseph like some sort of cat insult, as he stalked off towards the food bowl in the galley.

The DI focused on the radio alarm clock and saw it had only just edged past eight. He still had a good thirty minutes of kip left before he needed to think about heading back to work.

His phone warbled, putting paid to that notion. When he checked the screen he realised he'd missed a previous call, which he figured was what had probably woken him. Maybe it would be Kate, he thought hopefully. But instead of her name on the screen, it was an unknown number.

If it was a spammer telling him he'd been involved in a car crash and he could get compensation, God help him, he would be hard-pressed not to track the bastard down and to ring their scrawny neck. He pressed the call accept button, ready to give the person at the other end an earful.

'Inspector Stone, is that you?' Anita asked.

His mind snapped into sharp focus. 'Jesus, where the hell are you? Are you okay?' Then he heard sobbing at the other end of the line. 'Okay, take a breath and talk to me'

'I'm fine,' she said between shuddering gasps. 'You sound like you already know about the trouble I'm in?'

'If you mean about being a member of the Hidden Hand club, then yes, I do. We've seen your journal.'

'Then you know I wasn't involved in Gabby or Eddie's murders?'

'Not until we can go over everything together, I don't. You need to turn yourself in to St Aldates as quickly as possible for questioning.'

A shuddering breath. 'Not when Ryan could be waiting for me. He sent me a text saying he knew what I'd done, and he was coming for me.'

Any remnants of sleep were swept away as Joseph's thoughts raced. 'Okay, we'll come and pick you up,' Joseph replied. 'Where exactly are you right now?'

'In the artist studio in Wytham Woods.'

'Why the hell would... Because that's where your secret liaisons with Ryan were?'

'Yes, and I assumed it would be the last place he'd think to look for me. But now I'm here, I realise I wasn't thinking straight. Ryan also knows this place is out of the way, and might come here to double-check that I'm not hiding here.'

'Hang on, you're not saying Ryan's been the murderer all along, are you?'

Anita took another shuddering breath. 'That's exactly what I'm saying, and now he has his sights set on me.'

Confusion filled Joseph's mind. So much here didn't add up.

To start with, Ryan couldn't exactly have shot himself. Even now, could Anita still be trying to frame the art student? All Joseph knew for sure was he needed answers before time ran out.

Anita filled in Joseph's silence. 'I'm really scared Ryan's going to work out where I am and turn up at any moment.'

Lie or not, Joseph couldn't take the risk.

'Then hide yourself in the woods until we get there and keep your mobile on you. Don't worry, we'll be there as quickly as possible.'

'Please hurry, but come alone,' Anita said, her tone tight with stress. 'I don't trust anyone else.'

The line clicked off before Joseph could ask why. He immediately tried ringing back, but the call went straight to voicemail. If she really was the victim here, she still wasn't thinking straight. Either way, he was going to send in the cavalry.

Joseph was already ringing Chris as he pulled his clothes on. The SIO picked up in a single ring.

'What is it?' the DCI said, his tone tense.

'Anita just rang me. She's hiding out in the artist studio in Wytham. We need to go there right now and bring her in.'

'Oh, thank Christ, she's made contact. But there's a snag. Someone just called in a bomb threat about an abandoned car on the hard shoulder of the A34. Hoax or not, we've had to take it seriously and have already closed the road. But thanks to that, all the traffic trying to avoid it is picking its way through Oxford, and has snarled the whole city up. Even with blue lights, it will take us a while to get to Wytham. I'll get a helicopter dispatched, but that will still take about twenty minutes.'

'Do what you can, but traffic or not, I can probably beat you all to Wytham on my mountain bike. If Anita really is the victim here, every second counts whilst Ryan and our mystery organiser are still at large.'

'Okay, do that. I'm heading out right now with Megan. But looking on the bright side, hopefully, we'll have a lot more answers to pick through once we have Anita safely in custody.'

'I certainly hope so. This whole investigation is absolutely doing my bloody head in.'

'You're not the only one, Joseph. I'll see you there.'

The DI ended the call as he grabbed his jacket and rushed outside. Then he headed back in a split second later to grab a canister of PAVA spray issued for his discretionary use, along with his telescopic baton. He also popped a set of plastic zip ties used for restraining prisoners into his pocket. He was going to go into this situation with his eyes open. Then he headed outside again, ready to deal with whatever was waiting for him in the woods.

Joseph pedalled like a maniac, weaving in and out of the stationary traffic jamming up every road across the city. The DI was rewarded for his efforts with the occasional indignant hoot as he got dangerously close to the odd wing mirror of the stationary and often very frustrated drivers. He really needed to consider having a blue light fitted to his mountain bike if this was to become a regular occurrence.

Even though he was painfully aware of every second ticking past with Anita alone in the woods, the ride had also given him the space to consider what was happening. Anita had said she hadn't been thinking straight, hiding in Wytham. But something definitely felt off about it all. Why ask him to come alone when her life was on the line? That didn't make any sort of sense. He was certainly looking forward to hearing her explanation for everything in a nice, cosy interview room back at St Aldates.

At last, the traffic evaporated as the DI neared the outskirts of the city. Before long, he was cycling frantically through Lower Wolvercote, and racing past one of his favourite gastro pubs, The Trout.

He was pedalling so fast up the old humped-back stone bridge next to it, he almost had air beneath his wheels as he reached the top. That was much to the surprise of a car heading towards him from the opposite direction.

The vehicle slammed on its brakes on the narrow section of the road, shuddering to a stop as the crazed cyclist refused to give way. The DI was briefly aware of the V-sign flicked his way. The driver also leaned on the horn for good measure as Joseph skimmed past the vehicle through the smallest of gaps. Miraculously, he somehow avoided leaving a scratch down the side of the vehicle as a memento of the close call.

Less than a mile away ahead, the forest-covered hill of Wytham Woods was just a black silhouette in the darkness. Unfortunately, there were no flashing blue lights dancing on the trees lining the small approach road, or any helicopter hovering over the scene, yet. It looked like he was going to be the first officer to arrive.

Joseph made the most of the flat open road, making rapid progress under a sliver of a new moon. He briefly registered all the stationary car headlights on the A34 above him as he raced through the underpass. It looked like it was going to be a long night for the traffic patrol team, cleaning up that mess and getting the road moving again after the suspect car had been dealt with.

Within five minutes, and after breaking a few personal records, he was climbing the hill up into the utter darkness of Wytham Woods. Not much call for street lights on a small road leading up to an isolated place like that. Still, his *burn your retinas out* bike headlight did a good job turning night to day and illuminating his way.

By the time the DI reached the top, having navigated his bike through a super-sized kissing gate, his legs were screaming at him. He raced past the Swiss Chalet. With what had happened to Gabby, he still thought Anita was crazy to seek sanctuary up here, even if she hadn't been thinking straight.

The tarmac road suddenly turned into a bumpy track, but it was nothing his mountain bike's suspension couldn't easily soak up.

A short while later, Joseph skidded to a stop at the gateway leading to the artist cabin. Letting his bike drop as he leapt off it, he grabbed his torch, baton, and PAVA spray from his bag.

Ahead of him, less than fifty metres along the path leading into the woods, he could see the windows of the artist cabin were dark. That hopefully meant Anita had followed his advice and was hiding somewhere nearby in the woods. He took out his mobile and tried to ring her, but his call went to voicemail.

Where are you, lass? Then a darker thought hit him. *But what if...* A lead weight filled his stomach. He headed straight towards the cabin and was already ringing Chris. He spoke immediately as the SIO picked up.

'I'm already here, Boss, but there's no sign of Anita and she isn't answering her phone. I'm just going to check in the cabin in case Ryan has beaten us to her.'

'Bloody hell, okay, keep us on speaker phone,' Chris replied, over the sound of their police siren wailing in the background. 'I'm with Megan and we're on our way to you now. But as predicted, we're stuck in traffic despite the DC's best efforts to bully everyone out of her way. The motorbike team were doing better, but John, who was on a call out to a burglary in Eynsham, was nearer still. He's just parked up at the bottom of the west gate entrance into the woods and is heading up the hill on foot to your location. He's less than ten minutes out. I'm afraid the helicopter is still a good fifteen, though.'

'It's good to know backup is on its way at least,' Joseph said, as he headed around to the back of the studio to the entrance. The blinds were down so he couldn't just check through the window to see what had happened inside. A bad feeling was growing stronger by the second as he rapped his knuckles on the door.

'Anita, are you in there?' Only silence answered him.

'Okay, I'm coming in,' Joseph said into his phone.

'You should at least wait until John reaches you,' Megan said at the other end of the line.

'But Anita could be bleeding out in there. Besides, if Ryan was here, he's almost certainly long gone by now.'

'Then just keep your wits about you,' Chris said.

'I'll do my best.' Joseph extended the telescopic baton. Megan would be so proud if she could see what he was doing right then. It bordered on the responsible, entering a potentially dangerous crime scene, albeit once again by himself, with some preparation.

Joseph tried the door. It swung open with a squeak, announcing his presence as well as any doorbell. But when he didn't spot Anita lying dead inside, he let out the long breath.

'Okay, the good news is there's no sign of her inside,' the DI said into his phone. 'The bad news is, there's no sign of—'

His words were cut off by a sharp scream echoing through the woods.

'Shite!' He raced out of the cabin and cupped his hands around his mouth. 'Anita, where are you?'

A second scream came in answer off to his right. Before Joseph could even think about what he was doing, he broke into a run, heading towards the source of the sound as it faded away.

'Hang on, I'm coming, Anita!' he bellowed into the dark woods ahead of him.

'You'll do no such bloody thing,' Chris said over the phone. 'You're going to wait for John—'

Joseph slapped his hand against his phone's mic a couple of times. 'Sorry, you're breaking up, Boss. Reception is awful in these woods.'

'I said you're to stay—'

Joseph pressed the power button on his phone, killing the call. *Will you look at that,* he thought, glancing at his phone's darkened screen as he pocketed it.

A third scream came again as he directed his torch into the murk of the woods, casting a kaleidoscope of shadows from the trees' boughs.

'Ryan, give it up, son. There's no escape for you. And if you harm a hair on Anita's head, so help me God.' There was much more bravado in Joseph's voice than he actually felt.

The thing was, Chris had a point. He was basically one man with a baton, getting ready to take on a murderer potentially armed with a crossbow. Sometimes, even Joseph knew he was too impulsive for his own good. But there was no way he could stand around listening to the sound of someone getting murdered. Not on his watch.

'Detective Stone, please help me,' Anita called out from somewhere ahead in the trees. 'I've managed to get away from Ryan.'

If there had been any waver in the DI's resolve, it was swept away in that moment. 'Okay, make your way to the sound of my voice,' he called back, increasing his pace, half sliding on the carpet of leaves as he descended down a slope.

Then he spotted Anita in a camouflaged jacket, dragging a leg as she headed towards him and looking back over her shoulder like she was being followed. When he reached her, she practically threw herself into his arms, sobbing.

'It's okay, but we need to get moving,' Joseph said as he

wrapped an arm around her to support her. 'If we head back to the Swiss Chalet, we can barricade ourselves in there until the cavalry gets here.' He glanced down at her leg. 'Are you okay to walk?'

'I just turned an ankle, but no way can I run, either.'

'Don't worry, just lean on me.'

She nodded and did as instructed, as he turned and headed back the way he'd just come.

'Is Ryan on your trail?'

'I managed to hit him on the head and knock him out. That's how I got away. But he could still come round at any moment.'

'Then well done. Is he armed?'

'Yes, and I didn't even think to take the crossbow off him,' she replied.

'Don't worry. It's hard to think straight in an extreme situation...' Joseph spotted a figure move into the torchlight ahead of them, a crossbow in their hands.

A splinter of ice ran up Joseph's spine.

'Stop right there, Ryan!' the DI bellowed at the figure.

But then Anita stepped away from Joseph, her injured ankle miraculously forgotten. She took several strides towards Ryan before the DI could stop her.

'What the feck do you think you're doing?' he said.

She glanced back over her shoulder, grim-faced. 'I've done what I needed to and played my part. I'm so sorry, Inspector Stone.'

Joseph stared, dumbfounded, as his brain caught up with the sudden change in reality. He was painfully aware of just how alone and vulnerable he was.

'You lured me into a trap?'

'I'm afraid so,' Ryan said, squinting into the torch beam Joseph was shining in his face.

Still not sure exactly what he was dealing with here other

than the two students were obviously working together, the DI reached for the phone in his pocket only to find a space where it should have been. Hang on, there was something. He took out a small plastic yellow Eliminator game token, identical to the others they'd discovered during their investigation.

Ryan turned on an action camera clipped to his jacket. 'Welcome to the Hidden Hand game, Detective Stone.'

Anita held up his phone. 'Sorry, we couldn't have you calling for backup.'

'So you're working together?' Joseph asked, painfully aware that he was on his own. John was probably still five minutes out. Chris and Megan were stuck in traffic.

'We always have been.'

The DI's mind raced. 'So you could win the prize money and split it between you, probably pretending one of you had murdered the other...' A darker thought struck him. 'Hang on, why exactly did you bring me here, then?'

Ryan nodded. 'I wish with my whole heart we didn't have to, but yes, as I said, you're now a player in the game.'

'So you're going to kill me, is that the measure of it?' Joseph asked, staring at them both with a rising sense of disbelief.

'You have to understand we're not behind any of this,' Anita said, her face looking ashen as Ryan handed her a second crossbow. 'Just know how sorry we both are.'

Joseph's brain was racing now. 'So someone is making you do this? The person who set up the Hidden Hand club?'

Ryan nodded. 'And they've left us with no choice.' He raised his crossbow to eye level, ready to fire.

Adrenaline coursed through Joseph's body, preparing him for fight or flight. But it was the latter that made the greatest sense in the split second he had left to decide. He ducked to the left, turning as he did so and breaking into a run, switching off his torch so hopefully they would find it harder to follow him.

That hope died as a crossbow bolt whistled past his ear and thudded into a tree trunk nearby.

If he was going to stand a chance at surviving, Joseph needed to find somewhere to hide until help arrived—just as he'd advised Anita to do. But what about John, who was on his way into this shite show? If the young officer stumbled upon the couple by himself, would they try to kill him as well? The DI putting his own life on the line was one thing, but not a colleague's, especially when that officer was someone going out with his daughter.

For feck's sake!

Whatever else he did tonight, Joseph knew he had to warn John before it was too late. The only problem was that Ryan and Anita were between him and the track the PC would be using from the west gate. Somehow he needed to draw Ryan and Anita away, before circling back and warning the young officer.

The DI kept his head down, stumbling several times over hidden tree roots in the darkness. He couldn't hear any sign of pursuit, but his heart hadn't got the message as it continued to thump away in his chest. With every step, he half expected the burning pain of a crossbow bolt slamming into his back.

Senses heightened, every crackle of leaves sounded like a gunshot. The tapestry of forest shadows seemed to swirl around Joseph. The scent of rich earth cloyed in his nostrils.

This was what a hunted animal must feel like. And that was exactly what Ryan and Anita were trying to reduce him to. Prey. But his mind kept screaming at him: where is the *why* in any of this?

The DI ran as quietly as he could, approaching the edge of the woods bounded by a tall fence. If he was trapped against it, he didn't fancy his chances.

Then Joseph spotted a hollowed-out root from a toppled tree. He ducked down into it, his feet squelching in the soft mud at the bottom as he hunkered down into the depression in the ground.

A torch beam threaded the darkness coming down the slope after him and waved around as he heard footsteps approaching. A stone filled Joseph's throat and he clutched his baton tighter as the footsteps drew closer. Then Ryan crept past, heading towards the fence line. But where the hell was Anita? Had they separated so they could cover more of the wood? If so, then he knew he might still have a chance of picking them off separately.

Before Joseph had a chance to second-guess himself, he acted. His hand closed on one of the stones buried in the mud beneath his feet in the root bowl. He worked it loose as quietly as he could as Ryan headed away.

As soon as it was free, Joseph lobbed the stone at a tree between him and the other man.

Ryan's head whipped around at the sound, the torch beam once again piercing the darkness over Joseph's head.

The DI had one single idea in his head—the *hunted* must become the *hunter*. He needed to lure Ryan into his trap.

Joseph's fingers closed around a second stone and this time he threw it hard at a tree trunk five metres away to his right. His projectile smacked into it with a satisfying thud.

The torch beam immediately swivelled towards it as Ryan doubled back, aiming the crossbow towards the tree where the sound had come from.

That's it, keep on coming, lad, Joseph thought to himself as the figure closed.

His heart was crowding his throat by the time the art student passed his hiding place, towards the tree trunk.

This was the DI's one and only chance.

Joseph didn't waste a second. He began crawling out of his hiding place with the third and final rock he had prised free clutched in his hand. The next moment he was edging forward on the balls of his feet, breathing through his nose and trying not to make a sound. Then the inevitable happened.

A twig he hadn't spotted in the darkness, snapped under his foot.

As Ryan whirled around. The DI didn't so much leap as launch himself like a human cannonball straight at the student, just like he'd once done to save this same lad's life. He crashed into Ryan, sending the crossbow flying, and the student tumbling backwards into a tree trunk.

Joseph got ready to bring his rock crashing down onto the lad's head. But when the student didn't move, he checked himself. Ryan's eyes were closed, and he had a gash to the back of his head where he'd slammed it into the tree, knocking him out cold.

That will do nicely.

But taking no chances, the DI set to work pulling Ryan into a sitting position with his back resting against the tree and then pulling the lad's arms back around the trunk to bind his wrists together with a zip tie.

Let's see you get yourself out of that, you little arsewipe.

Joseph picked up the crossbow, still loaded with the bolt that had been intended for him. Then he looked at the rock in his other hand. He stood there, weighing which was the better option. The crossbow might be the more effective weapon, but having to shoot someone with it... Then his thoughts returned to John, who could stumble into Anita at any moment.

Oh, feck it. The DI dropped the stone and, holding the crossbow, set off in a direction he hoped would lead to the track that John would be using. He just prayed he would be in time to stop all this madness in its tracks before it went any further.

CHAPTER TWENTY-NINE

The sense of dread grew inside Joseph as he desperately tried to get to John in time. His colleague had no idea of the danger he was in. The DI crashed through the woods like a rampaging bear, saplings slapping his face as he shoved them aside, not caring how much sound he made. Much better that if anyone was going to put their life on the line, it would be him. In fact...

Joseph stopped for a moment and cupped his hands around his mouth. 'If you want me, here I bloody am!' he bellowed at the top of his voice.

He strained his ears to hear even the slightest of responses, but beyond the rustle of branches in the gentle wind stirring the wood, he couldn't hear a thing.

The DI set off again, seriously tempted to call John by name. But doing that would only alert Anita to the presence of another officer in the wood. Instead, every so often, he would stop and bellow out a challenge, crossbow ready to fire if he heard so much as a mouse fart.

The wood felt like it was closing in around him, and even though he had a weapon in his hands, a primordial fear was sinking its claws into his soul. Would this be the night he died? And for what reason exactly? So some students could get their rocks off playing their twisted idea of a bloody game?

At last, he spotted the track ahead on a ridge rising through the woods. But then he noticed a figure prowling silently along it, peering into the darkness on either side. It was Anita, her torch off, crossbow in hand and ready to shoot.

Joseph's mind raced. There were so many ways he could handle this: fire a shot without a warning, or alternatively, call out a challenge and risk being killed. But could he really bring himself to shoot Anita in the back? However, there was one other alternative.

Keeping low, and creeping forward, his own weapon ready just in case, the DI edged through the woodland towards Anita, stopping dead whenever she threatened to even vaguely look in his direction.

But then she glanced around and looked down right at where he was standing.

The DI quickly ducked behind a tree, hoping the darkness would hide his presence. With his back pressed against the trunk, he couldn't see Anita, but he could certainly hear her. Her breathing was coming with the panting breaths of someone on the edge of hyperventilating and sounding close to panic. Not exactly what he would have expected from someone who had been working with Ryan to assassinate other players. So maybe they'd both been telling him the truth about not having any choice. The question growing more urgent by the second was, who was the real genius behind this nightmare?

Her breathing grew quiet, and the minutes stretched on. Then the DI heard the softest of footfalls nearby.

Joseph looked down at the crossbow in his hand. He could spring out and try to shoot Anita before she could do the same to him. But there was something about this whole situation that didn't sit right with him. His instinct was screaming at him that Anita and Ryan might be many things, but even now, despite everything that had happened, were they murderers?

The DI reversed his grip so, rather than holding the crossbow by the grip, his hands were clamped around the arms of the weapon at the opposite end.

A trickle of cold sweat ran down his back as he got ready to swing it with everything he had.

His senses went electric as the nose of her raised crossbow edged into view past the bough of the tree. Without hesitating, he swung his own weapon straight into where her stomach should be.

A shudder shot through Joseph's arms as his improvised club made contact with Anita's midriff and she let out a startled cry. Without hesitating, the DI followed through, shoving his crossbow before him like a battering ram as he emerged from behind the tree.

Anita toppled backwards, her crossbow bolt flying harmlessly into the canopy as she squeezed the trigger by accident.

Even as the woman crashed onto the ground, Joseph didn't waste a moment and had already discarded his crossbow in favour of the PAVA spray. He leapt on top of her, using his knees to pin the woman down, as he sprayed the artificial pepper spray straight into her face.

Anita screamed as the fluid flooded her eyes, her weapon falling from her hands as she desperately tried to wipe it away. Within moments, Joseph, panting hard himself now, had her arms zip-tied behind her back as the woman sobbed uncontrollably.

'Okay, calm down, you'll bloody live,' Joseph said.

He turned on his torch and shone it in her face. Her bloodshot eyes were ringed by bright red where the PAVA spray had done its job. But rather than looking up at him, she was frantically looking around them at the shadow-filled wood.

'Let me go!' Anita said, weeping.

'Like that's going to happen anytime soon,' the DI replied, as he pulled her up into a standing position.

'You don't understand. We're both in danger—'

A hiss whistled through the wood and a crossbow bolt buried itself in Anita's leg. Her scream echoed throughout the wood as spittle flew from her mouth.

Heart racing at the shocking turn of events, Joseph was already hauling Anita with him back behind the tree.

He stared down at the arrow sticking out of Anita's thigh. As her eyes fluttered shut, Joseph had a flashback of trying to staunch the blood flow after a similar bolt hit Ryan outside the police station.

Joseph pressed his fingers to her neck, feeling a pulse thumping away there. Not dead, but the pain and shock had made her pass out. He quickly slipped his jacket off, using it as an improvised tourniquet.

What the hell am I going to do now?

The DI's gaze fell upon Ryan's still-loaded crossbow, just out of reach beyond the cover of the tree trunk and in the direct line of fire.

Whoever was out there, it was highly unlikely to be Ryan, as Joseph still had the student's weapon. Then he noticed the action camera clipped onto Anita's jacket, just like Ryan had been wearing.

This had to be related to what was happening and the genius behind this sick game. Whoever it was had somehow manipulated people, managing to set friends and even lovers against each other. They'd even got their victims to film what they were doing so they could get their kicks out of rewatching what their players had done.

Whoever it was, was out there right now and had just taken a shot at Anita. Was this all about making sure there were no witnesses left to pull the pieces of the puzzle together? Was he a target too, and if so, why? The one thing the DI knew for sure was the PAVA spray wasn't going to be much good for defending Anita and himself against an assailant who had a weapon that could be used at range.

His eyes locked onto Ryan's crossbow, so tantalisingly close, but still out of reach.

It was near total darkness, so he hoped whoever was out there would have a hard time seeing what he was up to.

Gathering his courage, bitterness filling the back of his throat, Joseph reached out slowly towards the dropped weapon. But the moment his hand broke cover, he heard a hiss. He had just enough time to snatch his hand back as a crossbow bolt buried itself into the ground where his wrist had been.

'Bloody gobshite!' he bellowed into the woods.

But whoever was out there was also one hell of a shot. They could obviously clearly see him, even though it was nearly pitch black. Night vision, it had to be. Whoever they were, they were very well prepared, and they meant business.

Joseph spotted a flicker of a torch through the trees, a fluorescent jacket just visible as someone ran up the track.

'John, get down!' Joseph called out.

But he was already too late. Another hiss of a bolt being fired sped away, and the PC dropped out of sight like a fallen stone.

Fury blazed through the DI, and knowing the shooter had to reload, he leapt out from behind the tree, grabbing Ryan's crossbow as he emerged. He ran, weaving from side to side as he headed towards where he guessed the bolts had been shot from. With nothing left to lose as the shooter could obviously see him,

Joseph turned on the torch again, clamping it to the stock of the crossbow with his hand as he ran.

Trunks rose like ghostly fingers from the ground, but there was still no sign of whoever was out there.

Another bolt hissed past him, skidding away over the leaf litter covering the ground behind him.

'You'll have to do better than that, you festering bag of pus,' Joseph shouted.

Twenty seconds later, another bolt sparked as it hit a pebble at his feet, forcing the DI to duck sideways. But this time, he'd heard the sound of the crossbow arms releasing with its distinctive *thunk*, coming from almost dead ahead of him. Joseph focused, sweeping the torch over the spot where the sound had come from, but he still couldn't see anything other than the trees. Who was the shooter, a bloody ghost?

Then he caught the barest of movement, not at ground level, but up one of the trees. There was a strange bulge on the trunk and it shifted slightly. Joseph swept his torch up. A camo net hung over some sort of framework bolted into the tree's trunk about three metres up. A metal ladder protruded from the bottom.

Dylan had shown him one of these when they'd first come for a walk up here. The tree blinds were used by the research students as hides to study the deer, birds, and other animals in the woods.

The camo net fluttered and another arrow burst from it. This one hissed close enough for one of the flight feathers to sting the top of his ear.

Even as his heart roared, Joseph ducked to his knee and raised his crossbow, aiming it straight at the spot where the bolt had been fired from.

'Stop! I know you have to be reloading right now. So help

me God, I will put an arrow right between your eyes if you keep this up.'

There was no reply, but based on the way the camo net kept moving, the person inside wasn't listening.

Despite his warning, Joseph aimed the arrow at where he guessed the person's leg would be hidden.

'Don't say I didn't warn you.' The DI pulled the trigger.

The problem was police firearm training was not something Joseph had ever done. Even if he had, as far as he knew, it certainly didn't cover crossbows, especially when you were trying to hold on to a torch at the same time, to illuminate your target. As a result, when he fired, the moment the bolt left the crossbow, the weapon kicked into his shoulder. Joseph already knew he'd missed. Sure enough, the bolt flew past the hide and away into the woods.

'Bloody hell!' Joseph cursed. He ducked behind a fallen trunk, realising at the same moment that was his one and only shot.

Then he heard exactly what he'd been dreading—the sound of a person dropping down from the hide and landing on the ground. He briefly peered over the top of the log to see a man stalking towards him wearing combat fatigues, his face smeared with camo paint, and image-intensifying goggles strapped to a helmet covering his eyes. The guy aimed straight at Joseph. He had a split second to duck before the projectile whistled over his head.

'Give it up,' Joseph shouted. 'Reinforcements will be here any moment.'

'Just like the officer who's lying dead on the track right now?' a familiar voice said.

The DI immediately knew exactly where he'd heard it before. 'Geoff Goldsmith?' he said, staring at the figure advancing on him.

'Well, as you're going to be dead in a moment, it hardly matters, but yes.'

'You're the one running the Hidden Hand club?' Joseph asked, slightly incredulously, even as his finger sought out the button on the PAVA canister. He'd already realised his only real chance was to lure the man within range of it.

The man stopped ten metres away. The crossbow had already been reloaded and was once again ready to fire. The problem for Joseph was that Goldsmith was still well out of range of the pepper spray.

'Yes, and they all danced as I pulled their strings in my little game,' Goldsmith replied, a note of actual pride in his voice.

Joseph realised there might be an in for him with Goldsmith here. Keep the guy talking, letting him crow about what he'd done. That might buy him some precious minutes for Chris, Megan, and the others to get here.

'I still don't understand how you convinced any of them to commit murder in the first place?' he asked.

Goldsmith laughed. 'You're as gullible as my recruits are.'

'What do you mean?'

'I mean, they were meant to think they were killing each other, so I could fuel their paranoia. The fun was watching each of them break as they became convinced that what had meant to be an innocent game, like the Assassins' Syndicate, was anything but. What's more entertaining than watching them play my far more interesting game and realise too late, exactly what they'd been caught up in?'

'So you suckered them in at first with the prize money, because you knew about their financial problems.'

Geoff nodded. 'You learn a lot when you hang out in the student union bar after an Assassins' Syndicate game. People don't tend to keep their voices down when they're going on about how hard up they are. Ryan, Gabby, Anita, and Eddie were some of the loudest. Anyway, it's astonishing what you can get people to do if you find the right buttons to push. But even then, they needed some proper motivation to take the game seriously. That's why I murdered Gabby, to prove that one of their number was a psychopath.'

'But you had an alibi for the time of her death. You live streamed that interview with those board game designers on YouTube.'

Goldsmith grinned at the detective. 'Oh yes, "live streamed" is certainly what it says on the YouTube page.'

Joseph gave him a confused look. 'It wasn't?'

'No, it's actually very easy to fake when you already have a recording ready to go. I even faked the questions from viewers to make it look really authentic. Then all I had to do when I started the stream was to run my prepared recording to make it look like a live broadcast. Just so you know, although you never got round to checking, I also had similar fake alibis set up for the time of Eddie's death, as well as for tonight's grand finale. According to the video going out right now, I'm talking to several gamers about their top five board games.'

'Bloody hell. But I still don't understand. Why didn't Ryan and Anita just tell us what was going on?'

'Because once I'd recruited them, I sent them all texts from a burner phone at the start of the game, promising to target their families if they tried to withdraw or tell anyone. When none of them took that risk, from that moment on, I knew I had them all under my control. Then all I had to do was sit back and watch the fun unfold.'

'In other words, to get them to murder each other?'

Geoff sighed. 'That was the plan, but sadly I quickly discovered, even after I murdered Gabby, they couldn't bring themselves to do it.'

'Hang on, are you saying that none of them tried to actually murder each other?'

'No, they just thought one of the others had, which I believed would be enough to tip them over the edge into the depravity. You see, that's what lurks just beneath the surface of all human beings, and you can get them to act on it under the right circumstances. There's a famous case of that called the Stanford Prison Experiment. We covered it in a sociology lecture. It's about how the people involved were consumed by the parts they were meant to play. It was certainly an enlightening lecture into human behaviour and inspired me to create my own little experiment in the form of this game.'

'So you're saying you're the one who murdered Eddie as well?'

'Yes, by slipping a dose of Rohypnol into his drink when he met Anita in the King's Arms. The idiot didn't even realise I was standing right next to him at the bar when I did it. But you did manage to stop some of my fun with your heroics when you managed to save Ryan. Of course, I'd had to gather all my courage together to be up there at all. I hate heights. But I needed you all to believe you were dealing with another freerunner so I could frame Eddie. Anyway, tonight was meant to be the culmination of my little game, setting the stage for Ryan or Anita, believing the other was responsible for all the other murders, to try to kill the other. Then, of course, I planned to serve up a coup de grâce by murdering the remaining player.'

'But something went wrong, didn't it, based on the fact I'm here at all?'

'I hadn't anticipated that Ryan and Anita were having an affair. He *talked* to her, rather than just shooting her like I'd planned.'

'So they agreed not to murder each other?'

'Exactly, and when I discovered what had happened, I

realised I needed to pull the final lever on my insurance policy and blackmail them into luring you here and killing you as part of my grand finale. Then with that hanging over them, I planned to use that to keep pushing them tonight until one of them finally cracked and murdered the other.'

Joseph glowered at the student. 'Only a depraved mind would come up with something as twisted as that.'

Goldsmith shrugged. 'You might say that, but I like to think of it as a very elegant piece of game design.'

'Okay, we're going to have to disagree about that. But what I still don't understand is how you could guarantee that only I would turn...' Joseph realised exactly what had happened. 'The bomb threat—that was you, wasn't it?'

Goldsmith grinned. 'I leave nothing to chance. You see, I actually saw you out on your bike one day, which formed a little plan in my mind. Reading about how you handled yourself during previous cases, and how you seemed to always be there at pivotal moments like this one, I knew you couldn't resist playing the hero yet again and charging in alone. As you know, I love my games and I relished the challenge of taking you on as part of my grand finale. Cue one phone call from Anita, a damsel in distress. But of course I knew that with the roads blocked, you'd attempt to get to Wytham on your trusty bike. You see, I do like to be very thorough in researching my chosen targets.'

'But why would either of them agree to help you?' Joseph asked, painfully aware that he was running out of time.

'Just to underline how serious I was, I sent them photos of their families, saying I would follow through with my original threat to murder them unless they drew you here and killed you. As I said, it's amazing what you can get even the most decent people to do with the right motivation...' He cocked his head.

Then Joseph heard it as well, the distant sound of a helicopter getting louder.

Goldsmith shook his head. 'Too little, too late. And I'm afraid as nice as it's been chatting to you, it's time to tidy up my loose ends. Ryan and Anita, along with your good self, are going to die tonight before anyone else shows up to spoil my fun.'

'So that was always your intention all along? To murder whoever was left?'

'Of course. I'm the game master and they are just my players in a dungeon of my making. If I do say so myself, it really is the best game I've ever played, and I've played a lot. Maybe I'll even do this again someday. Anyway, enough talk. It's time to die, Detective Stone. Thank you for playing.'

The detective found himself looking straight at the arrowhead of the bolt, loaded and ready to end his life.

'Lower your weapon,' John's voice called out.

In disbelief, the DI looked past Geoff to see the PC, standing just behind the student, his Taser already raised and ready to fire.

The DI smiled up at Goldsmith standing over him. 'What is it you say in that other precious game of yours? Oh yes, checkmate!'

'You think?' Goldsmith replied with a smirk. He whirled around, bringing the crossbow to bear on John.

John didn't hesitate to fire. Two electrodes leapt up from the Taser and buried themselves into the man's chest. Goldsmith jerked violently as the charge surged through him, and he dropped to the ground. Even before Joseph had a chance to move to assist his colleague, John had already kicked the crossbow away and was cuffing Geoff's hands behind his back.

The helicopter roared overhead, hovering, its searchlight lancing down through the canopy almost directly on top of them. Almost at the same moment, torches appeared on the ridge above them as figures ran along it.

'Looks like the cavalry has arrived,' John said as he finished securing his prisoner.

'I think they'd already arrived, and now I owe you a pint.'

'You better make that several,' John replied, grinning at him.

'Done. Now contact the others to let them know what's happened. Ryan and Anita have both been injured and need urgent medical attention.'

'You sound like you've had a busy night of it.'

'Like you wouldn't believe,' Joseph said, standing as Goldsmith moaned.

CHAPTER THIRTY

EVEN THOUGH JOSEPH was running on empty and was fit to drop, a celebratory breakfast was underway the following morning at Wallace's, something of a rock star of greasy spoons in Oxford. Of course, after the events of the previous night, Joseph had insisted on dragging John out with the rest of the team. The only person missing was Chris, who was currently interrogating Goldsmith, trying to extract as much information as possible before formally charging him with the murders of Gabby and Eddie.

'To the man of the hour,' the DI said, raising a cup of tea to John. 'If it hadn't been for you, last night would have turned out very differently, and I'd now be very dead.'

'Just a shame you didn't wait for me and went steaming in there alone,' John said.

Megan grinned. 'Exactly, John. But try telling him that.'

Joseph shrugged. 'As they say, you can't teach an old dog new tricks—it's just the way I am.'

'Tell us about it,' Ian said, shaking his head, as he tucked into his bacon sandwich oozing Oxford brown sauce, threatening to spill down his shirt. 'Anyway, here's to John for saving our DI from his death wish.' He raised his orange juice as the others did the same with their drinks.

'To John,' everyone echoed.

The PC looked decidedly embarrassed as he shook his head. 'Thanks, but I was just in the right place at the right time, and luckily his aim was off. If anyone should be praised, it's Joseph. He single-handedly managed to deal with Anita and Ryan, without getting himself shot.'

'But you're the man who brought Goldsmith down,' Joseph replied. 'I don't think I've ever been so keen on a fellow officer turning up. But talking of Ryan and Anita, what's the latest? Are they still in hospital?'

'Ryan's already discharged and is on his way back to be interviewed back at St Aldates, as we speak,' Sue said. 'As far as Anita goes, she would have died if you hadn't put that tourniquet round her leg. But the paramedic helicopter managed to get to her in time and airlift her out to the JR, so it looks like she's not going to lose her leg either.'

'Thank God for small mercies. She's too young for that to happen to her.'

'That's very magnanimous of you, considering that she and Ryan were trying to murder you,' Megan said.

'Yes, but she'd been blackmailed and manipulated into it by Goldsmith. He boasted to me that he'd been inspired by a lecture covering something called the Stanford Prison Experiment.'

'And what's that when it's at home?' Ian asked, as a big dollop of sauce finally escaped his bacon sandwich and landed on his tie.

'Actually, I know something about that,' Megan replied. 'It was a week-long psychology experiment at Stanford University, where students pretended to be guards and prisoners. But even though they were meant to be roleplaying, the power went to the student-guards' heads. It all quickly got out of hand when the students playing the prisoners were psychologically tortured. The experiment had to be terminated early. It famously demonstrated how quickly even decent people can start to do the wrong thing under the right circumstances.'

Joseph nodded. 'So, inspired by that, Goldsmith wanted to create what he's been calling his ultimate game. He created a real-life version of the Hidden Hand club to manipulate the players to do the unthinkable, with him as their puppet master.'

'Yes, but even so, to be prepared to commit murder says a lot about Ryan and Anita's characters,' Sue said.

'I wouldn't be too quick to judge,' Megan replied. 'Who knows what any of us would be capable of if someone found the right buttons to press, like Goldsmith did?'

'Exactly. Although I suspect the CPS won't quite see it this way,' Joseph said, 'in many ways, Anita and Ryan were victims as much as Gabby and Eddie were, albeit not ones who lost their lives in what was meant to be a game.'

'I actually agree,' Chris said, as he appeared at their table.

'So all done back at the nick?' Ian asked, trying to wipe off a fresh brown sauce stain, but only succeeding in making it even bigger.

Chris nodded as he sat down at the table. 'Goldsmith hasn't so much sung like a canary, but more like a whole aviary of the bloody things. I almost couldn't get him to stop boasting about how he exploited the others to do whatever he wanted. I tell you, it was as much as I could do not to wipe the smug grin off his face. Apart from the murders, he even admitted to framing Ryan, Anita, and Eddie by leaving the falsified evidence for us, including the paintbrush bolts, the Rohypnol in Anita's bathroom, and the crossbow and action cam footage in Eddie's bedroom. Of course, that wasn't just to frame the players, but to convince them they had a killer in their ranks and fuel their paranoia.'

'So we were right. Goldsmith was the one in that video from on the roof?' Megan asked.

'In one. As Joseph guessed, Goldsmith used AI to dub Eddie's voice over the top of footage. That was actually Goldsmith firing at Ryan from the rooftop. Apparently, he learnt how to do that from a YouTube video. But this man was as sly as any hardened criminal I've ever dealt with. When the remaining players still hadn't taken the bait, he set about framing Anita by slipping Rohypnol into Eddie's drink at the pub. So, when Ryan learned that Eddie had been killed, believing it was Anita, he did a bunk from the hospital to talk to her, because he couldn't believe she'd done it. He was desperate to get to her before we did.'

'So none of this was about money, then?' John asked.

'Maybe to start with it was, and I'll get to that in a moment. But the key thing Goldsmith went out of his way to do once they'd been suckered into playing his game, was to fuel their paranoia in any way he could. The bastard even boasted to me about how he'd sent Ryan and Anita anonymous texts only a couple of days ago, threatening them. But what he hadn't counted on was those two having an affair, and actually deciding to talk, rather than just murder each other in Wytham Woods like he wanted them to. But even then he had an insurance policy in place.'

'By hiding out there himself to make sure that the game was concluded to his satisfaction?' Joseph asked.

'Exactly. When he saw Ryan and Anita were heading off script, he sent the final texts from the burner phone we found on him, saying that unless they worked together to draw you into the woods to kill you, then their families would be murdered.'

'That's pretty much what he told me,' the DI replied.

'Bloody hell, that borders on evil,' Ian said.

Megan nodded, and looked at Chris. 'So, did Goldsmith say anything about his motive for doing all of this?'

'Oh, I've heard some petty reasons in my time, but nothing gets even close to this. Apparently, it started when Ryan shot him with a Nerf gun in the student union during an Assassins' Syndicate game. Goldsmith, someone who saw himself as the "king of games," took it especially badly because Gabby, Eddie, and Anita took the piss out of him. After that, the guy seems to have stewed in his own juices, becoming increasingly convinced they were always laughing behind his back. The final straw was when Ryan accidentally hurt Anita during an Assassins' Syndicate game, a club Goldsmith ran and felt very protective towards. That's when he began to plan his revenge and created his own real-life game based on the myth of the Hidden Hand club. Then, knowing how hard up they were, he lured them in with the offer of a cash prize that didn't actually exist.'

'Because he was always going to be the last person standing?' Megan asked.

'Precisely,' Chris replied. 'Even now, he continues to see those four, and even our illustrious DI, at the end, as pawns to be played as he saw fit.'

'Well, I could certainly have done without him luring me into the woods,' Joseph said.

'Unfortunately, Goldsmith got a taste for doing that from all the false trails he left us. But he was also very aware of how our investigation was closing in. In the end, he convinced himself that you, Joseph, were his nemesis, and might still bring him down. So in his sick mind, what better finale to his rigged game than to take out someone he was growing increasingly paranoid about?'

'I think I'll take that as a compliment, but really he could have fixated on any one of us.'

'Well, I'm certainly glad it wasn't me,' Megan said.

'Yes, it sounds like you picked up a psycho fan there,' Ian said.

The DI pulled a face. 'That, I can really do without, any day of the week.'

Chris nodded. 'The one thing for certain is that Goldsmith has very much condemned himself to a very long stretch indeed. He even waved away the defence strategy his solicitor was trying to angle for, a plea of diminished responsibility due to his mental health.'

'He deserves everything that's coming to him,' Sue said. 'So what are the CPS saying about Ryan and Anita?'

'Even if their defence goes with the argument they were acting under extreme duress, they are still likely to serve jail time, albeit with a heavily reduced sentence.'

'That sounds about right to me,' the DI said.

'Says the man who was nearly killed by both of them,' Sue added.

'Yes, but you weren't there. Neither of them wanted to do it, but they'd been backed into a corner. I know we would all like to think we would have acted differently in their position, but I'm personally not so sure. Imagine if someone you loved was threatened like that. How far might you be prepared to go?'

Everyone nodded, even Sue, as they turned that particular gem over in their minds.

'With that cheery thought, can I tempt anyone with a fresh brew?' Chris asked.

Everyone else nodded, but Joseph was checking his phone again.

'That must be the umpteenth time I've seen you do that,' Megan said. 'Expecting an Amazon delivery of another fancy part for your bike?'

'Something like that,' Joseph replied, deliberately not meeting her eye.

The truth was, despite the fact he should be celebrating the conclusion of the case, he still hadn't heard from Kate. As every hour ticked past, his worry had started to ratchet up again. Surely if she'd been delayed heading back from Cheltenham for whatever reason, she would have let him know, if only to stop him fretting. Especially after last time.

But it was only a few moments later, as Chris was getting the orders in, that the DI's phone finally pinged. He opened it to see a photo of Kate's driving licence. Then his blood iced as he read the attached message.

'We have her. If you want to see her alive ever again, you'll cease all your investigations into the Night Watchmen and Derrick Walker immediately. We're always watching.'

A feeling of cold dread writhed inside him as his mind locked up. The moment he had been dreading with his whole being had finally arrived.

'Joseph, are you okay?' Megan said, picking up on his pale expression.

He stared at her, and then, without saying a word, stood.

'Going somewhere?' Chris asked with a smile, as he returned with two mugs of tea for Sue and Ian.

All Joseph could do was manage a vague nod as he grabbed his jacket and headed to the door, leaving them looking after him. But Joseph barely registered any of that because his feeling of dread was already morphing into one of hot fury. He was going to have it out with Derrick, right then and there.

Joseph didn't so much as walk, as storm into Derrick's glass office.

'What happened to knocking first?' the superintendent asked, looking up from his screen.

But the DI ignored him as he closed the blinds on the windows. He didn't want any witnesses for what was about to happen.

'What do you think you're doing?' Derrick asked, as Joseph closed the door behind him.

'What I should have done months ago when I first had my suspicions about you, you little fecking cockroach.'

Derrick tucked his chin in. 'How dare you talk to your commanding officer like that?'

'Oh, I'm going to do a lot more than *talk* if you don't tell me the bloody truth.' Joseph headed to the man's desk and shoved his phone into the DSU's face to show him the photo he'd just been sent.

Derrick shot him a confused look. 'Why have you got a photo of Kate's driving licence?'

'As though you don't fecking know already. Read the message, you little arsewipe, and then we can stop with all this pretending. Then I'm going to knock seven shades of shite out of you.'

Derrick's expression became flintlike. 'Lay one hand on me and it will be the end of your fucking career, Stone.'

'You've held that threat over me for far too many years now, but not anymore. Throw me out, but I'm still going to tear a pound of flesh from you first.'

The superintendent blinked. 'What the hell has got into you?'

Joseph did a slow handclap. 'I have to give it to you, such a great performance, pretending you don't know why I'm here. Now read that fecking message before I ram my phone up your arse!' The DI planted his fists on the DSU's desk and loomed over him, making the other man cower back.

The DI jerked his finger towards the phone as his eyebrows knitted together.

Derrick glanced back at the phone, and then his eyes widened and his face grew pale. 'Oh my God, not this. What has Kate done...' His eyes swivelled up to Joseph glaring down at him. 'What have you done?'

'What do you mean, what have I done?'

'This bit about you still investigating the Night Watchmen.'

'Of course I bloody have been. That's how I know you've been working for them. Tipping the crime syndicate off about Daryl Manning's prisoner transfer during the Burning Man case to start with, and God knows what else.'

Derrick didn't so much slouch as crumple into himself, staring up at Joseph, his expression drawn.

'So what happened when Kate told you she thought you were involved with the Night Watchmen?' Joseph continued. 'You told them? And I bet you even knew all about the threatening email they sent her last time, warning her off?'

The DSU closed his eyes for a moment as he pinched the bridge of his nose. When he opened them again, Joseph was taken aback to see tears in them.

'You've got this so back to front, Joseph,' Derrick said in the barest whisper.

'What do you mean?'

'I mean to start with, it was me who sent Kate that warning email.'

Joseph gaped at the man as his cold fury dropped to arctic levels. 'You did what, you little gobshite?' he replied, every syllable dripping with threat.

Derrick quickly held up his hands, clearly realising just how dangerous Joseph's mood was becoming. 'I was trying to protect her from them.'

Joseph breathed through his nose, trying to maintain control before he ripped the hypocrite's head clean off his neck. 'What do you fecking mean?'

'I mean, that's what this has all been about. When I was approached by Kennan to do some favours for her when she asked me for them, I didn't think anything of it at first. Just small things like countersigning the application for an officer she wanted to fast track. I didn't realise it was a test. But then she offered me a bribe to do something more.'

'Which was?'

'It doesn't matter, because I refused point-blank, threatening to report her to the Counter Corruption Unit. That's when she made it very clear the group of people she was working with wouldn't hesitate to murder Kate if I tried anything.'

It was like a switch had been thrown within Joseph. Suddenly, all the rage and fury that had been threatening to erupt dissolved away as he stared down at Derrick.

'So you started to do whatever they asked you for?'

The DSU shook his head. 'Only once, and that was about Manning's transfer.'

The anger sparked again within Joseph. 'You little fecker, because of that betrayal, two officers were nearly killed, not to mention the prisoner lost his life.'

Derrick put his head in his hands and he looked down at the table. 'I know, but you must believe me, I had no idea they were going to do that. If I had, I would never have told them anything.'

'But the problem is you did, and you crossed the line.'

'Yes, but it was a mistake I've never made again. You must believe me,' Derrick said, his tone pleading.

Joseph peered at the man, trying to work him out. 'Is that why I saw you throw that envelope of cash back at Kennan in the Old Ink Press car park, when she tried to give it to you?'

Derrick glanced up, his brow smoothing out. 'If you witnessed that, then you know I'm telling you the truth.'

The ember of anger threatening to take hold again in Joseph's gut flickered out. 'Maybe. But what about that threatening email to Kate?'

'Do you think the Night Watchmen would have even hesitated for a moment to kill Kate if they'd learned she was investigating them?'

The summary execution of one of their own, Darryl Manning, flashed through Joseph's mind. 'Aye, I don't suppose they would.' He stared at the DSU as his assumptions about the big man melted away. 'So you're trying to tell me this was all about protecting Kate and never about taking backhanders?'

'I promise you with every fibre of my being that's the utter truth. When Kennan first took an interest in my career and fast tracked me, I had no idea the price she was going to ask for doing me that favour, especially when we both knew it should have been you who got that promotion.'

The thought Megan had just shared back in the café flashed into his mind. *Who knows what any of us would be capable of if someone found the right buttons to press?*

He slowly nodded. 'So by threatening Kate, they forced you to work with them?'

'Exactly. It sounds like you're beginning to understand. That's why I couldn't just go to the CCU myself and report Kennan. Do that, and...' He swallowed hard.

Joseph nodded. 'And they would have killed Kate.'

'Exactly. They didn't leave me any choice. And now they have my wife. What the hell are we going to do, Joseph?'

'What do you mean, *we?*'

'You still care for Kate, don't you?'

Joseph felt like laughing in the man's face. He had no idea

just how far he'd go to protect the woman he was still very much in love with.

'Tell me why I shouldn't just go ahead and report you?' the DI asked, instead.

'We both know the reason. Could you really live with Kate's blood on your hands?'

Joseph shook his head. 'You already know the answer. So, *we* it is. But tell me this, if they wanted me to back off, why not just have me killed already?'

Derrick gave him a drawn look. 'Because they probably think that under their thumb, you're more useful to them alive than dead.'

'So let me get this straight. Not only do they expect me to back off my own investigation into the Night Watchmen, but they are also going to want me to be in their pocket to secure Kate's freedom?'

'I think that's about the sum of it. The question is, are you prepared to do it? Because I'm begging you, for Kate's sake, at least, you have to. If it was just about throwing me under the bus, I'd say go ahead, but not when her life is on the line. Once we have her safely back, we can think again about what our next step is.'

There was that idea of them working together again, but for now, Joseph knew he had to accept that this was the only way to move forward if they were going to secure her release.

'Looks like I've no other choice. But we can't let things go on like this afterwards. One way or another, we need to come up with a plan to bring Amanda Kennan and the Night Watchmen down. What do you say, Derrick? Or is the man who was once a committed police officer, long dead and buried under a pile of corruption?'

'I think he's still alive inside me somewhere,' the DSU replied, a small smile curling the corners of his mouth.

'So what happens now?'

'I'll let Kennan know I've spoken to you and you've seen sense. Then, as long as Kate promises to stop investigating them, they've got no reason to hold her.'

'We're talking about Kate here—the word stubborn is her middle name.'

Derrick actually chuckled. 'Don't I know it? Anyway, maybe if you talk to her, you can persuade her to stop. The Night Watchmen rarely give anyone a second chance.'

'And you'll work on Kate as well?'

'Of course, but she listens to you in a way she never has with me.' Derrick shrugged. 'I might not like how close you two still are, but that's just the way it is and has always been.'

Joseph met the other man's eye. 'She will always mean everything to me, just like our daughter does.'

'Of course,' Derrick replied, with no hint of annoyance or even jealousy in his voice.

Joseph realised for the first time just how accepting the superintendent had been over the years about his continuing close relationship with his wife.

'You really think they will release her just like that?' Joseph asked, not wanting to pursue that line of conversation with the DSU any longer than he had to.

'Oh, there will be a price to pay, I just don't know what yet. Hell, if it means I can secure Kate's freedom, I'm prepared to dance naked on top of Castle Mound.'

'Please don't. That would just frighten the tourists away.'

Derrick burst out laughing, and just like that, the tension in the room between the two men evaporated. 'You might have a point there.' He glanced at his screen and then back at Joseph. 'I just also wanted to say well done on helping to catch Goldsmith last night, not to mention rounding up Ryan and Anita.'

'What, no lectures on charging in without waiting for backup?'

'Would it make any difference?'

'Nah.'

The DSU snorted. 'I thought as much.' Then his expression grew serious again. 'So, it looks like we're going to be unlikely allies in this.'

'It does, doesn't it?' Joseph replied. 'But once we've secured Kate's freedom, whatever it takes, we bring all those Night Watchmen feckers down. What do you say?'

To his credit, Derrick didn't even hesitate. 'Count me in. You don't know the relief I feel finally being able to talk to someone on the right side of the law about this.'

But Joseph could easily imagine the weight of guilt that had been weighing the man down over the last year. Not even able to discuss it with his own wife, whom he'd been trying to protect, must have hollowed the man out from the inside. How much of the brittle edge that had crept into Derrick had been due to that guilt?

'Then we'll work it out together, and the bastards won't know what's hit them,' the DI said.

'I certainly hope so.'

Joseph nodded and turned to go.

'Thank you for this, seriously,' Derrick said. 'I realise now I should have spoken to you about this years ago.'

'Aye, maybe you should have.' With a nod to the superintendent, the DI headed out of the door, still not quite believing how in a heartbeat everything had changed between him and the big man. They might be unlikely allies, and he wasn't sure he would ever call the man a friend again, but if that was what it took to bring Kate home, so be it.

CHAPTER THIRTY-ONE

WHEN CHRIS HAD EVENTUALLY RUN into Joseph in St Aldates, he'd immediately sent him home to catch up on some much-needed sleep, not that there was a lot of that going on currently for Joseph. Until the DI received a phone call from Derrick to say Kate was safe, he wasn't going to be able to relax.

As Joseph sat on board *Tús Nua* gazing out of the window, he couldn't help but feel sceptical that the Night Watchmen would be ready to release a woman who gave them such serious leverage over both the DSU and himself.

Also, the phrase that kept circling his mind was, *we're always watching*, which he thought was rather apt for a crime syndicate called the Night Watchmen. It also suggested that there might be another member of the team at St Aldates who'd been corrupted and was keeping not only a close eye on Derrick, but now himself as well. But if true, who?

Derrick had told Joseph his own promotion had been fast tracked by Chief Superintendent Kennan. So could it be that another senior officer enjoyed a similar leg up and was now working for the Night Watchmen? Unfortunately, that led him to one inevitable conclusion. He hated to even consider it because he viewed the man very much as a friend these days. But as much as he was loathed to believe it, could it be Chris Faulkner? The more he thought about it, where did the money come from? Hadn't the man bought himself an Aston Martin DB5, that even wrecked must have cost a small fortune?

The thought that someone like Chris might be a bent cop made Joseph feel physically sick to his stomach. But if someone like him could be corrupted, how many other officers who'd been fast-tracked into senior positions were open to doing the crime syndicate's bidding whenever required?

A knock came at the door, pulling him out of the pit of his own thoughts. He could hear Tux, who'd been busy watching the squirrel hanging from the bird feeder designed to defeat it, miaow in welcome.

Joseph stood and headed to the door. When he opened it, he saw Amy standing there.

'God, you look pale,' she said, cutting straight to the point like she always did.

'I need to sleep, but can't seem to drift off.'

'From what I hear, after the busy night you had, you should be exhausted by all rights. Anyway, I just thought I'd pop over during my lunch break to see how you were doing.'

Just for a moment, he considered telling her everything. But part of him couldn't go there. He didn't want to drag anyone else into his mess.

'Okay, apart from that lack of shut-eye,' he said instead.

'Good. But what's all this about you nearly getting yourself shot with a crossbow?'

'Three times actually, but those are the breaks—'

'Of once again charging into a situation alone,' Amy said, finishing his sentence for him.

'I know, I know, but please don't lecture me. Everyone else already has.'

'Then I won't, but if I lost you...' Amy stepped into the cabin, pushing the door closed behind her with her foot. She wrapped herself around him, drawing him into a passionate, fill-your-boots kiss.

'What are you trying to do, seduce me?' he asked.

'Absolutely, because apart from anything else, it will help you switch your brain off and get that sleep afterwards, like a typical man,' Amy said.

'Afterwards?'

In answer, Amy, grinning, kicked off her boots and shimmied out of her trousers. 'But we have to be quick because I need to get back to work.'

'Then a quickie it is,' Joseph said, smiling as he pulled the blind closed on the window looking out onto the towpath and the view of the squirrel leaping onto the feeder and scaring the birds away again.

Amy's version of a sleeping pill had certainly done the trick, because when another knock came from the cabin door, the DI's eyes snapped open to see that night had settled. He fumbled with the bedside light switch and, as his eyes came into focus, he saw that it was already seven p.m. The next thing he did was check his phone, but there was no sign of a message from Derrick about Kate. His heart fell. But maybe this was the DSU himself, who'd come in person to give him an update.

'Just give me a moment,' Joseph called out, pulling on some jogging bottoms, along with a T-shirt.

Tux did his usual at trying to trip him by winding around his legs as he made his way past the cat's food bowl. But despite the cat's best efforts to waylay him, the DI made it to the cabin door and opened it.

His heart sank seeing it was Dylan carrying a picnic hamper, along with White Fang and Max standing there, rather than Derrick. The dogs immediately set to work on the serious business of greeting Tux, who was now rubbing himself along their flanks.

'I know you haven't eaten since at least breakfast, so I come bearing sustenance.'

'And you would know that because?'

'Amy swung by after she left you snoring your head off and asked me to keep an eye on you.'

'Did she now?' Joseph said, standing aside and gesturing into the cabin for Dylan to enter.

The insanely good smell of ginger, garlic, and possibly chicken caught his nostrils as the professor headed past him towards the galley.

'So, what have you got in the picnic hamper?' he asked.

Steam swirled around Dylan's head as he took a pot out of the basket, giving the grey-bearded man a resemblance to Merlin looking into a cauldron containing a magic potion—at least in Joseph's mind.

'Vietnamese Phở. I think I've finally perfected the recipe,' the professor said.

'Oh, like from that rooftop restaurant in the Westgate Shopping Centre?'

'That's the one, although if it's not too immodest a thing to say, I think mine may be even better.'

'Well, if anyone could pull it off, it's you.'

Dylan smiled at his friend as he set to work locating two of Joseph's more substantial bowls, along with his chopsticks from the bottom of the cutlery drawer. Soon, both men were adding in the fresh bean sprouts, coriander, and chopped red chillies, to the already delicious-smelling broth with its shredded chicken and chopped pak choi.

Joseph used the Japanese-style wooden ladle Dylan had brought with him to try his first mouthful. A beautiful rich spicy broth immediately hit his taste buds.

The DI looked at his friend with a certain level of awe. 'Once again, that's off the roof, spectacularly good, and yes, I think you really could give that restaurant a run for its money. I honestly don't know why you don't open one, with these culinary skills of yours.'

'Ah, that's a whole different level of pressure to run your own restaurant. Don't forget, I cook to relax, along with being able to feed my friends.'

'Well, this particular friend certainly appreciates your selfless dedication to your art.'

'So do I,' Dylan said, smiling. 'Anyway, I thought we should celebrate the successful conclusion of your latest case with some good food.'

'What, no special gin to match the Phở?'

Dylan raised an eyebrow at his friend, leaned down into the picnic hamper, and withdrew a black bottle with what looked like Japanese writing on it.

'May I present for your appreciation, a bottle of Ki No Bi Kyoto,' Dylan said. 'Lots of botanicals and notes of the gyokuro tea and green sanshō peppercorns they use in the distilling process. They even draw the water from a well.'

Joseph smiled at his friend. 'Only you could come up with a gin for Phở.'

'Some might say that, along with cooking, it's one of my callings.'

'And I would be at the front of them,' Joseph said, as Dylan poured both of them a generous measure.

'What, no tonic or aromatics?'

'No, this gin is one of those that can be enjoyed neat. Besides, the Phở has more than enough smell to cover the aromatics side.'

'You're not wrong,' Joseph said, raising his glass to his friend. 'Thank you for your help, as usual, with this latest case, Dylan. You really made all the difference at a crucial time, coming up with the name of the Hidden Hand club.'

'Always glad to be of assistance. Amy gave me a brief update before she headed off. Sounds like a bit of a close-run thing up in Wytham?'

'The cases I'm involved in always seem to end up like that. But at least we have the genius behind it all securely locked up. Anyway, let's try this intriguing gin before it has time to evaporate from our glasses.'

'I doubt there's going to be much danger of that,' the professor said, as he took a sip from his own glass and pulled an appreciative face. 'Oh, now that's rather splendid.'

Joseph followed his friend's lead and took his first taste. The gin was immediately warming and grew to a spicy finish. 'Oh, I like that and you're right, the perfect accompaniment to the Phở. You really are like some mad food and spirit scientist with your ability to put these flavours together.'

'Like I said, it's my calling.' Dylan took a second sip and then his eyes widened. 'I almost forgot.' He dug his hand into his jacket pocket slung over the back of his chair. He withdrew a small envelope and handed it to Joseph. 'This was stuck under the railing on *Tús Nua's* roof.'

Joseph looked at it and the distinct lack of writing on it. 'Probably some sort of charity flyer...' His words trailed away as he opened the envelope to see the edge of a photo.

'Doesn't look like a charity flyer to me,' Dylan said, peering across as Joseph pulled the photo out.

Nausea rushed through him when he saw it was a photo of

Ellie, her bag slung over her shoulder as she emerged from the main entrance of the Blavatnik School of Government. Heart hammering, he quickly turned the photo over to see no message written there. But there didn't need to be. The meaning was clear. This was exactly the same trick Goldsmith had used with Ryan and Anita to bend them to his will.

The professor's eyes flicked between the photo and the DI. 'Okay, what's that all about?' Dylan asked gently.

Joseph didn't say anything, glancing at the turned-over evidence board. That was all the hint Dylan needed.

'This is something to do with the Night Watchmen?'

Joseph nodded. 'I think it's some sort of warning, unless they've already taken her.'

'Oh, good God, they know you're looking into them?'

'Yes, and Kate, too. They snatched her and now they've gone after my—' A sharp knock came from the door.

Joseph sprang to his feet. He rushed to the cabin door to see Kate standing there, tears running down her face. Without saying a word, Joseph pulled her into his arms, his own eyes filling as they clung to each other.

After a few moments had passed, Joseph finally pulled away to look into her face. 'Have they taken Ellie?'

Kate quickly shook her head. 'No, but they told me they will if either of us so much as breathes a word about this...' Her words trailed away.

Joseph felt like he had been physically punched in the stomach and half sat, half collapsed onto a bench next to the door. 'No, not that,' he said, realising in that instant that the Night Watchmen knew exactly how to find anyone's weakness and use it to their advantage.

Kate knelt by him. 'We've got to stop looking into them.'

'I know...'

Dylan was staring at the two of them. 'First of all, I'm so

sorry, but have I got this right? The Night Watchmen are threatening Ellie's life if you don't back off?'

'That's about the measure of it,' Joseph replied. 'That's how they've made Derrick do their bidding all these years, although in his case, it was all about protecting you, Kate.'

'What?' Kate asked, staring at him.

'You need to talk to your husband. But make no mistake about how dangerous these people are. We either comply with their wishes or there will be serious consequences.'

'But you can't,' Dylan said.

Kate and Joseph both turned to stare at him.

'What choice do we have?' Joseph asked.

'This is an awful situation, particularly right now. However, I'm telling you, there will be a heavy price to be paid if you don't stand up to them.'

'Do we really care if it means keeping our daughter safe?' Kate said.

Dylan sighed. 'Look, I know you both well enough to know that neither of you can live with being under their control. It will eat you from the inside out. The only thing you can do is find a way to stop them. Permanently.'

'And endanger Ellie, I don't think so,' Joseph said.

'I didn't say it would be easy, and obviously you will need to play along for now. Act as though you've been suitably cowed by their threat. But whilst doing so, you both gather all the evidence you can and bring the whole stinking edifice of that crime organisation, and all the bent senior officers along with it, crashing down. For now, you bide your time and strike when the time is right. And I will be right here to help you, every step of the way.'

For a few seconds, Joseph and Kate both stared at him, mute. But it was Kate who crossed to the professor first and drew him into a tight hug. 'Thank God for your no-nonsense brand of common sense in a crisis, Dylan.'

Joseph reached out and shook the professor's hand. 'Aye, we were a bit lost there for a moment.' He turned to his wife. 'I'm up for this if you are, Kate?'

'God yes, but the first sign of any real danger, we send Ellie packing on a round-the-world tour, or something like that.'

'Sounds expensive, but agreed. Not a hair on our golden girl's head is going to be harmed in this,' Joseph replied. 'Oh, and there is someone else who will help us as well in this—Derrick.'

Kate stared at him. 'So you've already spoken to him about this?'

'Yes, although I went in ready to tear his head off his shoulders when I thought he'd been involved with your abduction. But then I quickly discovered it was nothing of the sort. He was trying to protect you from them all along.'

His ex-wife stared at him, wide-eyed. 'Really?'

'So it would seem. But like I said, you really need to speak to him yourself. You know I've not been his biggest fan for years, and I can't believe I'm going to say this, but you need to cut Derrick some slack here. I'm surprised he didn't tell you any of this himself, after my conversation with him earlier today.'

'That's only because I came straight here to talk to you first.'

'You did?'

Kate took his hand in hers as she turned to Dylan. 'I need to have a quiet word with Joseph alone.'

'Of course,' Dylan said, starting to rise from his chair.

But Kate was already shaking her head. 'No, you stay there and we'll pop outside before I head off home.' She blew Dylan a kiss, and then walked outside onto the deck with Joseph, making sure she had closed the door behind her.

'What's this about, Kate?' the DI asked as she gazed intently into his eyes.

'It's just I had a lot of time to think after they snatched me.'

'Did you see their faces?'

'No. They both had balaclavas on and they bundled me into the boot of their car. The next thing I knew, they threw me into a dark room and locked me in.'

'For feck's sake.'

'Exactly. And like I said, I had plenty of time to think. I thought of what I would regret most if I was going to end up dying in that place, and it was this.' She reached out and drew Joseph towards her, kissing him gently on the mouth, before pulling away again.

An impossibly huge tidal wave of love swelled up through Joseph's chest as he stared, dumbfounded, back at her.

'I know I have no right to say this as you're involved with Amy, but I still love you, Joseph, with every fibre of my being—I always have and I always will,' she whispered.

A storm of emotion flooded through Joseph, but as he opened his mouth to answer, Kate put her fingers on his lips and shook her head. 'Don't say anything, because what can you? It was maybe unfair of me to even show you how I still feel, but there it is. I just knew that I needed to do it, even if you never want to see me again.'

'Of course, I do. But Kate...'

She pressed her finger deeper into his lips. 'Shush. Anyway, I'm going to love you and leave you, whilst I go have a heart-to-heart with my husband.'

'What's that meant to mean?'

'I don't know yet, so we'll just have to see, won't we?' Kate leaned in again, but this time kissed Joseph on the cheek, before turning and jumping across to the towpath and quickly walking away. She didn't turn around once as she stepped out with a sense of determination in her stride.

Joseph lingered there for a moment, numb and not sure what he was going to do about any of this. As Kate disappeared into the darkness, he turned back to the cabin where his good friend was waiting for him, because goodness knew he needed his advice now more than ever. And just this once, it had nothing to do with an investigation.

JOIN THE J.R. SINCLAIR VIP CLUB

To get instant access to exclusive photos of locations used from the series, and the latest news from J.R. Sinclair, just subscribe here to start receiving your free content: https://www.subscribepage.com/n4zom8

ORDER A HARVEST OF SOULS

DI Joseph Stone will return in
A Harvest of Souls

Order now: https://geni.us/AHarvestofSouls